THE LAST PARTY AT SILVERTON HALL

Rachel Burton

An Aria Book

This edition first published in the UK in 2023
by Head of Zeus, part of Bloomsbury Publishing Plc

9 7 5 3 1 2 4 6 8

A catalogue record for this book is available from the British Library.

ISBN (PB): 9781803287256
ISBN (E): 9781803287232

Cover design: Leah Jacobs-Gordon

Typeset by Siliconchips Services Ltd UK

Printed and bound in Great Britain by
CPI Group (UK) Ltd, Croydon CR0 4YY

Head of Zeus
First Floor East
5–8 Hardwick Street
London EC1R 4RG

WWW.HEADOFZEUS.COM

In memory of Vesper, the ginger cat who sat at my feet as I worked.

Look at that sea, girls – all silver and shadow and vision of things not seen. We couldn't enjoy its loveliness any more if we had millions of dollars and ropes of diamonds.

—L. M. Montgomery, *Anne of Green Gables*

Prologue

Norfolk, England – June 1953

She sat on the beach in her bathing suit, towel wrapped around her, knees tucked up to her chest. Her head ached from the champagne the previous night and her eyes felt gritty from lack of sleep. Her husband was at home, asleep now, resting from the night before, from the party at Silverton Hall, the most glamorous evening of her life, and from the revelations that came afterwards.

I'll explain everything tomorrow.

But she hadn't let him wait until tomorrow. She'd demanded he tell her everything then and there.

'Let's get some sleep,' he'd said.

But she'd refused and so he'd told her as they stood in the kitchen next to the twin tub washing machine, dressed in their evening clothes. She could still feel the sensation of the countertop beneath her fingers, the countertop she'd gripped harder and harder as he'd told her the truth, quietly and calmly as though what he was saying was completely ordinary and routine.

When he'd finished, she'd walked away. He had called her name, tried to reach for her, but she'd gone upstairs, taken off the midnight-blue dress and packed it carefully away, wrapping it in tissue paper. Then she'd gathered her swimming things and left for the beach. As she passed through the living room she saw him asleep on the couch, snoring gently, his bow tie undone.

It was the morning after midsummer and the sun was already climbing in the sky. She could feel its warmth on her skin as she sat on the sand and waited for her friend. She wouldn't have got through these last months without her, without their morning swims in the salt water. But she wondered now how much longer this early morning ritual could continue, or if she even wanted it to.

Because how could anything ever be the same now?

I

Norfolk – July 2019

'I still can't believe she left me Little Clarion,' Isobel said, staring up at the house in front of her. 'I always thought she'd leave it to my mother.'

'These were Vivien's instructions,' the lawyer replied in clipped tones. 'She was very specific.' He paused for a moment. 'Has your mother said something?' he asked, fidgeting with concern. It was the most animated Isobel had seen her grandmother's lawyer all morning. He was scratching his ear and squinting in the bright summer sunshine.

She smiled. 'Don't worry,' she said. 'Mum doesn't want the house.' Isobel wondered if her mother, Gina, wanted anything that reminded her of Vivien or Silverton Bay. Gina and Vivien had never seen eye to eye and Isobel had never really understood the reasons why. Knowing the stubbornness of both her mother and grandmother it was probably something petty that had got lost in the murkiness of the passing years.

'I see,' Mr Brecher said, shifting from one foot to the other, probably embarrassed by the flaws of other people's families. 'Well, perhaps it's time to give you the keys.' He held them out to her, explaining which key was for which lock. As she took them from him, she noticed that her hands were shaking.

Mr Brecher stayed at the bottom of the steps as Isobel walked up to the front door, looking up once again at the three-storey, late Victorian house that she couldn't quite believe was now hers. She put the correct key in the lock and turned it until it clicked. The click brought back memories of when she used to live here – the last time she'd had her own front door key. She swallowed as the door swung open.

'I'll be on my way,' Mr Brecher said as he backed down the garden path towards his car, which was parked behind Isobel's battered Citroën on the road in front of the house.

'Is there anything else I need to know?' Isobel asked. She suddenly didn't want to be left alone with this huge five-bedroomed house. It felt like too much of a responsibility.

'There's still some paperwork to go through,' he said. He seemed small and faraway at the bottom of the steps and Isobel started to walk towards him again, away from the house. 'Some things I need you to sign, but I'll call you about those.'

'OK,' Isobel said as Mr Brecher opened the garden gate and stepped through.

As he closed the gate behind him he turned around, leaning slightly on the wrought iron. 'Don't forget Vivien's wishes,' he said quietly. 'I don't know why, but they were very important to her.'

'I won't,' Isobel said as the lawyer unlocked his Rover.

*

Isobel hadn't really thought about what would happen to the house at all until the funeral – she'd been too wrapped up in her grief and her guilt. She'd loved her grandmother and had spent so much of her childhood in Silverton Bay with her, but she hadn't been back to the village much over the last few years. She'd known Vivien was getting older, known she wasn't really coping with the upkeep of the house anymore. She should have visited more often. She should have spent more time with her grandmother – more than just the odd day here and there, taking her out for lunch, or for a drive along the coast. Isobel had never wanted to stay in the house for very long when she visited – it had smelled musty, the beautiful garden had become overgrown, and Vivien was only living in the downstairs rooms. It was no longer the house Isobel had grown up in, and the sight of it slowly falling apart was too much of a reminder of her grandmother's age. So she'd avoided it completely by taking Vivien out instead. Vivien had loved to go out for a drive, to get away from the Bay for a while. It had reminded her, she'd told Isobel once, of when she and her late husband, Max, had gone out in his open-top car – the first car she'd ever been in. It was one of only a handful of times Vivien ever mentioned Max.

When Isobel had taken the phone call back in April telling her that her grandmother had died – a heart attack, fatal and immediate, whilst shopping in the village – she'd felt her knees buckle beneath her from the shock. She hadn't been expecting it, even though she should have been. Vivien had always been such a strong presence in Isobel's life. It seemed almost impossible to imagine that she wasn't there anymore, that she would never be there again.

'But she seemed so well,' she'd said to Spencer, who had called her to break the news. But as soon as Isobel said the words, she knew they weren't true. Vivien hadn't really been looking well for months – each time Isobel had visited her grandmother she'd seemed smaller, frailer.

'I should have done more, seen her more often.'

'There was nothing you could have done, love,' Spencer had replied soothingly. 'We all have our time and your grandmother had lived a good life.'

Isobel had gone to the funeral with her flatmate, Mattie, who'd insisted on coming for moral support. Gina, Isobel's mother, hadn't been able to come – the thought of getting on a flight from New York was too much for her still. She hadn't flown since 2001.

'You don't understand,' she'd told Isobel on numerous occasions. 'You weren't here, you didn't see those planes fly into that building.'

Isobel's father had offered to fly over to go with her, but she'd told him she was OK. She didn't want to trouble him and, even more than that, she didn't want to have a conversation about what she was going to do with her life. Not now.

So she'd gone to her grandmother's funeral with Mattie and afterwards had been taken to one side by Mr Brecher. She'd thought she'd known what was coming, that the house would be left to Gina, who didn't fly of course, so Isobel would have to deal with it all. She hadn't been expecting Vivien to miss Gina out altogether.

She had been in a daze as Mattie drove them both back to

Cambridge afterwards. She had been in a daze all day, truth be told, barely talking to anybody at the funeral, desperate to get back in Mattie's car and away from the reminders of her grandmother. And so it had been Mattie who had presented the case, just as she would have done in court, for what became known as 'Isobel's New Start'.

'A house in a village you love, no rent or mortgage, big enough to turn one room into a studio,' she'd said, listing out the points on her fingers. 'You could start painting again, Isobel, you could give up the job you hate. Have you any idea how many people dream of this?'

But it didn't feel like a dream, not now Vivien was dead.

Leaving the job she hated was a good start, though, and she'd started back at St Swithin's School after the Easter holidays by handing in her term's notice.

'But you're the best art teacher this school has ever had,' the head had said.

Too damn good for this place. Something both she and her father could agree on, but she didn't say it out loud.

Three months after her grandmother's funeral, on a warm and sunny July morning, Isobel stood in the hallway of the house that was now hers as Mr Brecher's Rover drove away, leaving her alone. The house felt full of memories, emotions, potential. She could feel them all floating around her like the dust motes in the sun, but she felt reluctant to step further into the house for fear of disturbing ghosts. She could smell the musty smell of unused rooms and dirty upholstery that had put her off staying here too long for the last few years and she was sure she could smell damp. She touched the faded Strawberry Thief wallpaper in the hallway.

You're being ridiculous, she told herself. *It just needs a good airing, that's all. It's been shut up for months.*

She took a breath and walked purposefully into the house, leaving the front door open behind her. She walked through to the dining room at the back of the house – it had large windows overlooking the garden and if she opened them she could get a through breeze. That would sort everything out.

The dining room window was stiff at first and seemed to be caught up in something that was growing up the back wall – a vine or ivy, perhaps? Isobel put her shoulder against it and pushed as hard as she could.

And watched as the bottom part of the window frame crumbled to dust.

'How did I not notice how dilapidated everything had become?' Isobel asked. On the other end of the phone she heard Mattie sigh a little bit.

'I don't know, Izzy, you told me it was ready to move into.'

'I…I thought it was…' Isobel hesitated. Had she really? Or had she been kidding herself, remembering the house of her childhood rather than the house of now?

The window frame had just been the start of it – she'd managed to get the window closed again so at least the house was secure, or as secure as she was going to get it. As she'd started walking around she'd noticed problem after problem – blown electric sockets, damp walls, dried mouse droppings on the top floor – and she realised she had no idea how to deal with any of it.

'I knew the whole house was in need of modernisation,' she said to Mattie. 'I'm fairly sure it needs rewiring and the plumbing has been making a clanging noise for as long as I can remember. But I thought it was liveable. Nana had been living here after all.'

'And you hadn't noticed anything about the way she was living?' Mattie asked. There was no malice or judgement in her question, she just wanted to know in that simple, straightforward way of hers. Suddenly Isobel just wanted to be back in Cambridge, sitting in the living room of Mattie's flat, drinking too much tea and putting the world to rights.

'No,' she replied hesitantly. 'But...well... I never really stayed long. Recently I'd taken to staying only long enough to pick Nana up and take her out for the day and then settle her back again afterwards. I'm not sure why.'

But she did know why. Just as she'd known, deep down, that the house was in worse repair than she was willing to admit. She couldn't bear the thought of her grandmother, the person she loved most in the whole world, getting old, of her not being the woman she'd always been. So she'd ignored it, just as she'd ignored the cracks in the walls and the faint smell of must and damp in all the parts of the house that Vivien hadn't lived in anymore.

And in her head Isobel had preserved the version of the house that had last existed during that one perfect summer before she went to university.

'Come back,' Mattie said now. 'Come back to Cambridge and we'll sort something out.'

It was so tempting, but... 'No, I can't. This was meant to be a second chance. I can't give up at the first hurdle.

I haven't even been back in Silverton Bay for twenty-four hours!'

'You don't have to go back to teaching or anything. Just come back and put the house on the market. I know how much houses along the Norfolk coast sell for these days, even the dilapidated ones. Sell it and even after taxes the money will be enough to help you start again.' A few years ago, just before Silverton Hall had reopened as a hotel, the gardens were used to portray Sotherton in a TV production of *Mansfield Park*. Ever since then, the village and the surrounding area kept appearing in the Sunday papers as a highly desirable place to live. House prices had shot through the roof.

'I can't sell it.'

'I know how much you want this, Izzy, but—'

'No, I can't. Not for thirteen months from the day I get the keys. Nana stipulated it in her will.'

'Can she do that? It doesn't sound legally binding to me.'

'You're a criminal barrister not a probate lawyer, Mattie. Mr Brecher said I had to abide by her codicil.'

'Hmmm…' Mattie mumbled. She hadn't liked Mr Brecher when she'd met him at the funeral. She'd called him 'an old, fussy lawyer holding the profession back' but Isobel suspected that he knew what he was talking about. 'I'm going to ask around and find out how legally binding that request is.'

'OK,' Isobel replied, knowing there was little point in arguing. 'And I'm going to stay here, for a day or so at least.'

'In the house?'

Isobel thought for a moment. She thought about the bedrooms upstairs that seemed to have been closed off for years. She hadn't wanted to open another window and she wasn't sure if they could be slept in without being aired. She thought about the new sheets and duvet cover in the back of her car that she'd brought with her, ready for her new room in her new house – the bedroom on the top floor that she'd slept in when she was younger that now seemed to be home to a family of mice.

'No, not in the house. Not for tonight at least.' It wouldn't take that much to get the house liveable in, would it? A dehumidifier, a pest control expert, someone to fix the windows…how much would all that cost? 'I'll stay at Silverton Hall again tonight.' She'd stayed there the night before and could barely afford that, let alone a second night, but what else could she do right now?

'If you're sure.'

'I'm sure,' Isobel said with renewed vigour, pushing away the nagging voice that kept telling her she hadn't really thought this plan through at all. 'It'll be fine, everything will be fine. I'm just tired and missing Nana. I'll call you tomorrow.'

Besides, she couldn't go running back to Cambridge until she'd fulfilled her grandmother's second request.

2

Isobel sat in the lounge bar of Silverton Hall the next morning, sipping her second cup of coffee and putting off going to see Spencer.

The hotel had reopened to much fanfare three years before, quite rightly as it was truly magnificent. The new owner had held on to as many of the features of the original building as possible whilst still allowing for the luxuries of a modern hotel. The rooms came with a price tag to match the grandeur.

The Jacobean manor house had belonged to the Harrington family for centuries – the family tree and the village itself could be traced back to William the Conqueror – but more recently the Harringtons had been known for their small chain of luxury department stores in London, Cambridge and Oxford and the wild parties that were held at the Hall during the 1920s and 30s. In the early 50s the last of the family line had died suddenly, the department stores were sold to a rival chain, and a distant cousin who had inherited everything else sold the Hall to pay off debt and taxes.

How the mighty fall.

Silverton Hall was then sold in the 1950s to an American

financier who specialised in turning old, crumbling, bankrupt country houses into fashionable country house hotels. Hotel guests saved the English country house as Britain recovered from the war and rationing. That second incarnation of Silverton Hall was a huge success until the early 1990s, when cheaper hotels started popping up all over the place, at which point the Hall closed and the windows were boarded up. The gardens, however, had been kept open, maintained by a team of volunteers from the village. It had been part of the contract between the American financier and the mysterious distant cousin of the Harringtons that the gardens of Silverton Hall remained open to the public, just as they had been when the family lived in the Hall.

Despite all the time that Isobel had spent in the Bay, this was the first time she had ever set foot inside Silverton Hall. She'd often suggested to her grandmother that they go there for Sunday lunch or for afternoon tea, but Vivien had always refused and Isobel had never really understood why. Another stubborn family mystery.

'Can I get you anything else?'

Isobel looked up at a woman wearing a smart suit and a badge that read 'Ella Williams – Duty Manager'. Tempting as it was to sit here all morning drinking coffee and looking out across the beautiful gardens of Silverton Hall, bathed in summer sunshine, Isobel knew she had to leave. This was going to be a huge hit on her credit card as it was.

'No, thank you.'

'Are you staying in the area for long?' Ella asked.

'I'm actually moving here,' Isobel replied, and, despite everything, the thought of living here in this seaside village made her feel warm and content. 'I've inherited my grandmother's house. Her name was Vivien Chambers and she lived—'

'Of course!' Ella interrupted, a look of recognition passing over her face. 'Vivien mentioned you.' She stopped, the smile fading from her face. 'I'm so sorry for your loss,' she said quietly. 'Vivien was very popular in the village and here at the hotel.'

Isobel nodded slowly, thinking about what Ella had said. Vivien was very popular in the village – yes, that was certainly true. But at the hotel?

'You knew her?' she asked.

'Oh yes,' Ella replied. 'She used to come up here for morning coffee at least once a week.'

'She did?' Isobel felt her brow furrow as she said the words. As far as Isobel was aware, her grandmother had never set foot in Silverton Hall and never would. Much like the conflict between Vivien and Gina, she had no idea why.

'She used to tell us stories about when the Hall was a country house hotel in the 50s and 60s,' Ella went on. 'And all the parties that she used to attend here. It sounded ever so glamourous.' Ella smiled and Isobel tried not to appear too shocked. She wondered why Vivien had never told her about these parties, why she'd always shrugged and smiled whenever Isobel brought the subject of the Hall up. And she wondered why her grandmother had never told her about her morning coffees and chats with Ella and the other staff. Vivien was allowed a private life, Isobel reminded herself. But still.

'I've never been inside the Hall before,' Isobel replied, trying to keep her grandmother out of the conversation.

'When I lived here as a teenager it was boarded up, but I do remember coming up here with my...' She paused, remembering briefly that wonderful summer eighteen years ago. 'I used to walk my friend's dog in the gardens here,' she finished, pushing the memories away.

'The gardens are still open to the public,' Ella said. 'And there are guided garden walks a few times a month. That was stipulated in the contracts when the new owners bought the hotel.'

'Then I'll look forward to enjoying them once I'm settled in.' Isobel smiled, standing up and shouldering her overnight bag. She really did have to go. She couldn't put off seeing Spencer any longer.

'I don't know if you have time now,' Ella began. 'But we've got a display of photographs in the ballroom at the moment. It's a sort of history of the Hall over the years going right back to when the Harrington family lived here. Your grandmother gave us a few photographs from the 1950s to display and I wondered... I'm sorry, are you all right? You suddenly look a bit pale.'

Isobel had dropped her bag and sat down again rather abruptly as Ella told her about Vivien's photographs. Her grandmother had not only attended parties here, but had contributed photographs to an exhibition? Why then did she never want to talk about it? Why did she never visit the Hall? Did the memories of it upset her? Did it remind her of the husband she lost long before Isobel was born?

'I'm sorry,' she said to Ella, trying to smile. 'It's just been a long few weeks. Could I possibly get a glass of water?'

3

Isobel had put off going to see Spencer for far too long already but once she'd drunk her water, curiosity took over from surprise.

'Could I possibly see these photographs?' she asked, standing up again.

'Of course,' Ella replied. 'If you're sure you're feeling OK.'

'I'm fine, honestly. A little embarrassed, but—'

'Oh please don't be.' Ella smiled. 'I can take you to see the photographs now if you like. The ballroom will be empty this morning. We mostly use it for functions; conferences and weddings and so forth, but we've nothing on until the weekend.' She started to walk away and Isobel followed her along a corridor, the heels of Ella's shoes clicking on the wooden floor. 'How much do you know about the history of the Hall?' she asked.

'Well I know it was owned for years by the Harringtons of department store fame,' Isobel replied. 'Everyone in Silverton Bay knows that, I think.'

Ella nodded. 'Yes, that's right. But, well…' Ella paused. 'Things changed after the war, I suppose. There wasn't much money and the department stores were sold to pay the debts. Then in the 1950s the Hall was sold off too – that was when it first became a hotel.'

'When I was here as a teenager the Hall was empty,' Isobel said. She'd found it creepy at the time.

'Yes, the country house hotel fell out of favour for a while there,' Ella replied, pushing open the doors to the ballroom. 'We're trying to take a slightly different angle by keeping the hotel family and dog friendly. Golf weekends are popular too. And we focus on using this amazing ballroom for functions as well, of course.'

'It's beautiful,' Isobel breathed, looking around her. So many of the original features had been kept, including the painted ceiling. She could almost imagine parties taking place here in the 1930s, men dressed up like Bertie Wooster, women in their finest gowns, their hair freshly bobbed, a band playing jazz...

'The photographs are over here,' Ella said, interrupting her thoughts and walking towards a gallery-style wall. 'These are from when the Hall was still privately owned.' She pointed at a set of sepia photographs. 'This rather dour-looking couple is Lord and Lady Harrington between the wars. They would have been the parents of the final Lord Harrington.'

'Did they just run out of heirs?' Isobel asked.

Ella nodded. 'Two wars in fairly close succession will do that and I believe the house could only be inherited down the male line. It went to a cousin in the end and it was him who sold it to the hotelier.'

Isobel nodded, her eyes flicking over the photographs – pictures of what looked like all the staff – maids, footmen, cooks and butlers – standing on the steps of the Hall. She wondered why on earth anyone needed so many staff. Could they not do anything for themselves?

'That's my grandmother,' Ella said, pointing at one of the blurry figures in a maid's uniform. 'She was one of the very last housemaids at the Hall before it was sold. She started working here when she was fifteen, just after the Second World War.'

'I didn't realise the English country house was still a thing after World War Two,' Isobel said. Although, to be fair, she knew very little about the English country house at all apart from the handful of episodes of *Downton Abbey* she'd seen over the years.

'It was definitely on its last legs,' Ella smiled. 'You can see that there were far fewer staff by then.'

'Is that why you started working here?' Isobel asked. 'Because it was where your grandmother had worked?'

'Actually, I didn't know about my grandmother when I started working here. I was sent by head office and it was only when I told my mum where I was going that she told me Granny used to work here.' Ella turned towards a different set of photographs. 'This is the last Lord Harrington, just before he died,' she said, pointing at a photograph of a man who looked to be in his early twenties, standing outside the Hall wearing plus fours, a cigarette between his fingers. 'Big golfer, apparently.'

'How old was he when he died?'

'About twenty-five, I think. He'd had a weak heart since childhood.'

Twenty-five is no age, Isobel thought sadly.

'And this set are the parties in the 50s and 60s.' Ella pointed to another group of black and white photographs. 'Vivien gave us three of these and that's her there, see?'

Isobel looked at the pictures. They were almost exactly as she'd imagined when she'd walked into the ballroom – men in black tie, women in evening dresses. But the suits were cut differently, in a mid-century style, and the dresses were full-skirted with tiny waists – very clearly the 1950s. And then she spotted a very young-looking Vivien wearing a dark dress that plunged at the back, looking over her shoulder into the camera and smiling at whoever was taking the photograph. Isobel gasped. She recognised the photograph, even though she knew she had never seen it before. The posture and the dress was exactly the same as a portrait of Vivien that hung on the top landing at Little Clarion. Her grandfather had painted it the summer before her mother had been born.

'Is Max, my grandfather, in any of these pictures?' she asked.

Ella shook her head. 'No, he took them apparently. It was the inaugural midsummer party, which was held in the summer of 1953 just after the hotel opened. They held the ball annually, right up until the early 1980s. We've been thinking of reviving it, but it won't be until next year now, obviously.'

Isobel turned to stare at the photograph of her grandmother again, the photograph that was exactly the same as the portrait.

Max Chambers must have painted it as a memory of this night.

Ella moved down the row of photographs to a set that were taken in the gardens.

'These are all of the end-of-season garden party,' she said. 'That was another tradition that dated right back to when the Harringtons owned the Hall and the gardens were opened up for the whole village to enjoy.'

Isobel nodded, but her attention was still with the photograph of Vivien. She felt as though her grandmother was looking straight at her and she felt once again the strong stab of grief in her gut as she remembered that Vivien would never look at her again. She wished she could go back to Little Clarion now and ask her grandmother about these photographs. She wished…

'…in September,' Ella was saying.

'Sorry,' Isobel said, tearing her attention away from the photograph. 'What was that?'

'We're starting up the garden party again in September. You must come.'

'That would be lovely.' Isobel glanced at the photograph again and a shiver went through her. It proved that Vivien had been here, had attended at least one of the glamorous parties at Silverton Hall when she was young and that it was probably something to do with Max who had been the son of a banker and had introduced Vivien to a whole new life.

'It's a beautiful photograph, isn't it?' Ella said. 'Would you like to have it back?'

Isobel tore her eyes from her grandmother's picture. 'How do you mean?' she asked.

'Well, as you've inherited Vivien's house, it's up to you whether or not we can still display the photographs.'

'Oh of course you can display them,' Isobel answered. It hadn't even crossed her mind to take the photograph away. 'But once you change the exhibition it would be nice to have it back.'

'That goes without saying.'

'Did you say that Nana told you she'd been to several of these parties?'

Ella nodded. 'Yes, but this was the one she told me about. It was the first time she'd been anywhere so glamorous, she said. It was quite a big deal at the time.'

Isobel felt a stab of jealousy. Why had Vivien told Ella all of this and not her?

'It's funny,' she said, trying to keep that envy out of her voice. 'But I never remember Nana talking about parties here at Silverton Hall.'

'It was a long time ago,' Ella replied.

'I suppose so. She always had so much going on.' Logically, Isobel almost believed herself. Vivien had had a full and satisfying life after her husband died and Gina left home. She'd studied a history degree with the Open University and gone on to become a teacher at the local school. She and Isobel had always had so much to talk about and perhaps Vivien hadn't wanted to dig up ancient history. She hardly talked about Max, after all, so perhaps remembering the parties upset her too much. And perhaps she had only got talking to Ella because she was lonely, because Isobel didn't visit enough.

But when she looked back at the photograph of her grandmother in her ballgown, smiling over her shoulder at the camera, exactly as she was in the portrait that Max had painted of her, she felt as though there was something else. Something more.

She shook her head. She was hot and tired and being ridiculous. 'I should leave you to it,' she said to Ella. 'I should probably get on myself.'

'You must have a lot to do at the house,' Ella said and Isobel remembered the windows and the damp and the family of mice.

'You could say that,' she replied.

As Isobel walked down the hill and back towards the village, she couldn't stop thinking about the photograph, about Ella and Vivien and the parties. She wondered if her grandmother had ever told Spencer about it.

Vivien and Spencer had been friends for years and Isobel had spent many happy days in Spencer's antiques shop, Odds & Ends. But it had been a long time since she'd last set foot in it, only seeing Spencer when he'd joined them for a trip down the coast. Odds & Ends was so wrapped up in that summer, the summer before university, that Isobel had always been reluctant to go back, to face the memories, the smell of the past, the history that pervaded the very air.

But today she had to go back, because as well as stipulating that the house couldn't be sold for thirteen months, Vivien had also insisted in the codicil to her will that the only person who was to help Isobel clear the house was Spencer Hargreaves.

Spencer was younger than Vivien had been, but only by a few years – he must be well into his eighties now – and Isobel wondered if he still did the house clearances himself or if he had someone to help him. As she approached the shop, she saw that the door was wide-open, just as it always had been during opening hours, and the shelves of second-hand books were standing outside waiting to be rummaged through.

She stepped inside and smelled the familiar aroma of

furniture polish, mothballs and history. Nobody seemed to be about.

'Hello,' she called as she watched sunbeams flicker through the dusty windows.

There was a pause and then from somewhere in the back of the shop the words 'be with you in a minute' floated through. It was a man's voice, but not Spencer's. A voice that reminded her of being young, of drinking beer in the garden of The Two Bells, of walks on the beach and the best kiss she'd ever had. She touched her lips, just for a moment.

And then suddenly he was there, filling the gap between the doorway at the back of the shop that led to the storage room and the flat above. It had been over eighteen years, but it still felt like yesterday.

Nick Hargreaves was back in Silverton Bay too. What were the chances?

4

London – October 1952

As Vivien stepped out of the offices of Musgrove & Mortimer and on to Tottenham Court Road, she could barely see her hand in front of her face. It was the fourth day in a row that the smog had been so thick that she had to feel her way along, hoping that her knowledge of the streets would be enough to get her safely home.

'A real pea-souper,' Mr Musgrove (Mr Mortimer or any descendant had long since stopped practicing law, it seemed) had said as she'd left. 'Be careful out there.' But he hadn't lifted his eyes from his ledger and Vivien wondered, not for the first time, whether her boss would notice if she was careful or not or even if she returned the next morning. He probably only knew how bad the smog was because this time it had infiltrated the inside of the building like so many ghostly fingers.

Messrs Musgrove & Mortimer (whoever Mortimer might have been) had been practicing law on this site for over a hundred years and the current Mr Musgrove, as he delighted in telling anyone who would listen, was a direct descendant of the man who set the practice up all those decades ago. Vivien had been working at the solicitor's office for nearly three years now, since she was eighteen, and had found out about the typist's job from a friend of her father's. It was better than being stuck at the dressmaker's with her mother day in and day out where she had poked herself with the needle far too often. She was much better at typing than she ever had been at sewing – 'Fast and accurate,' Mrs Blanche, the senior secretary, had said. 'And a good telephone manner.'

But oh, it was boring. Dull, dreary letters about dull, dreary legal matters day after day, trying not to drift off during shorthand, counting down the hours and minutes until five o'clock.

Vivien had a habit of daydreaming. 'You'll dream yourself off the edge of the world one day,' her father had told her when she was a little girl, but the thought hadn't frightened her or warned her off her daydreams as her father had probably hoped. Instead she wondered what it would be like to drift off the edge of the world and what she might find there.

These days her daydreams took on a less fairy tale-like character, although they were no less distracting for it. Vivien often found chunks of her shorthand missing and had to guess what she was meant to be typing. Most of the time Mr Musgrove couldn't remember what he'd said anyway and would sign the letter off without comment.

It was her daydreaming that had caused the problem tonight, of course. When the smog was this bad, when she could hardly breathe or see for it, Vivien knew she needed to keep her wits about her, or she would get run over by a bus. Thick smog always happened after a period of very cold, still weather, when tiny particles from the coal smoke that pervaded London would gather to form this thick, sticky, smelly fog that clung to your clothes. At least that was what Vivien's father had told her and he always seemed to know about these things. She was always in awe of his knowledge, his love of learning – especially as he had left school at the age of fourteen. She wished she had half his brains. Anyway, he had always warned her to keep her hand against the wall of the building on nights like this and to count her footsteps so she could find the station, but at some point her mind had slipped, as it often did, to an alternate reality – a place where Vivien Burke wasn't a typist at a solicitor's office but a tightrope walker in a travelling circus or dancer in a New York club.

Tonight Vivien was an actress in a musical in the West End, making audiences cry as she sang the grand finale each night.

And tonight Vivien was also lost. Somewhere along the way she'd stopped counting, stopped touching the wall beside her and now, where the station was supposed to be it just wasn't.

Don't panic, Viv, you've got through worse, she reminded herself, thinking of the air raid sirens that haunted her childhood sleep, the bomb shelter at the end of the road and the brown paper label tied to the coats of almost every other child she'd known as they were sent away from London while her own parents had decided that Vivien was safer at home with them.

'I don't trust strangers, especially not ones from the countryside,' her father, Robert, had said.

There you go again, Viv, getting lost in the past when you need to concentrate. She knew the smog had killed people and she didn't want to be another statistic. *Now, if I can just find—*

She didn't see him coming, didn't even sense his presence until she'd walked slap bang into him, knocking him sideways and knocking the hat off her own head. As it fell to the floor she knew she'd never find it again in this smog. No one could ever find anything in this.

'Excuse me,' the man said as he stepped slightly away from her, disappearing into the gloom. 'I should have looked where I was going.'

'It's my fault,' Vivien replied. 'I was miles away and now I'm a little lost…' She wondered how much she should be saying to a strange man that she could barely see. She ran a hand over her hair, wondering about the whereabouts of her hat. 'I didn't realise I'd gone off course,' she rambled on. 'Until the station wasn't where I thought it should be.'

She couldn't see the man, but she heard him chuckle.

'Well, why don't we see if we can get you back on course,' he said.

He took her to one of the new Italian coffee bars in Soho, guiding her through the smog with his hand resting gently on her elbow. He introduced himself as Max and he made her feel so much better about getting lost on a road she knew so well.

'I feel like a bit of a fool,' she said, but he assured her she wasn't, that the smog was disorientating for everyone and it had taken him a lot of concentration just to find his way around the little streets of Soho, despite knowing them well.

Once she had been able to sit down and take a breath, she looked at him properly for the first time in the light of the coffee bar as opposed to the looming shadows that the smog created outside. He was so handsome she felt her heart contract like a ridiculous heroine in a sentimental novel. Vivien Burke was a lot of things, but sentimental was not one of them. Nor was she ever particularly enamoured of the opposite sex – her daydreams always featured her being successful on her own terms. But this man, who'd rescued her when she was lost, was something to look at – like a film star with his chiselled bone structure, twinkling blue eyes and devastating smile.

'What sort of coffee would you like?' he asked as she looked around her in awe.

'I'm not sure,' she replied, feeling ridiculous again. 'I've never drunk coffee before.' She turned towards the counter where the busy waiters collecting impossibly small cups and taking them to the crowded tables as the huge, gilded Gaggia machine belched out steam like a dragon. She'd heard of these coffee bars, of course, and the spectacular coffee machines imported recently from Italy, but she'd never met anyone who'd been in one. Her friends and family went to Lyons' Corner House if they wanted to celebrate anything, but the people in here – dressed so casually that Vivien felt horribly frumpy and old fashioned in her office attire – looked like they spent all day here, lounging at the tables, drinking from their tiny cups, listening to the American music blaring from the jukebox.

'Max!' a woman called as she approached their table. She was wearing the tightest jumper Vivien had ever seen, her hair was short, and her waist tiny. Again Vivien felt small and frumpy. 'Haven't seen you in ages.' The woman leaned a hand proprietorially on the back of Max's chair whilst completely ignoring Vivien. 'Look at you, all trussed up like the Christmas turkey.'

'I've come from the bank,' Max said. His voice sounded expressionless, his face blank, as though he didn't want to see this woman or talk to her.

'And who's your friend?' she asked, finally acknowledging Vivien's presence.

'This is Vivien,' Max said. He didn't mention the smog or getting lost, for which Vivien was very grateful. She smiled at the woman and held out her hand. 'Pleased to meet you,' she said, but the woman ignored her, turned around, walked away.

'Maybe see you sometime,' she called to Max over her shoulder.

'I'm sorry about that,' Max said. 'Now, let me get you a coffee.'

He brought back a cappuccino for her, creamy and bitter, and a tiny cup of thick, dark coffee for himself.

'Do you like it?' he asked as she took a sip and she nodded, wiping the foam from her top lip even though she wasn't sure she liked it at all.

He was an artist, he told her, a recent graduate of the Slade – a place Vivien had heard of only vaguely, not that she let Max know that. She nodded along as though talking about schools of fine art was an everyday occurrence for her. She knew how to fit in; she'd had to learn that skill quickly at Musgrove & Mortimer.

'So what do you paint?' she asked.

'Portraits are my favourite,' he replied. 'In oils, mostly.'

Vivien had remembered an afternoon just after the war, when the artworks had been brought back to London from their wartime locations in Bath and Buckinghamshire. Her aunt had taken her to the National Portrait Gallery, thinking it would be a treat, but she hadn't liked the portraits very much – they'd all been big and dark and a little frightening. When she'd thought about Max painting portraits, that was what she imagined. Later, when he painted her, she had found out how wrong she'd been that afternoon.

But painting must, for now, take a back seat.

'I work at my father's bank however,' he said, rolling his eyes as though it was the most boring thing in the world. Vivien had raised an eyebrow at this man whose father owned a bank and who had probably never had to worry about where the next meal was coming from.

Some people don't know they're born, she thought to herself.

'Well that explains why you're trussed up like the Christmas turkey,' she said out loud, smiling at him from behind her coffee cup.

'That was Charlotte,' Max explained, glancing toward the table she was now sitting at with a group of similarly casually dressed people, engulfed in a cloud of cigarette smoke. 'She was in my year at the Slade, most of the people she's sitting with were.'

'Do you not want to go and sit with them?'

He shook his head. 'Not when I'm trussed up,' he said, smiling, but the smile didn't reach his eyes.

Vivien realised then that she liked this man sitting opposite her – he seemed honest and authentic and Vivien didn't think many people were like that – and she was disappointed when, after she finished her coffee, he walked her to the station, feeling his way through the thickening green smog, and put her on her train to Newbury Park but hadn't asked to see her again.

She was disappointed but, as the train pulled slowly away from the platform, she wasn't surprised. He was posh and rich and she...well...she wasn't. And however hard she tried to hide it, her background came off her in waves in the cut of her clothes and the intonations of her speech.

What had surprised her was to find him waiting outside the offices of Musgrove & Mortimer two weeks later. She'd told him she worked there but she hadn't expected to ever see him again. He was dressed as though he'd come straight from his father's bank again and he tipped his hat at her in an old-fashioned way as she walked down the steps outside the office.

'No smog tonight,' he said with a smile.

'No,' she replied. 'I haven't needed to be rescued by handsome strangers for a while.'

'Does it happen often?'

'Maybe.' She grinned at him.

'How about a bite to eat?' he asked. 'And some dancing?'

He started meeting her from work for dinner and dancing once or twice a week. He told her about himself, about the house in Surrey and the boarding school, about his father's bank and his childhood summers at the seaside. And in return Vivien told him about the little two-up-two-down where she'd been born, and the morning in 1941 when she and her mother had come out of the bomb shelter to find it wasn't there anymore, like a missing tooth in a row of other identical houses.

'Were you not evacuated?' he asked and she shook her head and admitted that she had never left London in her life – had never been evacuated to Kent with a brown label tied to her coat and her gasmask in her hand like so many of the boys and girls in her street. Her dream, she told him – her realistic dream anyway, when she wasn't dreaming about being a film star – was to see the sea. It had been all she wanted since those same boys and girls had come back from Kent full of stories of sea air and salt water.

'My parents wouldn't hear of me being sent away. They didn't trust strangers, or the government or anyone who lived in the countryside, and they hated the way they weren't told where the children would be going. They said it was like the Pied Piper of Hamelin.'

Families need to stick together, her father had said. And then he'd been called up and sent to France along with Uncle Brian and it was just her and her mother at home, until they didn't have a home at all.

Max raised an eyebrow. 'You know the government called the evacuation plans "Operation Pied Piper"?' he said.

'I didn't know that,' Vivien replied. 'How crass.' She immediately put her hand over her mouth. She hadn't meant to say it, hadn't meant to criticise the government, but she'd never really liked Churchill that much – his face and pointing index finger telling her to 'Deserve Victory' from posters all over the place had scared her and made her want to disobey him all at the same time. Vivien had never been much of a rule follower, but she did suddenly understand her parents' concerns about sending her away.

'And your house,' Max asked. 'Where did you live?'

'We moved in with my aunt and my four cousins,' she replied, remembering how her mother and Aunt Nora had shared the big double bed while she'd slept on a mattress on the floor of her cousins' room. Where else could they go, after all? It wasn't as though the government did anything to help. 'We stayed there until the war was over and then, when my father came home, we rented a flat above a shop for a while before we moved to a new flat in Newbury Park.'

She was honest with Max because she felt she could be. For the first time in her life she felt as though she wasn't being judged for coming from nothing.

'Nobody can help where they're born, Vivien,' he said.

They never planned their meetings – sometimes he was waiting for her outside work and other times he wasn't – but for the next month she saw him once or twice a week.

And then he disappeared.

Three weeks passed and he just wasn't there. The smog came back at the beginning of December – worse than ever; thick and green and smelly and lasting for days – and it felt as though Max had disappeared into it.

'Too good to be true, love,' her mother said cynically. But Vivien didn't believe he would just disappear like that. There must be a reason.

Thousands of people died in the smog of December 1952, killed by accidents with vehicles they couldn't see, fatal falls into the smoggy gloom, or because they simply couldn't breathe in the filthy air. Vivien had just begun to think the worst, begun to think that Max might be one of those thousands, when he reappeared, standing outside her offices tipping his hat.

After that he always made arrangements for when he would next see her and he was always on time, exactly where he promised to be. Vivien knew things were changing between them when he asked to meet her parents.

'I thought perhaps we could take them to The Dorchester for tea,' he said, but Vivien shook her head.

'No,' she said firmly, that would be too much for Robert and Flo, they'd be nervous and who knows what they would say then. It was bad enough that Max insisted on meeting them. 'Not The Dorchester.'

In the end they went to the Lyons' Corner House on Coventry Street for afternoon tea, or what passed for afternoon tea in these late days of rationing – tea itself was no longer rationed at least, but you would never know it was so weak.

'Well this is wonderful,' Flo announced loudly over the teapot as she poured. 'Shall I be mother?' she'd asked as she'd picked it up and Vivien had tried not to die of embarrassment right there on her chair. 'I said to Viv that you were a good 'un, didn't I. Viv? Didn't I say?'

Vivien smiled and nodded and thought about the coffee bars in Soho that she and Max went to and wondered what her parents would think of them, or of coffee for that matter. She didn't mention the time her mother had told her that Max was too good to be true, and when she looked over at her father – who was all dressed up in his Sunday best, his round, red face beaming, his tie looking as though it might strangle him – he winked at her knowingly.

And she tried not to wonder too much about why it was that Max was meeting her parents when he hadn't even kissed her yet.

5

Norfolk – July 2019

Nick knew who it was as soon as he heard her call out that tentative 'hello'. He felt his abdomen tighten just as it had done eighteen years before when he'd first seen her in this very shop. Part of him had been waiting for her.

He'd first met her the day after he arrived for his summer in England – a summer his parents had been talking about for months as though they couldn't wait to be rid of him, couldn't wait for him to be on the other side of the world, to be somebody else's problem. He didn't mind a summer at his grandfather's shop, he'd loved visiting as a child before his father had accepted the job offer that had taken the family to Singapore where Nick had attended the International School, which he'd hated more than anything else in the world.

He'd always loved his grandfather's shop though and it hadn't felt like a hardship to spend a summer there. Odds

& Ends was full of curiosities and antiques – what some people would call junk, Nick supposed. It hadn't felt like junk to him though. It still didn't. To this day he loved the smell of the old things, the sensation of their history, the quiet of the shop.

But the morning after he'd arrived in Silverton Bay eighteen years ago, taking a taxi from the airport to the village where his grandfather had been waiting anxiously for him, the shop hadn't been quiet. He'd heard her long before he'd seen her, her laugh ringing out like a bell as she'd chatted to his grandfather. As soon as he'd heard that laugh he'd become self-conscious in his own skin, very aware of his height; his skinny, rangy build; his too-long arms and legs. And he'd felt something unfurl in his abdomen in a way he'd never felt before, in a way that made him embarrassed to be there. Instead of walking out into the shop, instead of saying 'good morning', he'd hidden behind the partition that divided the shop floor from the stairs that led to the flat above, and he'd watched her.

She had a lot of blonde hair, piled up on top of her head and a long, slim neck. Her lips were full and constantly moving, smiling, laughing. She'd been sitting on top of an antique cabinet, swinging her long, tanned legs as she spoke, and she'd been holding a pad of paper. He could have fallen in love with her then and there, if he'd believed in that sort of thing.

'Good morning, Nick,' his grandfather had called. He clearly hadn't hidden very well. When Nick had stepped out onto the shop floor, the girl jumped down from the cabinet and walked towards him. For a moment he'd thought she was going to hug him and he'd frozen, scared like a rabbit in the headlights.

'I'm Isobel and you must be Nick,' she'd said, her voice just like her laugh, clear and sweet. 'Spencer's been telling me all about you,' she'd nodded towards his grandfather, 'and he says you're here for the whole summer. I live here, with my grandmother in one of the Victorian houses on the edge of the village.' She'd waved ink-stained fingers vaguely in the direction of the scattering of large detached houses that had been built in the late 1800s. 'My parents live in New York and I stayed here when they moved.'

He'd nodded then, finding his voice. 'My parents live in Singapore,' he'd said. 'That's where I was until I came here.'

'It's so good to meet you. I can't wait to show you around!' He'd taken the hand she was holding out to him as though he was in a dream. He'd held on to it for far too long. He hadn't been able to keep his eyes off her.

They'd been so young then, so full of plans. She was off to art school in London – Central St Martin's – and he had a place to study medicine at Sheffield. She'd sketched him one afternoon while he was helping his grandfather in the shop. He'd never seen anyone so focused, her hand moving quickly across the page, the pencil held loosely in her fingers. When she showed him the sketch it had taken his breath away. He'd kept it in his wallet for years. Long after they'd lost touch.

And now she was back and his memories of that summer seemed as clear as if they had happened yesterday.

He stood just out of sight for a moment, as he had done on that morning years ago, and leaned his head against the wall. Why now? Why today when his grandfather had left the shop for the morning?

'Be with you in a minute,' he called, giving himself a moment to collect his breath, collect himself before he turned around to look at her.

She was the same but different – long, graceful neck, hair piled on top of her head, but subdued somehow, as though the joy she'd exuded when she was younger had been sucked out of her. *Of course she looks subdued*, he thought to himself, *Vivien's dead. She's grieving.* But there was more to it than that, he was sure of it.

'Isobel,' he said, barely more than a whisper, barely more than an exhale. She'd once told him that he and Spencer were the only people who never shortened her name. She liked it when it wasn't shortened, she'd said.

'Nick,' she replied, her voice soft. She took a step back towards the entrance of the shop and shifted her bag on her shoulder.

He walked around the shop counter, leaning against it so that he was facing her but keeping his distance. He felt as though she would run off if he made any sudden movements. He realised that she hadn't known he would be here, which meant Spencer hadn't told her.

'I'm so sorry about Vivien,' he said.

She nodded, looked away. 'I didn't know you'd be here.' She ran a hand over her face, her left hand. No ring. And then he thought about the ring he'd taken off just a few weeks ago when he'd first come back to the Bay. It was hidden away in a drawer, almost as though he'd known Isobel would be coming.

Which he had done, of course, he just hadn't known when she'd arrive.

He shrugged now, very aware of the space he was taking up. He felt like a teenager again.

Pull yourself together.

'I'm helping Grandad out,' he said. 'Just for a while.'

He watched her nod slowly, her eyes glancing around the shop.

'He's not here right now,' Nick said.

'No…I…er…'

'Can I help?'

She let go of a breath as though she was deflating and leaned against a dark mahogany cupboard that, at a guess, Nick thought might be Edwardian. He was surprised how quickly it was all coming back to him.

'Vivien left me the house,' she said.

'I know—'

'It's all such a mess,' she interrupted. He could hear tears in her voice. She was standing in the shadows so he couldn't see her face and he wanted to put his arms around her, to tell her that everything would be OK. He crossed his arms firmly across his chest to stop himself.

'What is?' he asked.

'The house. It's falling apart. The window frames are crumbling, it smells of damp, I think there are mice living there and…' She stopped. Her breath hitched. 'I didn't notice. I should have noticed.'

When had things got so bad, he wondered. Why had nobody been keeping an eye on Vivien?

'Houses can be fixed,' he said authoritatively. Because he knew it was true. It might take a lot of time, a lot of patience and, sometimes, a lot of money. But houses could be fixed, there was a certainty to them. Unlike people.

'Nana wanted Spencer to help,' she said, her voice steadier. She stepped away from the Edwardian cupboard and the morning light caught the side of her face. Nick was staring again, like he used to when he was eighteen. He looked away. 'That's why I'm here, to ask for Spencer's help. I don't really know what to do.'

Nick opened his mouth to tell her that he'd help, that he'd shut the shop right away and do anything she needed him to do.

'Nana left a stipulation in her will that I had to ask Spencer,' Isobel explained before he could offer, as though she was reading his mind. She didn't need his help, which was probably for the best.

'He won't be gone long,' he said instead. 'He's just gone to look at a house in King's Lynn.' His grandfather specialised in house clearances, had done for years. He had a knack for knowing what was rubbish, what could be sold on, and what was valuable. 'Shall I get him to call you?'

She nodded, shifted her bag again. He wanted to ask her if it was heavy, if he could carry it home for her. Instead he crossed his arms a little tighter.

'I should go. He's got my number.'

Nick watched as Isobel walked away. Suddenly she turned back, the light silhouetting her in the doorway.

'How long have you been here?' she asked.

'A few weeks. Like I said, I'm helping Grandad out. He's not getting any younger and there's a lot of heavy lifting in this job...' He didn't tell her that he'd moved here to help himself as much as Spencer and that he had no idea how long he'd be here or where he'd go next.

'What about the hospital?' Isobel asked him.

'Which hospital?' For a moment he had no idea what she was talking about. Who was in hospital? And then he realised that she meant the hospital he was supposed to be working in.

She didn't know. Spencer hadn't told her that either.

'The hospital can survive without me,' he said, with a shrug and a smile as though it was no big deal. She hesitated for a moment, looking like she was going to say something else and then she changed her mind.

'I guess I'll see you around then,' he said to her as she started to turn away.

'I guess you will,' she replied.

'How did she seem?' Spencer asked later, when he returned from King's Lynn. ('A good house clearance,' he'd said. 'Lots to get our teeth into.')

'Quiet, subdued... I guess it's normal. She must miss Vivien.' Nick paused. 'Did you know about Vivien's will? Did you know about this clause in it saying only you could help her with the house?'

'I knew she was leaving the house to Isobel and she asked me to keep an eye on her. I suppose this is what she meant.' He smiled. 'Typical Vivien, bossing me about from beyond the grave.'

Nick knew that his grandfather missed Vivien too, that

her death had been a blow to him, had knocked the stuffing out of him. With Vivien's death, Spencer's eighty-two years suddenly seemed more real, to Nick at least, and he had started to notice his grandfather look frail for the first time. It was why he'd moved back, to help him in the shop and with the house clearances. That and the fact that he had nowhere else to go. It was like rewinding the clock eighteen years and he was that lost kid learning the difference between Victorian and Edwardian furniture while waiting to go to medical school.

'I got the impression that Vivien's house is in a bit of a state,' Nick said as gently and diplomatically as he could. He'd got the impression that it was falling down around Isobel's ears. 'It's damp, apparently, and she says there are mice.'

Spencer didn't say anything for a moment.

'Did you not know?' Nick asked.

'Not know what?'

'That the house was falling apart?'

'A little bit of damp and a few mice isn't falling apart, Nick, you know that.'

'I got the impression it might be worse than that.'

Spencer exhaled and turned towards Nick.

'I had a feeling that things weren't great at the house,' he said quietly. 'But Vivien never let me have a proper look around. She was living mostly on the ground floor I think, had shut up the rest of the house. I don't know why. She never talked about it.'

Nick nodded, turning back the chest of drawers he was fixing up.

'Did you tell Isobel about—?' Spencer began.

'No, I didn't tell her anything. She wasn't here for long.'

'I'd have thought the two of you would have wanted to catch up.'

'It's been eighteen years,' Nick said. 'It felt awkward and she doesn't need to hear a litany of my failures when she's grieving her grandmother and trying to settle into that house.'

There was a moment of silence and Nick heard his grandfather's footsteps behind him and his hand on his shoulder. 'They aren't failures, Nick,' Spencer said quietly. 'It's just life.'

Nick grunted. 'She didn't know about the hospital,' he said. 'You didn't tell her.'

'It's not my story to tell.' He paused, moving away again. 'I think I'll go to the house to see her, try to get the lay of the land, see how bad things really are.'

'Good idea.'

'Do you want to come with me?'

'Not a good idea,' Nick said, not taking his eyes off the chest of drawers. He needed to get himself together before he saw her again. Needed to be prepared.

'I can value the furniture Isobel might want to sell, but you know more about fixing up a house than I do.'

'Have a look around,' Nick replied. 'Let me know. I can always go up there another day if she wants me to.'

'Do you want me to tell her?'

'No, just leave it for now. If the house is as bad as she seems to think it is, I doubt she'll stay for long.'

But he wanted her to stay, even if that would mean having to tell her everything.

6

How long had he been back? Had Vivien known he'd be here? What was he doing back in Norfolk instead of some disinfected surgical ward in a city hospital?

The hospital can survive without me.

Isobel took a breath, hitching the bag higher onto her shoulder again as she walked up the hill back to Vivien's house. Except it wasn't Vivien's house anymore, it was her house – damp smells, mouse infestations and all.

Nick had seemed taller than he used to be, more sure of himself, as though he had finally grown into those long limbs. She'd had to force herself to tear her eyes away from him, from the breadth of his shoulders, the t-shirt stretched tight around the muscles of his arms when he crossed them across his chest. She knew she'd made a fool of herself, getting all breathless and upset at the sight of him. But seeing him again had been a shock and a reminder of everything that had happened, everything that had gone wrong.

She had to stop thinking about him, she had to concentrate on Little Clarion…her house. She had to get at least some of it liveable in by this evening – it was either that or give up and go back to Cambridge. Another night at Silverton Hall was out of the question.

As she walked, she remembered that she'd wanted to ask Spencer if he had a dehumidifier she could borrow. It was the sort of thing he'd have stored away somewhere. But seeing Nick had thrown her completely, turned her brain into even more of a stuttering mess than it already was, and she'd completely forgotten. She stopped, hesitating at the top of the High Street. Should she go back or wait until she saw Spencer?

In the end she decided to wait. She couldn't face him again, with his folded arms and his cryptic answers and his 'I guess I'll see you around'. Around where? How long was he staying? Nick being here changed everything. She could still remember his kiss on that warm September afternoon, right before her life turned upside down. The kiss which had inadvertently become the bar against which all other kisses had been held.

As she walked back up the hill, her mind swirling with thoughts of the house, of Nick, of the photographs taken at the party at Silverton Hall, she felt something, a familiar itching in her left hand, a desire to pick up her pencil and draw. She hadn't been able to draw a thing since Vivien had died; she'd stared at blank page after blank page of her sketchbook for months. It was the reason she had known handing in her notice at St Swithin's had been the right thing to do. How could she teach anyone else to draw when she couldn't draw herself?

But now, suddenly, she was desperate to pick up that pencil again. She felt her pace speeding up as she walked back towards the house, towards her sketchbook, which sat in the boot of her car, thrown in carelessly as though it was a sudden last-minute addition.

She was sitting in the narrow hallway of the Little Clarion when the doorbell rang.

At least the bell was working.

'It's open,' she called, not looking up from her sketchpad. She'd lost track of how long she'd been sitting there – back pressed against the bannisters, one foot braced on the wall in front of her, sketchbook resting on her thigh, pencil held lightly in her hand. She had sat there as soon as she'd walked through the front door, not even properly shutting it behind her, everything forgotten – the photographs, the damp, the mice – by her desire to put pencil to paper again. She wanted to start as soon as possible before the elusive feeling disappeared again. She'd thought it would be the sea that would help her start to draw and paint again, but she hadn't even been down to the beach yet. She wasn't quite ready to face it without Vivien.

'Hello, love,' said a soft voice that she recognised. She tore her eyes away from the drawing on her sketchpad.

'Spencer!' she squealed, jumping up and very aware of the relief in her voice. 'Thank god you're here.'

Spencer held out his arms and she practically fell into them as he hugged her. Somehow everything felt a bit better now he was here, a connection to Vivien, someone who knew what they were doing. Isobel realised, perhaps a little too late, that other than Spencer she didn't know anyone who could help her in any sort of practical sense – her father was useless at anything like that, even if he hadn't been on the other side of the Atlantic. Designing houses, rather than fixing them, was his speciality. Fixing up Vivien's old house seemed quite a big project to embark upon with only an octogenarian to assist.

'It's good to see you,' Spencer said as he stepped away from her. 'How are you?'

Isobel exhaled a puff of air. 'I… I don't know. Everything is a mess.' She gestured at the house around her. 'I hadn't noticed how bad everything had got, not until yesterday and…' She faltered, feeling as though she was going to cry.

'It's OK,' Spencer said reassuringly. 'Houses can be fixed.'

That's what Nick had said. Isobel opened her mouth to ask Spencer what his grandson was doing here, then she closed it again. It felt like too big a thing to talk about and, anyway, Spencer had picked up her sketchpad and was looking at what she had been drawing. Or rather who she had been drawing.

'Nick said he'd seen you,' Spencer said, looking at the sketch. 'He always was a good model.' When he chuckled to himself Isobel had to dig her fingernails into her palms to stop herself snatching the pad from him. When the feeling of needing to draw had almost overwhelmed her in the High Street she hadn't known what her subject matter was going to be. As soon as the pencil touched the paper it was the outline of Nick's features that had started to appear, just as they had over and over again during that summer eighteen years ago – the curve of his cheekbone, the shadow of stubble on his jaw, those hazel eyes that she used to think she could drown in. She hadn't thought about what she was drawing, she just went with it; relieved that she still had it in her. But now someone had seen what she was doing and she felt mortified.

'Good bone structure,' she muttered, trying to muster up a smile.

Spencer turned to her and put the sketch pad down. 'He told me you were upset, that you hadn't realised how bad the house was. Why don't you show me? I'm sure it's not as bad as you think.'

Leaving the front door open had aired the downstairs a little bit and the smell of damp wasn't as strong in the hallway as it had been.

'Let's start at the top of the house,' she said.

The dank, musty smell started to get stronger as they climbed the stairs. She let Spencer lead the way thinking he'd be slower on his feet, but he was as spritely as a man half his age and set a pace that left her breathless by the time they reached the top floor. She'd clearly been spoiled by the lift in Mattie's apartment building.

'Do you think there's a damp problem?' Isobel asked as Spencer crouched down – again seemingly defying ageing – in one of the guest bedrooms.

He shook his head. 'I don't think so,' he said, standing up. 'I think these rooms have just been shut up for a long time.'

'I can't remember when I last checked up on the house properly. These past few years I've just come up for the day to take Nana out.'

'Well, she did love a drive,' Spencer said. 'Reminded her of Max, I think.'

Max again. The grandfather nobody really talked about. The grandfather who had taken the photographs at the inaugural midsummer party at Silverton Hall all those years ago. How many other parties had her grandparents been to? Isobel thought again about how Vivien had never mentioned it, never wanted to go near the Hall. Did Spencer know anything about that?

'You do have a mouse problem though,' Spencer said before she got a chance to ask anything. 'And a lot of your window frames are rotting.'

'I know, one came apart in my hands yesterday.'

'Well, not to worry,' Spencer said. 'I'm here now. We can fix this.'

'I don't have anywhere else to go though. I quit my job, packed my things and left Cambridge. I had all these plans. I've been wanting to come back for years, dreaming of how I could make it happen and what it would be like...and then Nana died and suddenly it was possible, but in the worst possible circumstances. I just want to make things right.'

'We can make this right,' Spencer said, a comforting hand on her shoulder.

'Can we?'

'We'll get a couple of dehumidifiers in, dry the place out a bit, then we can find a pest control company and someone to fit new windows at a reasonable rate.' He paused. 'What's your budget?'

'For what?'

'For renovating the house. I assume you're intending to renovate if you're going to live here. Otherwise you could sell, I suppose – even properties that need work are selling for good money around here, but you'd have taxes to pay.'

'I can't sell,' Isobel said. 'Nana put it in her will that I had to keep the house for thirteen months and you were the only person I could ask for help.'

Spencer smiled and shook his head. 'I knew about that last one, Nick told me, but I didn't know she'd put an embargo on you selling. You know, nobody would say anything if you ignored her wishes.'

'She'd probably haunt me.'

'Ah well, she probably would.'

'Do you know why she did it?' Isobel asked. 'Why she put those clauses in her will?'

'No idea, love, but at a guess I'd say she asked you to ask me about the house because she wanted you to have someone you could trust to help you. Would you have asked me otherwise?'

Isobel shook her head. 'I wouldn't have wanted to bother you.'

'There you go then.'

'How much do you think it will all cost?'

'Weeeellll,' Spencer said slowly, drawing the word out like toffee. 'Like I said, we can get rid of the mice and get you some new windows relatively cheaply; Nick and I can call in a favour or two but the rest of it... I really don't know.'

'What do you mean by "the rest of it"?' she asked.

'Love, this place is old and, other than the top floor, Vivien hadn't done a thing to it since your grandfather died. The wiring is going to need to be modernised at some point, maybe the plumbing too. They are big jobs but it's not really my area you know.'

Isobel's stomach dropped and it must have shown in her face.

'Don't worry too much,' Spencer said. 'They're big jobs but they don't have to be done straight away. You just need to be aware of them and I'm sure Nick will be able to help.'

'Nick?' If it had been her heart or her nervous system she'd have understood asking Nick, but wiring and plumbing?

Spencer shrugged and turned away from her again. 'He's done up a few houses,' he said vaguely.

Isobel knew there was more to it, more than neither Spencer nor Nick were telling her. Not that any of it was her business. She hadn't spoken to Nick Hargreaves for nearly twenty years.

'Have you eaten?' Spencer asked.

'Not since breakfast but—'

'Let's go to the pub, love.'

The Two Bells hadn't changed at all and, with the exception that it was no longer filled with a haze of cigarette smoke, it looked exactly as it had done when Isobel worked here during her university holidays. Horse brasses and watercolours of seascapes adorned the walls and Brandon Lyons was still behind the bar serving a menu that consisted of various fried food with chips. Brandon was the landlord now, Spencer told her. When Isobel had worked here he'd just been the ever-present barman. *He must really love The Two Bells*, she thought to herself.

'Your dad could pay to get the whole place refurbished,' Spencer said as they settled into a familiar corner of the village pub after ordering scampi, chips and peas – the only vegetable ever available and, Isobel knew, always out of a tin.

'I don't want to ask him,' Isobel replied. 'You know how much he fusses about me. I just want to show him that I can do this, that I can stand on my own two feet.'

'How does your mum feel about it?'

'About me being left the house instead of her?'

Spencer nodded.

'I think she was expecting it.' Isobel smiled and Spencer's blue eyes twinkled. 'I'm not sure she would have wanted it and it's not like she could have seen it even if it was hers.'

'She's still not flying then?' Spencer asked, even though he knew the answer as Gina hadn't been able to get to Vivien's funeral.

Isobel shook her head. 'Says she'll never fly again.'

'Still,' Spencer said slowly as he looked out of the window to the village green beyond. 'That doesn't stop you asking your dad for help.'

'Nana left the house to me and I want to do it myself. It's what she would have wanted.'

'She wouldn't have wanted you to bankrupt yourself.'

'Is it really going to cost that much?'

Spencer shrugged and took a sip of his pint. 'Maybe, maybe not. Houses are funny like that.'

'Could you be any less cryptic?' Isobel asked, teasing him gently.

'There's no way of knowing yet but if we need to rewire, for example, it's not going to come cheap. We need to get people who know a lot more about houses than I do to have a look at it though.'

'People like Nick?' Isobel said, tentatively tyring to broach the subject again.

'Well, he knows all the good electricians.'

Spencer clearly wasn't going to be drawn in. Before she could ask any more questions he changed tack.

'You're absolutely sure you don't want to sell?' he asked. 'Not even after the thirteen months are up.'

'I thought I was sure. This house, this village… I've daydreamed about living here for years – pretty much since the day I left to be honest, but now I've seen the house…' She hadn't been expecting there to be so much work – redecorating was one thing, even a new kitchen and bathroom eventually, but it felt as though she'd be practically rebuilding the house from the ground up.

Vivien and her husband Max had moved to the village from London in the early 1950s after a whirlwind romance. 'We wanted to get away from the city,' Vivien had always said when she was asked. 'Away from the smoke and the endless smog. We wanted to be able to breathe again, especially after Gina.' Gina, who had been born just six months after Max and Vivien's wedding, not that Isobel would ever have dared to embarrass her grandmother by telling her she'd worked that out.

When she was eighteen Gina had moved in the opposite direction to her mother, back to the pollution and the smoke, first to university and then to work at an architect's office where she met Tim Malone – the American-born son of her boss. They'd fallen in love, married, and a few years later, in the autumn of 1982, Isobel had been born. And how in love they'd fallen – it was obvious to anyone with eyes how Isobel's parents felt about each other. Sometimes even Isobel felt like she was in the way of her parents' relationship and she'd always jumped at the chance to spend her summers with Vivien in Silverton Bay. Isobel was more like her grandmother and preferred the Norfolk coast to London any day. Then, when she was fifteen, Isobel's father wanted to move back to New York and she went to live in Norfolk permanently.

'She's not going to boarding school in London and that's final,' Vivien had said to Gina the summer before the move to America. Gina's plan had been for Isobel to become a boarder at the school she already attended as a day girl and then she could spend her holidays in New York or Norfolk – whichever she chose.

'It's easier this way, Mum,' Gina had insisted. 'Tim and I don't want to uproot her from her education at this stage.'

'Well, maybe Tim should have thought of that before he decided to go back to New York.' Isobel had listened to the conversation at the door. She hadn't been sure whether or not she wanted to go to boarding school, but she had known that she didn't want to go to New York. It had seemed so far away. She had wanted to burst into the room and tell her grandmother that it was OK, she didn't mind boarding school, especially if she still got to spend her summers in Norfolk.

'It's his home, Mum,' Gina had said. 'He's been wanting to go back for years.'

'Isobel can move here and live with me,' Vivien had replied decisively and Isobel's stomach had flipped with expectant excitement. She'd crossed her fingers and squeezed her eyes shut. Every summer she had spent in Silverton Bay had made it harder to leave, to go back to London. Now she had the opportunity to stay here for ever. *Please say yes, Mum*, she'd whispered to herself as she listened in.

After a lot of fuss about schools and holidays, Gina had said yes. Isobel's dreams had come true and she hadn't had to leave Silverton Bay that summer at all. She was finally home. Because Little Clarion had always been her home, for as long as she could remember, not the glass and chrome apartment building in West London that her father had designed and where they lived in the penthouse flat. She'd never have to see that monstrosity again.

She'd missed her parents, of course she had, but they came to Norfolk every Christmas and she spent a few weeks of every summer in New York where she got used to the hot, sticky city streets – although she much preferred the weekends they spent on the coast at Montauk. Isobel always preferred to be near the sea.

'Nana's house has always been my home,' Isobel said to Spencer now. 'I want to live here. It just feels like a huge job to make the house liveable in.'

'We'll talk to Nick,' Spencer said as their meals were put in front of them.

Isobel gave the older man a few moments to enjoy his scampi before venturing into Nick territory again.

'Are you going to tell me what's going on?' she asked

eventually. 'Why is Nick such an expert on houses all of sudden?'

Spencer swallowed. 'You didn't ask him when you saw him this morning?'

'He just said the hospital could survive without him. He's as cryptic as you.'

'Look, Isobel love, Nick doesn't work as a doctor anymore. He quit a couple of years ago. He's been going through a pretty hard time these last few years, but I suspect he'll tell you himself soon. Just give him time.'

Isobel stared at Spencer in shock. 'He quit?' she asked. 'But being a doctor was all he ever talked about, it was his dream, wasn't it? His calling?'

'I think perhaps it was his father's dream,' Spencer replied quietly, turning back to his scampi and chips.

'How long has he been back?' she asked.

'Well, he moved into the shop in the spring, not long after Vivien's funeral. He tells me I need help, that I can't do all the house clearances on my own anymore. While there's more than a little truth in that, I suspect he needs me as much as I need him.'

'And he knows about houses, you said?'

'He's flipped a few over the last couple of years. He's made quite a bit of money out of it. He'll help you too, you know that, don't you? All you have to do is ask.'

She nodded and went back to her meal, sure she'd got everything out of Spencer that he was willing to tell her for now.

'Where are you staying tonight, love?' he asked.

'At the house, I guess.'

Spencer shook his head. 'You can't stay there until we've

got the windows secure at least, and probably got rid of those mice. Come and stay at the shop for a couple of days.'

'I can't put you out, besides, you've got Nick staying—'

'Nick can sleep on the couch,' Spencer said. 'He won't mind, not for you.'

'I can't, Spencer. It's too much to expect. I can just stay at—'

'No arguments.'

Isobel agreed to stay even though she wasn't comfortable with the idea of making Nick sleep on the couch – the shop was Nick's home now, after all. And besides, did she want to stay in the same house as Nick? Would Nick want her to stay? The summer that they'd met had ended in that one kiss, and then…nothing. Life had changed for Isobel almost overnight when two planes flew into the World Trade Centre the day after Nick went to medical school. Could she explain why she'd never kept in touch? Was it too late?

As they were leaving the pub to go back to the house so Isobel could collect her overnight bag, they bumped into Ella.

'Hello,' she said to Isobel. 'Nice to see you again. How are you settling in?'

'Well there's a lot to do,' Isobel replied. 'But we'll get there. Ella, this is Spencer Hargreaves. He was a friend of Vivien's and he owns the antiques shop at the bottom of the village. He's helping me with the house. Spencer, this is Ella, she works up at the Hall.'

Ella and Spencer shook hands.

'I'll see you around then,' Isobel said.

'Yes, do pop into the hotel for a coffee and let us know how you're getting on. We miss Vivien so much, but it'll be nice to get to know her granddaughter.'

'What was that she said about missing Vivien?' Spencer asked as they walked back towards the house.

'It's a bit weird actually,' Isobel said, telling him, as they walked back up the hill, what Ella had said that morning – about Vivien going up to the Hall for coffee, about the stories she told, about the photographs in the ballroom. 'It's been bugging me all morning,' she went on. 'Along with a lot of other things.'

'But she never liked Silverton Hall,' Spencer replied, brow furrowing. 'I didn't really know why, but she would never go. Always turned her nose up at going there for a cup of tea.'

'That's exactly what I thought.'

'Didn't really bother me, mind,' Spencer went on. 'Always seems like the sort of place where I'd have to iron a shirt to go so…' He shrugged, looking down at his rather scruffy attire.

'So she never told you about any parties either?'

'No, never. Mind you, I only moved here in the 1980s and didn't know her before then. Perhaps things were different when your grandfather was alive?'

'Ella said that it was my grandfather who took the photographs. I wonder if perhaps the Hall made her miss him all over again. Perhaps it made her sad to go up there?'

'She never spoke about Max much,' Spencer said. 'At least not to me.'

'Nor me. And Mum hardly ever talks about him either.'

Isobel stopped outside the house that now belonged to her and looked up at it.

What had life been like when Max Chambers was alive? Maybe the house would be able to answer some of the questions she'd been asking about her grandfather for years.

7

London – Winter 1952

'Perhaps I could come and visit you soon,' Max said to Vivien's father outside Lyons' Corner House as he hailed a cab for her parents. 'In Newbury Park.'

'Well you'd be welcome any time, Mr Chambers, any time,' Robert replied, shaking Max's hand vigorously as a cab pulled up at the kerb.

'Call me Max, I insist.'

Max leaned in to talk to the driver, paying him in advance. Vivien looked down at her shoes to hide the burning in her cheeks. She didn't know what she was more embarrassed about; her father's loud exuberance, her mother's insistence that they could afford a cab even though Max knew they couldn't, or the thought of Max – beautiful, polished, perfect Max – seeing the horrible flat in Newbury Park. For a moment she wished the paving stones of the Strand would open up and swallow her.

'Are you coming with us, Viv?' her father called and she looked up, shook her head.

'I thought I'd take Vivien to an exhibition,' Max said. 'If that's all right with you, Mr Burke.'

'Robert,' her father corrected him, wagging a friendly finger at Max as though they were the firmest of friends. 'You're to call me Robert and that's more than all right if that's what Vivien wants.'

Vivien nodded, still unable to find her voice and she watched her parents exchange a glance, so subtle only someone who knew them very well would notice. A glance that asked each other how this was happening, unable to believe their daughter's luck.

She watched as Max shut the doors of the black cab and waved them off. And she watched him turn back to her and smile.

'I'm sorry,' she said.

'For what?' Max asked, his forehead crinkling in concern.

'For my parents, they can be a little—'

'Charming and entertaining,' he interrupted with a smile. 'Stop worrying, Vivien. Your parents are fine, everything is fine, I think.'

'You do?' she asked nervously, not sure what was going on or where she stood.

He nodded and she was suddenly very aware of how close she was standing to him, of the warmth of him, the smell of him. Something tightened like a rubber band inside her.

'Why do you want to visit my father?' she asked, her voice small, almost inaudible.

'Well,' Max replied, turning to walk towards Piccadilly and holding out his arm to her so she could slip her hand into the crook of his elbow. 'I was going to ask him something, ask his permission if you will. But it's a question I should probably ask you first.'

Vivien swallowed, her fingers pressing into the wool of the sleeve of Max's coat.

He didn't look at her or stop walking. He didn't get down on one knee or take a ring box out of his pocket. He just asked her then and there as they walked down the street. It was as though they were simply talking about the weather.

'I was wondering if perhaps we should marry,' he said. It sounded stiff and formal, nothing like the proposals Vivien had read about or heard about from the handful of friends she had who were married or engaged. But Max was different to anyone she'd ever met before – he was rich and from a completely different class. He hadn't grown up in the East End listening to German bombs falling every night and wondering if it was his house that would be gone tomorrow. Perhaps this was how people like Max proposed. How would she know?

He stopped walking then and turned to her. 'Vivien, are you all right?' he asked. 'You've gone ever so pale and you haven't said anything for a while.'

'I haven't?'

'No.' He smiled his kind, gentle smile. 'Did you hear my question or is this just your way of letting me down gently?'

'No,' she said. 'No. I mean, yes… I…sorry…'

'Shall I ask again?'

She nodded, heard him inhale as the sound of hurrying footsteps passed them by.

'Vivien, I know we haven't known each other very long but I can't stop thinking about you. Will you marry me?'

It hadn't been how she'd expected – not that she'd ever

expected anything or thought much about marriage at all – but she heard her mother's voice in her ear and saw her father's self-satisfied wink in her mind's eye and she knew this wasn't the sort of thing that happened to girls like her very often.

'Yes,' she said with a lot more conviction than she felt. How could she say 'no' after all? Or even 'can I think about it'?

'Are you sure you're all right?' he asked, his smile fading and his brow furrowing again. 'I'm sorry, I've done this all wrong, haven't I? I've sprung it on you in the middle of a busy street. I just couldn't wait any longer to ask.'

'Really?'

'Really.'

'But you haven't shown any signs of…well…you know… and I…'

He offered her his arm again then, pulling her close as they continued their walk. 'I've done all of this wrong,' he said. 'Meeting you from work, not asking your father. I'm not very good with rules. I'm not really sure what I'm doing.'

She felt the rubber band inside her loosen. She knew then that she didn't love him, not in that head over heels way her friend Essie had talked about. But she liked him a lot and she enjoyed his company and, given time, she'd grow to love him, wouldn't she? Besides, if she married him she could get away from the confines of her parents' flat in Newbury Park and the endless letters that needed typing at Musgrove & Mortimer. Falling head over heels wasn't all it was cracked up to be anyway. The young man Essie had fallen for had disappeared one Saturday morning, never to be seen again.

'It's all right,' she said, squeezing his arm with her fingers. 'My parents aren't that big on rule following either. They won't mind. But we should probably start doing things properly now.'

Max nodded next to her. 'The first thing I need to do is to get you a ring,' he said.

He took her to the Royal Academy that afternoon and they didn't talk again about what had just happened on Coventry Street. Instead Vivien told Max about the last time she'd been to an art gallery with her aunt and how she hadn't much liked the portraits she'd seen there.

'Art is less about what you see,' he said. 'And more about how you feel when you see it.'

The exhibition was by somebody Max had been at the Slade with. 'I think you'll like it,' he said and as she walked around the exhibition space, listening to the sound of her shoes on the polished floors, she realised that she was looking at painting after painting of the sea; calm seas and golden sands, rough waves crested with white foam, storms in the middle of the ocean with ships bobbing about like so many matchsticks. She stood in front of each painting, taking in all the detail and, as Max had told her, trying to understand how what she saw made her feel. What she saw was the raw power of the ocean and what she felt was a latent excitement because, perhaps, marrying Max might mean that she could finally see the sea, finally leave London, finally…

'What are you thinking about?' Max whispered quietly in her ear, his breath making the hairs on the back of her neck stand on end.

'The sea,' she said. 'How wonderful and terrifying it must be.'

'I shall take you to see the real thing. We could go to the coast for our honeymoon and wake up every morning to the sound of the sea.'

When he painted that picture of married life, of waking up together, of the sound of the sea on their honeymoon, she thought she could come to love him quite easily after all. She took his hand and squeezed it gently.

'I'd like that very much.'

8

Norfolk – July 2019

The easiest thing, Nick told himself, was to try not to think about Isobel at all. If he kept his distance and kept busy, he could manage it. After all, he wasn't going to live in this village forever and as soon as he'd worked out where he was going to go, he could get back to forgetting her.

Just like he'd forgotten that kiss eighteen summers ago.

He sighed. He was as likely to forget her as he was to forget his own name.

'Definitely mice,' the pest control expert said (was he called Bill? Nick couldn't remember – he hadn't really been listening). 'Lots of mice. No rats, though, which is good for you.'

'Can you get rid of them?' Nick asked.

'Course I can, that's what you pay me for.'

'And how much will it cost?'

The pest control expert who may or may not have been called Bill (or was it Will?) quoted a price and Nick agreed.

He wasn't going to wait to get the OK from Isobel, he wasn't even sure if she would be able to afford it, he just knew that he had to do what he could to get the house habitable for her, he'd pay Bill-or-whatever-his-name-was himself. Nick knew how much this house meant to Isobel, or at least he used to know, and if it meant even a fraction of what Odds & Ends meant to him then he was going to make this work for her.

Which was why he was here early in the morning while Isobel was still asleep in his bed in the flat above the shop. He'd used his grandfather's key to let himself in and his book of contractors to help him out, because the sooner he could get this house fixed up, the sooner she could move in.

And the sooner he could work on forgetting her.

'I'll leave you to it,' he said to the pest control man. 'I've got a few other bits to do.'

He went back downstairs to his truck to bring in the dehumidifiers that he'd borrowed from a friend. He hoped the electrics were up to it. Once he'd sorted that out he'd take a look at the window frames Spencer had told him about.

He had been in Norwich the night before – he'd had a property to look at there, but it hadn't been urgent, hadn't warranted him rushing off from dinner like that and it certainly hadn't required him to be out all night. But he'd sat in his truck after viewing the house and he'd known that he couldn't go back, that he couldn't sleep under the same roof as her. Not yet. So he'd called Scott, an old friend from medical school who lived nearby, and asked if he could borrow his sofa for the night. He was one of the only friends Nick still had after Jeannette. All their other friends had turned out to be her friends.

'She's back then?' Scott had asked, handing Nick a beer when he'd arrived.

'She's back,' Nick had said softly. He'd told Scott weeks before that Isobel would be coming back, that she'd inherited the house from her grandmother and that she'd mentioned to Spencer she wanted to live there, wanted to start again. He'd wondered what had happened that meant she needed to start again.

'You'll have to see her sometime,' Scott had pointed out. 'It's a tiny village, you're bound to bump into each other.'

'We've already seen each other but bumping into each other at Grandad's shop is a bit different to sleeping under the same roof. I'm not ready for that. I need to tell her about…well…everything first.'

'So she doesn't know?'

Nick had gulped down his beer. 'She doesn't know anything.'

But Nick knew about Isobel. He knew that she'd been working as an art teacher for the last ten years, he knew that after she'd won that award something had happened and she'd hidden her talents away. He knew how much she loved her grandmother's house, how it was the only real home she'd ever known, and he knew that he'd do anything he could to turn it into the house of her dreams. Just as long as he didn't have to tell her about what had happened to him.

He knew it wasn't fair, he knew he couldn't avoid her for ever, but just the thought of admitting his failures to Isobel, the one person he felt had ever understood him, was more than he could stand.

So he'd help from a distance, avoiding her for as long as he could.

Because he knew Spencer wouldn't let him avoid her for ever.

He'd been up with the lark this morning, on the phone to his contacts as soon as he'd got his first coffee inside him and now, just after nine o'clock, he was only waiting on the window contractor.

It wasn't a job he could do himself – he was pretty good at a lot of things, but he had no formal qualifications in the trade and Victorian sash windows were way out of his league. Nick was the man who put up the money, who bought the run-down houses and did as much as he could before calling in the experts. He was starting to get a reputation for paying well and on time and some of the local building firms often bumped him up to the top of the job list.

Then, when the work was done, he would sell at a profit and start looking for another project to work on. It stopped him thinking too much about who he could have been, about what he should be doing.

He'd bought the first house on a punt when he was still signed off sick, when he and Jeannette were still living under the illusion that he would go back to the hospital one day. It had been a two-up two-down just outside of Ipswich and Nick had had enough savings to buy it outright. He'd sold it for double what he'd bought it for and had immediately moved on to the next house. He'd known then that he'd never go back, although he hadn't admitted it to Jeannette.

Perhaps he should have done, perhaps things would have worked out differently if he had.

He looked at the third finger of his left hand. He'd worn that ring for ten years before he'd taken it off last month. If he looked closely he could see the mark where it used to be, the slight difference in the tone of his skin. In a few more weeks it wouldn't be noticeable at all, as though his marriage had never happened. Wasn't it strange how you could be with somebody, dedicate your life to them, and then, suddenly, they weren't there?

He hadn't started flipping houses for the money, although he knew the sick pay wouldn't last for ever. He just had to do something. He'd started doing it because the physical work allowed his brain to switch off, to stop catastrophising and thinking about what might have been. His therapist had told him it would be a good stopgap for him, something to keep him busy until he was ready to go back to work.

But he knew there was no stopgap, there was no back to work. This was his work now.

He'd thought about taking some courses, evening classes in Cambridge or Peterborough perhaps, where he could learn parts of the trade properly – carpentry, electrics, plumbing. He looked at his hands again, hands that had been destined to be surgeon's hands but never were. Could he do it?

As he waited for the window contractor he started to walk slowly around Vivien's house – except of course it wasn't Vivien's house anymore, it was Isobel's. But nothing had changed, it still looked almost exactly as it had done eighteen years before – from the William Morris wallpaper in the hallway to the faded, yellowing doilies on the dark furniture. The house felt eternally stuck in the 1950s and although he knew Isobel loved that, to Nick it was a big red flag.

When he'd first come here as a teenager he'd thought Vivien's house was just a bit out of date, but now he knew it could be a disaster waiting to happen. What was the state of the wiring? The plumbing? He'd need to look into that and it would be an expensive job. Did Isobel know what she was getting herself into? It might be easier if she sold it to a developer and used the money to buy somewhere else.

Or you could just do it yourself for her, he thought. *Mates rates, trade prices.*

The doorbell rang then, saving him from himself, his thoughts and his memories, and Nick went to let the window contractor in.

'There's two options,' he said after Nick had shown him around, shown him the disintegrating state of the window frames. 'The house isn't in a conservation area, I checked, so you can go with uPVC. I find that if you use one of the darker colours they go quite well with these Victorian houses and they're very secure. We do a dark grey that would look good I think.'

'And the second option?' Nick asked. He had a feeling Isobel wouldn't want uPVC windows, that she'd want the house to look like it used to look when she was younger.

'Bespoke wood. But it will cost you. I can do you a couple of quotes if you like, but if you're going to sell I'd go with the uPVC. Most buyers don't care.'

Nick looked at the living room window they were standing next to and nodded thoughtfully. 'Can you make them secure temporarily, Kev?' he asked. 'I'm trying to make the place liveable before any big work happens.'

'Sure, but that's not like you? Don't you usually want a quick flip and move on?'

'Usually, yeah, but this isn't my house. I'm doing this as a favour for a…' He hesitated. 'A friend.'

Kev grinned at Nick. 'Understood,' he said, although Nick was pretty sure he didn't understand at all. 'So who does it belong to?'

Nick opened his mouth to explain, but before he could say anything he heard a footstep behind him.

'It belongs to me,' Isobel said. 'What's going on?'

9

'He's there right now?' Mattie asked.

Isobel leaned back against the tree at the bottom of the garden, the tree she and Nick used to sit in as teenagers, smoking secret cigarettes that Vivien probably knew all about. She looked towards the house as she pressed the phone to her ear.

'Yeah, he's inside talking to the ratcatcher.'

'Ratcatcher? Jesus, Izzy, where have you moved to? Hamelin?'

'Mice not rats,' Isobel replied.

'What?'

'The house has an infestation of mice, but they're being dealt with.'

'Urgh. How?'

'I don't want to think about it, to be honest, Mattie, but he isn't going to pipe them away I don't think.'

'Well make sure you pay him so he doesn't do whatever it was to the children of the village.'

Isobel laughed then. 'Nick's paid him, the kids are safe.'

'Nick paid him?' Isobel could almost hear her friend raising a sceptical eyebrow.

'He insisted and I don't really have any money yet; I need to see Mr Brecher.'

'He can't withhold your grandmother's money, Izzy.'

'I know, and he isn't. I just haven't been to see him to sign the paperwork yet. I will, I promise.'

'So Nick's back,' Mattie said, changing the subject. 'This is like your dream come true!'

'What?'

'You've never stopped talking about how much you want to live in Silverton Bay,' Mattie said. 'You've wanted it since I first met you.'

'I've wanted to live in the Bay for a long time,' Isobel replied, trying not to think too much about Adam – the reason she'd stayed in London for so long – and all the years she'd wasted on him.

'And now you can, and the boy who kissed you the summer before university is there too. It's just as well you didn't come back to Cambridge like I suggested or you'd never have met him again. It's very romantic.' For someone who was perpetually single, Mattie was obsessed with romance.

'It really isn't,' Isobel replied. 'He hardly speaks to me and he can barely look at me. I'm not even sure he remembers the kiss, to be honest.'

'He must remember the kiss. It's the kiss against which all other kisses have been judged.'

'Only in my head. I doubt he's been thinking of it all these years.'

'Why's he back, anyway?' Mattie asked. 'Why isn't he saving lives somewhere?'

'Well that's the mystery. All I know is that he quit medicine a couple of years ago and flips houses for a living now.'

'What? Why?'

'I've no idea. Spencer – you remember him from Nana's funeral?'

'Yeah, old guy, Nick's grandfather?'

'Well Spencer seems to think Nick will tell me the truth in time but I don't know…he's changed. Everything's changed.'

'We've all changed in the last eighteen years. I can't get into my size ten jeans anymore and when was the last time you drew or painted for pleasure?'

'Yesterday, actually.'

Mattie paused. 'Oh wow, Izzy, that's huge. What did you draw?'

'Um…oh…just the scenery,' Isobel replied, thinking of the sketch of Nick. It wasn't quite a lie, she supposed.

'Going back to Norfolk is definitely doing you good if you're drawing again.'

'Hmm… I suppose,' Isobel replied, only half listening as she watched the ratcatcher leave by the backdoor and head towards his van. He must have finished whatever it was he was here to do. She shuddered at the thought.

'What is it?' Mattie asked. 'I thought you'd be more excited about drawing again.'

'I am, really I am, it's just…' She paused, looked up at the house where the man who'd come to quote for the windows was tapping the frames on the second floor. 'It's Nick, he's just taken over and this is meant to be my house, my project.' It wasn't just Nick of course. There was so much she wanted to talk to Mattie about that she didn't know where to begin, but Nick was foremost in her mind right now.

When Isobel had arrived back at the house that morning, she'd been full of plans and hope thanks to a long chat with Spencer over breakfast. They hadn't talked about Nick, about his sudden, rude disappearance halfway through dinner the night before, or his absence at breakfast – the neatly folded pile of blankets on the sofa indicating that he hadn't been home at all. Isobel was pretty sure she was the reason for him not being there and it made her more determined than ever to get Little Clarion to a point where she could live in it. She couldn't stay with Spencer for ever, especially not if it forced Nick out of his home.

'You'll stay tonight though, love, won't you?' Spencer had said as she got ready to go back to the house. 'These workmen will all get on with the job quickly, I promise you that, but they won't get it done today.'

She'd nodded reluctantly, promising to be back that evening.

She'd tried not to think too much about Nick or the reasons for his absence as she walked back up the High Street towards the house, but as soon as she turned into the driveway she saw his truck, a red pick-up with 'Hargreaves House Renovations' painted on the side. If he had a branded truck then his business must be more serious than he made out. She'd wondered where that truck had been parked the previous day when she'd seen him at the shop. It was a shame that it hadn't been outside to give her a bit of heads up before seeing him for the first time in eighteen years. Not that she'd have immediately associated it with him. Nick was meant to be a doctor.

Two vans had been parked either side of Nick's truck and judging from the decals on the sides of them, one was to do with pest control and the other to do with window fitting.

What the hell? What was Nick doing here?

As soon as she'd entered the house she'd heard the faint humming of the dehumidifiers and had looked at the list of contractors Spencer had given her that morning. Nick had got there before her, but why? How was it that he couldn't stand to sleep under the same roof as her, but was perfectly happy to interfere in her grandmother's house?

She told Mattie all of this as she leaned against the tree. 'And when I arrived he was deciding what sort of windows would be best,' she said indignantly.

'Well, from what you've said he might know a little bit more about renovating old houses than you do.'

'But I want to choose my own windows. Whose side are you on anyway?'

'Izzy, I'm not on anyone's side,' Mattie said soothingly. 'I think he's probably just trying to help.'

'If he'd hung around last night or joined Spencer and me for breakfast he could have given me the benefit of his wisdom then. But instead he takes Spencer's key and lets himself into my house without saying a word.'

'Yeah, that is weird,' Mattie admitted. 'What's all that about, do you think?'

'No idea.'

Isobel suddenly felt all the fight go out of her. If what Spencer had told her was true, renovating Little Clarion was going to be a huge job and she didn't know if she was up to it, certainly not without expert help that she was pretty sure she couldn't afford. 'Perhaps you're right,' she reluctantly admitted to Mattie. 'Perhaps I should at least see what Nick has to say.'

She looked up and, as if on cue, saw Nick heading down the garden towards her.

'I get that he's being a bit rude and secretive,' Mattie was saying. 'But it wouldn't hurt to hear him out. It does sound as though he's sorted out your immediate problems for you.'

Mattie was almost always right. 'I guess,' Isobel huffed. 'But I have to go, he's heading this way.'

'I'll call you later,' Mattie replied. 'But tell me something. Is he still devastatingly good-looking at least?'

Isobel sighed. 'You have no idea,' she said as she hung up the phone.

'Kev wants to know what windows you've decided on,' Nick said as he approached, looking exactly as devastatingly attractive as Mattie had clearly hoped. 'He's got another job on today but says if you want uPVC he can do it this week but bespoke wood will take a little longer to make up...'

'I haven't decided,' Isobel said quietly as Nick waved a piece of paper that she presumed had the window quotes on it. 'I have no idea what I can afford.' She took the piece of paper and her stomach sank when she saw the numbers. 'But I don't think I can afford this.'

When she looked up at Nick and he looked away, she felt angry all over again.

'I never asked you to do this,' she snapped. 'You've taken Spencer's key and are basically trespassing on my property.

Why are you doing this anyway? So I don't have to stay at Spencer's anymore because you can't bear to have me there?'

She watched the tic in his jaw. 'No, Isobel, that's not the reason. And that wasn't the reason I left last night either.'

'Then what is the reason?'

He rubbed his eyes and turned to her. 'I just wanted to help. I know how much this house means to you.'

'And the reason for leaving last night?' Isobel asked, but Nick didn't reply to that. He just started to walk back the way he came.

'Nick,' she called after him and he turned around. 'I'm sorry. Thank you for dealing with everything this morning. I do appreciate it, of course, it was just a shock to see you here and...well...' She hesitated, feeling awkward suddenly.

Nick stepped back towards her. 'Like I said, I know how much this house means to you but I need to tell you something. I had a long look around this morning while I was waiting for Kev to get here and Grandad's right, there is a hell of a lot of work needs doing. I hate to say it but if money is tight then you might be better off selling. These kind of properties, even in this condition, can sell for a fortune—'

'I can't sell it, Nick,' she interrupted, explaining her grandmother's conditions.

'Really? Is that even legal?'

'I don't know. Nana's lawyer says it is.'

'Bloody hell, Vivien,' Nick whispered to nobody in particular. 'What were you thinking?'

They stood in silence for a moment and Isobel didn't really know what to say. It all seemed so hopeless and on top of that she had a strange feeling that she hadn't known her grandmother as well as she'd thought she had. These strange secretive codicils to her will, the photographs at Silverton Hall…

Her phone rang, suddenly shattering the early morning quiet.

'I have to take this,' Isobel said. 'It's Mr Brecher – Nana's lawyer. I've been waiting for his call.'

Nick nodded. 'OK, but you need to decide what to do, Isobel, the sooner the better.'

She couldn't stop thinking about Nick as she drove her car along the winding country lanes towards King's Lynn and Mr Brecher's office. Would she ever be able to get him out of her head? Nick Hargreaves had been in the back of her mind for eighteen years and she'd never really understood how she had been unable to forget him.

All her memories of Silverton Bay and her grandmother and even the house itself were tied up with memories of Nick – even though the Bay had a lifetime of memories entwined in it whilst Nick had only been around for ten short weeks. But for those ten weeks Nick and Isobel had been inseparable – she had never had a friend like that before or since. She'd known, about halfway through that long hot summer, that she was falling in love with him, falling in love for the first time, and she'd been sure he had felt the same. When he'd kissed her on that last day she'd known that he was her one – she'd still believed in things like that back then.

And yet she had never seen him again.

But he'd been there all along, taking up free rent in her head. Three years ago when her fiancé Adam – who she'd been with since her final year at Central St Martins, who she'd made so many plans with – had told her that he was leaving her because she no longer had any ambition or drive, the first person she'd thought about had been Nick. When Adam had told her he didn't want to marry an art teacher she'd thought *Nick would never have said that to me.*

She'd packed up and moved out a few days later – sofa surfing for weeks until she'd found a new teaching job and a room to rent in Cambridge where she'd be closer to Silverton Bay than she had been in east London. She and Mattie, the perpetually single owner of the flat, had got on immediately and it was Mattie's friendship and common sense that had helped Isobel get through the last three years as her grandmother suddenly grew very old and her own life seemed to be going nowhere fast.

And it had been Mattie who had been there for her when Vivien had died, Mattie who had distracted her from her endless memories.

She heard a car beep, waking her from her reverie and stopping her from thinking about Nick's kiss. She had to stop daydreaming so much. She was almost at the King's Lynn roundabout now and she could barely remember getting there.

She parked outside Mr Brecher's offices in the spot she'd been told would be reserved for her and, as she got out of

thought about it.' Isobel paused. 'I don't really know anything about my grandfather,' she said.

'Like I say,' Mr Brecher went on, clearly not wanting to get side-tracked by questions about the mysterious Max Chambers. 'Some of the money is tied up in stocks and shares but I thought perhaps cash would be more useful to you if you intend to renovate the house?'

'Well, yes, I suppose it would. How much cash are you talking about, though?' Isobel couldn't imagine it amounting to more than a few thousand pounds at best.

'I've set it all out here for you.' The lawyer turned the folder around and pushed it across the desk towards her. She stared at the figures in front of her.

'There's well over a hundred thousand pounds here,' she said quietly.

'That's just according to today's market, of course. It may fluctuate depending on when you want to cash it in.'

'I had no idea...' Isobel began. 'I don't really know how much house renovation costs. I don't really know anything, do I? I feel as though I've come into all of this blindfolded.'

'I think you'll find it's enough to get a good chunk of work done. Do you know anyone who can help you? Because if not I have some contacts.'

Isobel thought of Nick and his red truck. 'I know someone who won't rip me off, if that's what you mean,' she said.

After that it was just a matter of signing all the paperwork.

'The money should clear into your account in a week or two,' Mr Brecher told her.

'Thank you so much. I'm still in a bit of shock, to be honest.'

'I know the money won't bring your grandmother back or heal the pain, but I hope it helps a little. It's what Vivien would have wanted.'

Isobel sniffed and looked away, determined not to cry in the lawyer's office.

'There is one more thing,' Mr Brecher said, taking a long white envelope out of the back of the folder. 'She wanted me to give you this once we'd dealt with everything else. I believe it's a letter so you may want to read it when you are alone.'

Isobel took the envelope and turned it over. She recognised the neat copperplate handwriting on the front of it as her grandmother's. Just one word: `Isobel`. She felt a tear roll down her cheek and brushed it away, blinking again.

'When did you last see her?' Isobel asked.

'She asked me to go to the house a few days before she died. That's when she gave me that envelope. She had finalised her will a few months before that.'

'It's almost as if she knew.'

'Perhaps,' Mr Brecher replied in the tone of voice one would use with an overly imaginative child.

Isobel stood up to leave and the lawyer followed her to the door. Before she opened it, she turned back.

'Did you know my grandfather?' she asked.

Mr Brecher chuckled. 'No, no I was still at school when he passed away, I'm afraid.'

'Oh god,' Isobel said, feeling rather mortified. Obviously Mr Brecher wasn't much older than her own mother. 'I'm sorry, I didn't mean—'

'It's quite all right. While I never met your grandfather,

this firm and my predecessor did act for him – for both him and Vivien in fact – for many years. My predecessor is no longer with us, sadly, but…' He paused and looked back towards his desk. 'Well, I wonder… Mr Chambers would have used this firm to buy the house in the first place, I suspect.'

'When was that?

'1953, I think, not long after he and Vivien married.'

'It's always been a bit of a mystery why they moved out of London,' Isobel said. 'Mum never seemed to know and Nana would never talk about it. She always just said they wanted to get away from the smog.'

'We have a strongroom on site,' Mr Brecher went on. 'In the basement. We keep important documentation there. I wonder if there's any information on when your grandfather bought the house, correspondence, letters, even which agent he used. There might be something of interest connected with your house there.'

Isobel felt that small, warm tingling sensation in her belly when Mr Brecher said 'your house'. This really was the beginning of something new.

'Would you like me to dig out the papers?' he asked.

'If you think there's something there I'd definitely be interested,' Isobel said. 'I know next to nothing about my grandfather. But there's no hurry, just next time you're in the basement.'

Isobel bid the lawyer goodbye and went back out into the street, clutching the letter in her hand.

*

My darling Isobel

By now you should have a full understanding of everything that I am leaving to you and I thought perhaps I should explain why, and why I have left some rather odd instructions from beyond the grave.

Don't worry, I'm not going to haunt you or anything if you don't follow them to the letter, (Isobel smiled to herself at that as she sat in her car outside the solicitor's office in King's Lynn, hearing her grandmother's voice in her ear and remembering talking to Spencer about Vivien haunting her.) *but hear me out at least before you make any final decisions*.

You're drifting, my love. I've been watching it happen for a while - watching you as you've stopped drawing, stopped painting, watching as you became a shell of who you used to be. I've seen it before in your mother - before she met your father - and in myself after Max died. I want you to be able to find yourself again, Isobel.

I've left you everything because I think, right now, you have nothing. Your mother has everything she needs, but you need an opportunity for a fresh start in a place I know you love.

I'm asking you not to sell for thirteen months for a reason. The number thirteen I plucked out of the air (unlucky for some, I suppose), but I do want you to wait before making any big decisions. It's tempting, I know, with today's property prices, to want to put the house on the market, to take the money and run but, in my experience, when people are at their lowest ebb they need more than money to haul themselves out of it.

Your mother would say that it's better to be miserable in comfort – and I suppose she's right in a way. If my plan doesn't work out then the house is yours to sell next year. Mr Brecher will help you with the conveyancing.

When your grandfather died I was beside myself – I'd never felt so low. Financially he left me very well off but it was living in the village that saved me in the end. Friendship and community brought me back to who I used to be and now I want to offer that same gift to you – a reason to stay in the village, a reason to find the person you used to be again.

Spencer will help you in any way you need, and he already knows that I've instructed you to ask him. And I think you'll find his grandson will be willing to lend a hand if you ask. He's grown into a very handsome young man! You remember Nick though, of course you do.

That's enough rambling from your old

nana, I think. What you do now is up to you, Isobel.

Sending you love from wherever I am now.

Isobel sniffed, wiping the tears from her cheeks with the back of her hand. She carefully folded the letter and put it back in the envelope. Then she turned the key in the ignition and headed back towards Silverton Bay.

She knew what she had to do now.

10

Meet me by the lighthouse at seven.

It had been over an hour since he'd texted those words, getting Isobel's mobile phone number from Spencer, and he'd heard nothing back. Now it was seven and he was waiting on the clifftop outside the lighthouse – the lighthouse that had become one of the most expensive Airbnbs Nick had ever heard of – with two portions of piping hot haddock and chips tucked under his arm. Did she still eat fish and chips? Would she want to come down to the beach with him? Would she come at all?

They'd met every morning at the lighthouse all those summers ago when he'd promised himself each day that he wouldn't fall in love with her and each day he'd fallen for her a little bit more. Hearing her voice again in his grandfather's shop had brought back so many memories that he'd tried so hard to forget, memories he'd only ever allowed himself to think about when he'd really needed to in those dark hours he'd spent in the desert, the sound of bombs falling somewhere in the distance. Those memories had got him through.

He wanted to help her, to restore her house to its former glory so she could live there happily ever after and he would know where she was, that she had the life she'd always wanted. But he'd found that he wanted to do it without actually talking to her, without asking her permission or advice, because it was easier to remember her as the eighteen-year-old that she used to be rather than the woman she'd become.

There was something about her now that made him think she was as unhappy as he was and he wasn't sure he would be able to cope with anyone else's unhappiness.

'Hey,' she said, appearing in front of him suddenly. She'd always had a habit of doing that, popping up from nowhere and interrupting his thoughts – which were usually about her. He never heard her coming.

'Hey,' he replied, dropping his eyes so he didn't have to look at her. He held up the fish and chips packages.

'Is that what I think it is?' she asked. When he looked at her again she was grinning. Hopefully that meant she still loved fish and chips as much as she used to.

'Haddock and chips,' he said. 'Think of it as a peace offering, an apology.'

She cocked her head on one side, blonde ponytail swinging behind her. She was wearing a flowing white top and dark trousers. She'd changed since he'd seen her earlier, since she'd come back from seeing the lawyer, and he noticed her toenails in her flips-flops were painted a pearly pink that matched her lip gloss. She suddenly seemed so much younger than she was, as though the years had disappeared.

'An apology for what?' she asked.

'For trespassing on your property. For trying to take over

a renovation you hadn't even decided on yet.' He knew it was the wrong thing to do, however much he might want to do it. He had to let her decide what to do about the house. He wondered what she'd talked about with the lawyer, whether they'd found a loophole that meant she could sell up and move on. He very much didn't want her to leave.

'You're forgiven.' She smiled, reaching for a packet of food.

'You still like fish and chips then?' he asked.

'Love them. I haven't had any in ages though. They always taste better by the sea, don't you think?'

'Would you like to walk down to the beach to eat them?'

He noticed her hesitate.

'Grandad said you hadn't been to the beach since you arrived.'

She shrugged. 'I've been busy and...' She paused. 'It sounds silly, but it feels strange going to the beach without Nana.'

'We can sit over there instead,' he said, pointing to the row of benches that looked out from the clifftop over the sea.

She shook her head. 'No, let's eat on the beach. I haven't moved to the seaside to avoid the beach for the rest of my life.' She started to walk away from him then, towards the cliff path, but then she stopped, looked back over her shoulder and smiled at him. The agitation he'd been feeling since he first sent her the text finally settled. He hadn't realised how nervous he'd been about seeing her properly again; about the offer he was going to make. But that smile made him think that perhaps everything would be all right.

It was a beautiful, calm summer's evening and the tide was out. Nick watched the light motes reflecting on the

the car, wished she'd taken the time to get changed before she left. Jeans and a t-shirt just didn't seem suitable attire for an appointment with a solicitor. She thought of Vivien again, of how she had always dressed smartly for every appointment, even putting on her signature red lipstick for a trip to the doctor's surgery.

'Hello, Ms Malone,' Mr Brecher said as Isobel arrived. 'Lovely to see you again. How are you getting on at the house?'

'It will need a bit of work,' Isobel replied diplomatically.

'Well come in and sit down. I have some news I think might help you.'

Isobel sat down opposite her grandmother's lawyer and rested her hands on the desk that sat between them.

'We just need to go through the final paperwork,' Mr Brecher said, opening a buff-coloured folder. 'Your grandmother's financials and then signing off the probate.'

'Her financials?' Isobel asked, curious. She hoped there weren't any nasty surprises lurking in there.

'Yes. Mrs Chambers had some substantial savings and a handful of rather successful stocks and shares.'

'She did?' Isobel had always known her grandmother had enough money to get by – a teaching pension and a mortgage-free house – but she certainly hadn't thought it to be in the region of 'substantial savings'.

Mr Brecher nodded. 'You never knew your grandfather, did you?' he asked.

'No, he died while my mother was still a child.'

'He came from a rather wealthy family. When he died he left your grandmother very well looked after.'

'I...well... I suppose that makes sense. I never really

surface of the sea as they walked down towards the beach. He took a deep lungful of the sea air and tried to imagine the ozone and negative ions washing away the last three years. He wanted to start again like his therapist had talked about, but he didn't know how.

Isobel sat down in the sand dunes and slid off her flip-flops, wiggling her bare feet in the sand as she unwrapped her fish and chips, and Nick followed suit. It was good to feel the sand between his toes and he wondered why he didn't come down to the beach more often. He passed her one of the little wooden forks the chip shop had given to him.

'Grandad says you're an art teacher,' he said.

She nodded, swallowed. 'Mmmm, was an art teacher. I quit when I found out about the house. I've just finished up my final term, although I'm starting to think it was a mistake.'

'Quitting?' he asked. 'Or teaching in the first place?' He couldn't imagine her as a teacher – he couldn't imagine all that creative energy being muffled by the confines of the National Curriculum.

'Maybe both,' she replied quietly.

'I was surprised to hear you went into teaching.'

'It was Dad's idea. He thought I should get a proper job so I went and did my PGCE.' She sighed as though she knew it had been a mistake back then and then she looked at him, squinting against the sun that hovered over the horizon. 'How do you know all this anyway?'

'Grandad told me in his letters.'

'He writes you letters?'

'He did until I moved in with him. One letter a week for the last god knows how many years – just village gossip and so on.' He shrugged, trying to sound nonchalant. He didn't want to give away how much those letters had meant to him over the years, a little bit of connection back to the Norfolk coast when he was miles away in the midst of unimaginable situations. He didn't want her to see how much he longed for those letters, for them to give him another snippet of Isobel's life. 'He told me about the portrait award.'

'Oh that,' Isobel said, turning to look out towards the sea. 'That was nothing.' But it hadn't been nothing, not if what Spencer had told him was correct. Vivien had been bursting with pride for her granddaughter, Spencer had said. It was a hugely prestigious award to win, especially for an artist as young as Isobel had been. What had happened to make her just brush it under the carpet like this? To turn to teaching, the 'proper job' her father wanted her to have instead? What wasn't she telling him?

Probably about as much as you're not telling her, he thought and decided to change the subject before she asked him again why he wasn't a doctor anymore.

'How did it go with the lawyer?' he asked.

Her face lit up then as she turned back towards him. 'Very surprising news,' she said. 'My grandmother had stocks and shares!'

'Really?'

'I know, can you imagine? I mean, I suppose she must have had money put away somewhere but I never really thought about it. Anyway, the good news is that she's passed them to me along with the house and...well...they'll definitely help with the renovations that I'm going to need to have done.'

She seemed more positive about the house than she had

been earlier, as though renovating it was a real possibility rather than a pipe dream. Nick wondered if she realised how much work was going to be involved.

'Well that's a relief,' he said.

'God, Nick, I was so worried when both you and Spencer told me what needed to be done. I've wanted to live in Silverton Bay for my whole life, I've dreamed of the day when I could move back for years, but now it's come at the sacrifice of losing Nana I wasn't sure if it was worth it, especially when I saw the state of the house. Be careful what you wish for, I guess.'

'Do you still want to live here?' he asked tentatively.

'As I was driving into King's Lynn this afternoon I really wasn't sure, everything felt as though it was falling apart. But then Mr Brecher, Nana's lawyer, gave me something else as well. A letter that she'd written to me.'

Nick thought, for a moment, about the letter he'd written to Isobel eighteen years ago. A letter to which she had never replied.

'What did it say?' he asked.

'It sort of explained why she'd left me the house. It was really helpful and made me realise that my doubts were just fears and that if I wanted to start again and make my dreams come true I had to step through the fears and get on with fixing up the house.'

'And you can afford to do that now too.'

'Absolutely and I don't have to beat myself up for quitting my job without considering the consequences. Dad wasn't very happy about that when he found out, but I hated that job so much…' She paused, looking out to sea again. 'I shouldn't have taken all of my worries and frustrations out on you this morning though,' she said after a while. 'I'm sorry, Nick, I know you were only trying to help.'

'It's OK,' he said, forgiving her instantly – not that there'd been anything to forgive. He'd been the one at fault after all, taking her keys and interfering like that. 'I can still help if you want me to.'

'I do want you to. But it's not a favour, OK? I want to pay my way. It's my house and my responsibility. You shouldn't be calling in favours for me.'

He wanted to tell her that he didn't mind, that he'd make the whole house beautiful for her and not charge her a bean, but how could he tell her that without telling her he still had feelings for her? So instead he offered her a compromise.

'At least let me do you mates rates,' he said. 'Grandad would kill me if I didn't.'

'Deal,' she replied, smiling and holding out her hand. He took it, holding it for a little too long, just as he had done on the morning he had first met her. 'What happens next?' she asked as he finally let her go.

'We look around the house together and you tell me what you want doing. I'll tell you if it's possible and then I'll work out a quote for you.'

'Sounds like a plan,' she said and he noticed her shiver. 'I'd forgotten how chilly it gets in the evenings on the beach when the sun starts to set. I should have brought a jumper.'

Nick untied the hoodie from around his waist and passed it to her. She tried to refuse but he pressed it into her hand.

'Thank you,' she said as she wrapped it around her shoulders.

They sat quietly together then, their fish and chips finished and for a moment it felt as though the intervening years had slipped away and they were eighteen again, their whole lives in front of them.

'I'm glad you're here,' Isobel said.

And suddenly he was glad he was here too, almost as glad as he had been eighteen years ago.

11

The next morning, Isobel and Nick stood outside Little Clarion trying to decide where to start.

It was a beautiful house, double-fronted and built from red brick sometime in the late 1880s. There were two huge bay windows either side of the front door. Isobel remembered that Vivien had always bought and decorated two Christmas trees to stand in those windows. 'We don't want one of them feeling left out, do we?' she used to say. It stood on a quarter acre of land with gravel pathways leading to the garden beyond.

During the summer months, when the dogwood that lined the front boundary of the property was in full bloom, the house was especially striking. The glorious scent of the flowers caught on the wind and reminded Isobel of summers past. She wondered if Nick felt the same.

Even from this distance though she was aware of how much the house had fallen into disrepair. The peeling blue paint on the front door and the crumbling window frames were easily visible from the driveway. The wisteria over the front door had grown out of control and Isobel already knew that there were vines creeping up the back of the house that were probably damaging the brickwork. She sighed at the thought of the work ahead of them.

'Don't worry,' Nick said. 'I know it seems like a lot, but houses have a certainty about them. With the right skills and equipment, they can be fixed.'

'Is that why you do what you do now?' Isobel asked.

'Sort of,' he replied, moving away from her as though telling her not to pursue that line of enquiry any further. She'd noticed how he dodged it whenever she so much as vaguely brought it up and she needed him on her side to get this huge project underway, so she dropped it, putting a pin in her questions until another time.

'Where do you want to start?' he asked.

'With the windows,' she replied. 'I haven't thanked you properly for all you did yesterday.'

Nick nodded and Isobel was grateful that he didn't remind her how defensive she had been. She'd made a decision the previous night as she lay in Nick's bed above Odds & Ends, after they'd eaten their fish and chips on the beach and had walked back to Spencer's together, not to fight him, not to try to control something she had no knowledge of. If what Spencer had told her was true, Nick knew what he was doing and he certainly had all the contacts she needed. She had to learn to go with it if she wanted to live in the house. She had to stop trying to keep Little Clarion exactly as it was, as some sort of shrine to her grandmother. The whole place was going to fall down around her ears otherwise.

'Now I've got more idea of the budget I'm working with,' she said. 'I'd like the bespoke windows, I think. They're more in keeping with the house.'

'I agree,' Nick replied, tapping something into his phone. 'I'll see when Kev can come back to us on that.'

Isobel walked up to the front door and ran her hand over the peeling paint. 'Will we need new doors as well?' she asked

'No, it's pretty sturdy that door. Just a fresh coat of paint should do the trick. Any ideas on a colour scheme?'

'I heard Kev suggesting a dark grey for the window frames, which sounded nice, so perhaps a lighter grey for the door.'

Nick tapped away on his phone again. 'Shall we go inside?' he asked, looking up at her.

Isobel took her key out of her handbag and slid it into the front door lock, as she had done every evening as a teenager when the school bus dropped her off on the corner of the lane. She was grateful that Nick was letting her unlock the door herself today – he hadn't even brought Spencer's key with him, she'd seen it hanging on a hook with the other keys in the kitchen when they'd left after breakfast. A breakfast that Nick had joined them for this morning – as though the fish and chips on the beach had been a truce for both of them.

'This house has so much potential,' Nick said as he followed Isobel into the hallway. He was standing so close she could feel his breath on her neck, and it made her shiver. She closed her eyes for a moment and breathed in the house. 'There's so much you could do to it,' he went on as he walked past her and started tapping on the walls. 'You could open up the whole back of the house, make it much lighter and airier or...' He stopped, turning around to look at her. 'I'm guessing by the look on your face that's not an option.'

She laughed and looked away. 'I'm sorry, is it that obvious?'

'Just a bit!'

'I know it needs modernising, Nick. I know I can't keep it exactly how Nana had it, but I don't want it to look too modern, you know? I don't want it to look like the flat my parents had in London, or their ghastly apartment in New York.'

'You want to keep some of the original features, keep it soft and slightly vintage-y,' Nick said, nodding. 'Old-fashioned taps and a butler sink in the kitchen, a range rather than a modern oven, a free-standing bath in the main bathroom?'

'Yes.' She turned and smiled at him. Perhaps he would understand, perhaps he would be able to help her. 'This is a house for me to live in, not a project to sell and make a profit.'

Nick opened his mouth and she held up her hand to stop him. 'I know what you're going to say, I know how much money I could make, but I'm not going to sell. OK?'

'OK.'

'I hadn't really thought about what I wanted to do to the house before I arrived because I hadn't thought it would need anything much doing to it other than a lick of paint or something. But last night, after we'd talked, I couldn't stop thinking about it. I have this idea of how I want it to look, but I don't know how to describe it.'

'Do you think you could draw it for me?' Nick asked.

Isobel thought about the sketchpad that she had only managed to open once since Vivien had died, and the sketch of Nick on the first page. She felt her face heat at the thought of it. 'I could try,' she said, although she had no idea if she'd be successful. She ran her hand over the old, faded William Morris wallpaper that lined the walls of the hallway. 'I'd like to keep some things like Nana had them though. I always loved this wallpaper but it looks so worn. Can you still get this design?'

Nick nodded. 'It's called "Strawberry Thief". You can still buy it, but it's not cheap.'

'It's only a small hallway though and it would be like remembering Nana every time I come home.'

Nick smiled warmly. 'Then your wish is my command,' he said. 'I guess that means we won't be knocking any of these walls through, then?'

'Not in the hallway, no, but that doesn't mean I'm completely averse to the idea.'

'Come into the kitchen then and let me show you what we could do there.'

But Isobel hesitated, standing in the hallway, her fingers still tracing the patterns of the Strawberry Thief wallpaper.

'Don't take this the wrong way,' she said quietly. 'But how long do you think it will be before I can move in? I don't want to stay at Spencer's indefinitely.'

He stepped away from her a little then, his smile fading. 'You don't have to move out until you're ready,' he said. 'I don't mind sleeping on the couch.' She had thought, considering how he'd spent the first night away from the shop because of her, that he would have been as eager for her to leave as she was. Even after their fish and chip truce, there was still an awkwardness between them like a kiss-shaped elephant in the room. Although it might only be her who remembered the kiss as anything other than a passing teenage moment.

'I don't want to be any trouble,' she said, turning her attention back to the crimson wallpaper, her fingers tracing the outlines of the birds and flowers that adorned it.

'You're no trouble, Isobel. Grandad loves having you around.'

And you, Nick? Isobel wondered. *What do you think?*

'It's not just that though,' she went on. 'I need to move in here properly, I need to feel as though I'm doing something with my life, as though I have some sort of direction.'

Nick laughed humourlessly. 'Well I do understand that,' he said, and Isobel turned to look at him, catching his eye. He held her gaze for a moment as though they were both daring each other to talk about the past, but neither of them did and Nick looked away first.

'We'd need to make sure the windows are secure for you,' he said.

'Is that really necessary?' Isobel asked. 'I mean, Nana was living here for years with the windows like this and it's not as though anyone will break in. I bet people still leave their front doors unlocked around here, don't they? And it's summer so I won't be cold.'

As if on cue, Nick's phone buzzed. 'Well you might be in luck,' he said as he looked at the screen. 'Kev's coming over later this morning.' He paused, putting the phone in the back pocket of his jeans. 'Where were you thinking of sleeping?'

'In my old room at the top of the house.'

'That will probably be OK now we've dealt with the mice

and the dehumidifiers are doing their work. Shall we go up and have a look? I can check the water pressure for you?'

As she followed him up the narrow stairs towards the top of the house, she couldn't help but remember her grandmother again. Vivien had never issued many rules whilst Isobel lived with her but during that summer when Isobel and Nick had first met – the first boy Isobel had ever been interested in, had ever brought home – she had been adamant that Nick was never to go up to Isobel's bedroom with her.

'Be careful,' she'd said, an edge of warning and fear in her voice. 'Don't do anything stupid that could get you in trouble. You have your whole life in front of you, Isobel, don't do anything you might regret.'

Isobel still wasn't sure whether she regretted that kiss or not.

The top floor was the only part of the house that Vivien had ever had any work done to. When it was decided that Isobel was to come and live with her, she announced that a teenaged girl needed her own space (although Isobel had always suspected that it was more a case of Vivien needing space from a teenage girl) and a builder was brought in from King's Lynn to do something with the top floor of the house that had barely been used since Gina had moved out over twenty years before. The builder turned the two empty rooms into a bedroom, a study and a bathroom and Isobel got to choose the colour scheme. It had felt like the most exciting, grown-up thing that had ever happened in her fifteen years on the planet.

'No one ever built me my own bathroom,' Gina had sniffed when she heard about it.

'I had to practically drag you to get washed as a teenager,' Vivien had bitten back. 'What would you have wanted with your own bathroom?' Isobel had winced at yet another row brewing and had immersed herself in the folder of paint colour sheets that the builder had given to her.

The rooms on the top floor remained virtually unchanged – still painted in shades of blue and purple and white that fifteen-year-old Isobel had chosen, although the colours were muted with age now. Isobel sat down on the bed and tried to think about the last time she'd slept here. She used to come back in the university holidays and then for occasional weekends after she had graduated until she and Adam had moved in together – something Vivien hadn't altogether approved of. On the few occasions that Isobel had visited Silverton Bay with Adam – few because Adam had never liked being away from London and his art studio – Vivien had made up separate rooms for them on the first floor, saying they'd be more comfortable there. But Isobel had suspected it was more to do with keeping an eye on them. She'd always been so strict about boys and bedrooms.

It must have been over a decade then since she'd last slept in this room. She took a breath as she remembered the dreams that she'd had, the future that she'd thought about in this room. If she closed her eyes she could still see the art prints she had put up on the walls, her old desk, the messy piles of books and CDs that littered every surface.

Did she really want to sleep up here surrounded by so many memories?

'Well the shower is working well,' Nick said, walking into the room and interrupting her thoughts. He stopped abruptly and stepped back a little so he was back on the landing.

'What?' Isobel asked.

'The shower's working,' he repeated.

'Not that. Why did you step back then?'

Nick smiled, his face colouring a little. 'Well I'm not supposed to come up here, am I?'

'I think we're both a bit old to worry about that.'

'Vivien wouldn't think so and she might be watching.' He shrugged. 'You never know.'

Isobel opened her mouth to tell him about how it wasn't just him, how Adam had been made to sleep in a separate room, but then she shut it again, realising she couldn't face telling Nick about Adam any more than she could face talking about the other failures in her life. The silence felt awkward again – that kiss-shaped elephant awkwardness.

'What will you do, Isobel?' he asked suddenly into the silence. He was leaning on the doorframe with his arms crossed again. 'Will you teach still?'

'I haven't decided yet,' she confessed quietly. 'I worked my term's notice in Cambridge and I packed up and came here.' She paused, thinking about how most of her stuff was still in the boot of her car. 'I probably should have thought about this whole thing more carefully – found a job, checked the house was habitable...' She put her hand to the back of her neck where strands of hair had fallen out of her bun. 'I feel like a bit of an idiot.'

'You're not an idiot,' Nick replied. 'You were just eager to move here – I can see that much in your face whenever you talk about it.' He relaxed a little. 'Something will turn up, it always does.'

'I've got some savings, and the money Vivien left of course, but most of that's going to get eaten up by the house.'

'Look, Isobel, you don't have to pay me upfront or anything. We can work out a payment plan if you want me to help renovate this house. It's fine, I'll be doing it at cost anyway and—'

'It's not fine, Nick.' Isobel sighed. She felt uncomfortable taking handouts from a man she hadn't seen for eighteen years. A man she knew virtually nothing about. Why was he being so secretive?

Nick shrugged, thrusting his hands into his pockets and turning away from her a little. 'Like I say, something will come up and once the windows are sorted out you can at least move in.'

'Tonight?' she asked.

'If that's what you want.' She could see the tension across his back and shoulders and she wondered why. He'd be glad to get his bed back, surely?

'I'd forgotten about this painting,' he said. 'It used to hang in the dining room, didn't it?'

Isobel stood and walked onto the small landing outside her bedroom door. This was where the portrait of Vivien hung. The one of her in the blue dress. The one that Isobel's grandfather, the man nobody ever spoke about, painted in the 1950s. Isobel wasn't a huge fan of oil paintings, but this had always captured her imagination and had taught her more about how portraits should be painted than any class she'd ever attended. Her grandfather had managed to paint so much more than an image of Vivien. When she looked at it, she almost felt as though her grandmother was in the room with her. Max had managed to preserve the very essence of Vivien, as though he had painted her soul on to the canvas.

Now Isobel knew that he had painted it from the photograph that he'd taken of Vivien at the Silverton Hall Midsummer Party and she knew that the photograph had been taken the summer before Gina had been born. That explained the angle that Vivien was standing at of course, with her back to the camera and looking over her shoulder, so that her pregnancy bump couldn't be seen. She wondered what the dress looked like from the front and if it had been cleverly cut to make the pregnancy as discreet as possible.

It had always been Vivien's smile that Isobel thought Max had captured so well in the portrait. There was something so bewitching about that smile and it always made Isobel wonder who or what Vivien was smiling at. It almost made her want to look over her own shoulder to see if she could catch sight of it herself.

'Nana had it hung up here a few years ago,' Isobel said. 'She claimed she didn't want to look at it anymore, didn't want to think about what she used to look like, so she had it brought up here. She never came to the top floor of the house.'

'That's so sad,' Nick said quietly.

'I thought so too,' Isobel replied. 'Nana never really talked about my grandfather no matter how much I asked. Something happened between them before he died, I'm sure of it, and I have no idea what.' She swallowed and looked at Nick's profile. His hands were still in his pockets and he looked straight ahead at the oil painting in front of him. It was an amazing likeness and captured so much of Vivien's spirit, of her energy – a certain something that she had never lost, even when she became very old.

'It's painted from a photograph my grandfather took at a party,' Isobel said quietly. She wanted to tell Nick what she'd seen in the ballroom at Silverton Hall. He'd known Vivien too and she wanted to know what he thought.

'I never knew that,' he replied.

'Nor did I, until Monday morning.'

12

Nick watched as Isobel gazed at the portrait of her grandmother and wondered again about Isobel's own painting career. She had twice the talent of her grandfather as far as he could tell – although, admittedly, what did he know? – but something had stopped her, something had made her lose her confidence and hide behind a career in teaching and he knew it wasn't her father who had done that. She'd told him, that summer, of her father's reservations about going to art school in the first place and she hadn't listened to him then.

She kept saying the move back to Silverton Bay was a fresh start, and he understood that. But it felt more as though she was retreating back into the nostalgic, rose-tinted memories of her childhood and he could tell she was finding it very hard to let go of the image of Vivien's house exactly as she remembered it. He'd seen this before when he'd helped other people renovate their homes. Other people's nostalgia got in the way of a house's potential and every house deserved to live up to its potential.

He had so many ideas of what could be done with Vivien's house – how it could be opened up and modernised without losing its charm, but it felt as though Isobel didn't want to think about that – all she wanted was new Strawberry Thief wallpaper. And he was breaking his own vow. He was working on somebody else's house.

But working with Isobel was different, wasn't it? She had the artistic vision to really see what this house could become if she could let go of the past. If he could just make her see it, he knew she'd be as excited as he was.

He'd been surprised when he'd realised that renovating houses excited him so much, that watching the new house rise phoenix-like from the ashes of the old could give him such a thrill, such a sense of purpose. And he'd been surprised to discover, when he'd finished his first house-flip, that he'd never felt that thrill or that sense of purpose during his medical career, not once. Not even when things had gone right, not even on the day that a woman had thrown herself into his arms after he'd saved her son's life.

He'd come to understand that you knew where you were with houses. As his grandfather said, houses could be fixed no matter how bad it all looked. He remembered the sixteenth-century cottage he'd bought in Suffolk a year or so ago. It had fallen into such disrepair that it was barely fit for housing livestock, but with the right contractors, with the help of specially skilled craftsman and the local thatcher, they'd brought it back to its former glory. It had ended up costing a small fortune and more than once Nick had rued the day he'd ever clapped eyes on the cottage, but it sold for over a million pounds to a family from London – a lawyer and his wife, and their two blonde children who were about to start private school in Cambridge – and he'd realised this was what lit him up, that perhaps Spencer had been right and medicine had been his father's dream after all.

There was a certainty about houses that you just didn't get in people. All too often people couldn't be fixed, no matter how hard you tried. Houses just stood benignly, looking beautiful or ugly, housing families or groups of itinerant tenants, storing up history in their walls.

People, on the other hand, were unpredictable, thankless, emotional.

People did despicable things to one another.

And people kept secrets – like the one he was keeping from Isobel, like the one he was almost certain she was keeping from him, and like the one Vivien seemed to have taken to her grave with her. He wondered if Isobel had any idea at all.

'I saw the photograph that my grandfather must have painted this portrait from up at Silverton Hall on Monday,' she said to him now.

'Silverton Hall?' he repeated quietly. His mouth felt dry saying the words. He hadn't been up to the old Hall in years – it was too full of memories for that. Memories of his mother holding his hand and teaching him about Jacobean architecture and the family who used to own it, memories of long walks with Bertha, his grandfather's old dog, and memories of a kiss that he'd carried with him for half his life.

She didn't say anything for a while, just stood and stared at the painting until she suddenly looked away and stepped aside, as though someone had clicked their fingers and she'd come out from a hypnotic trance.

'I remember Vivien not really liking the old Hall,' he said. 'Called it an eyesore, but it was all boarded up that summer that I lived with Grandad, so—'

'She never wanted to go there even after it reopened,' Isobel interrupted, turning towards him. 'Whenever I suggested afternoon tea or something, she refused, but—'

'But what?'

She turned to Nick and told him what she had learned about Vivien and Max at Silverton Hall, about the parties and the photographs.

'She never mentioned anything about it to you?'

'Never. I'd have loved to have heard glamorous stories like that, but…' She looked away from him. 'It was a long time ago, I suppose, when my grandfather was still alive. Perhaps Nana didn't want to remember.'

'Have you asked Grandad?' Nick asked, wondering if Spencer knew anything – if Vivien had ever told him.

'He seemed as surprised as I was when I told him,' Isobel replied. 'Like us, she always told him she didn't like the Hall. Found it all a bit stuffy. Which, now I've stayed there, turns out to also be untrue. It's really laidback and friendly.'

'When did your grandparents move to Norfolk?' Nick asked.

'In the early spring of 1953 I think, not long after they got married. They both wanted to get out of London and Nana had always dreamed of seeing the sea, so Max brought her here. What little I know about my grandparents is terribly romantic. They met during the Great Smog in the autumn of 1952 and were married by March. Mum was born in the August, so it doesn't take a maths genius to work out why they had such a short engagement.' Nick watched her pause for a moment, her index finger tapping against her top lip as she turned back towards the oil painting of Vivien. 'I wonder if that's the real reason they moved to Norfolk though – so people didn't ask too many questions about the due date.'

She didn't know.

A couple of years ago, when he'd been visiting Spencer, when he'd been at rock bottom with no idea what to do with himself and no idea whether or not his body would betray him again, he'd overheard a conversation – the tail end of it at least – between Vivien and his grandfather. Even now, when he remembered what he'd heard, it almost made him catch his breath.

He had still been waking up in the middle of the night then from dreams where he could hear the bombs as clearly as if he was back there. He would shift from sleep to wakefulness so swiftly that one moment he was dreaming and the next he was sitting up in bed screaming, covered in sweat, the sheets like ropes around his legs and so he'd questioned what he'd heard ever since. He couldn't trust his mind back then. Was it even real?

But now he realised that perhaps it had been.

'There's so much I wish I'd asked Nana before she died,' Isobel said wistfully. 'I tried but for some reason she would never be drawn into conversations about my grandfather.'

'Perhaps you should ask your mum. Maybe she knows something.' He couldn't tell her what he'd heard, could he? He wasn't even sure he'd heard it correctly.

He heard Isobel laugh, that bell-like sound that he'd always loved. He heard her say something about her mother never telling her anything. And he heard the wheels of a van on the gravel of the drive below.

Saved by the contractor.

'Looks like Kev's here already,' he said, glancing out of the landing window. 'Let's get these window frames sorted before we do anything else, shall we?'

13

London – Spring 1953

There was a lot Max didn't tell Vivien until after the wedding – he'd known that perhaps she would have thought twice about marrying him if he'd told her the full story. Perhaps she would have realised that it wasn't quite the life she'd been imagining.

But still, it was a very different world from the one she had left behind, so maybe she wouldn't have changed a thing. How can anyone know what choices they would have made if they had known what was going to happen?

Vivien's father had agreed to the engagement, of course. Vivien and her mother had known he would and were already planning her wedding dress before Max even came to tea – a tea that had been as excruciating as Vivien had feared it would be.

'I suppose you had better meet my parents,' Max said afterwards, reluctance in his voice as though it was the last thing he wanted.

'I don't have—' Vivien began in response.

'They'd like you to come for dinner on Saturday.'

He explained how formal it would be, which cutlery she should use, which wine glass, how she shouldn't help herself to breakfast, that one of the staff would do it.

'Staff?' she exclaimed. It was 1953, who had staff anymore? Vivien had thought that nonsense had ended after the war. The Great War.

'It's like the dark ages, I'm afraid,' he said. 'But it will only be for one night.'

'I'll be staying?' she asked.

'Afraid so, but look on the bright side. They'll probably never ask us again.'

Vivien didn't dwell too long on that cryptic statement for fear of working out what it might mean.

Things went badly from the start. Her clothes weren't right, she could see that as soon as she walked in, her handshake was wrong, the way she spoke, even the way she held her knife and fork – all of it screamed 'she's not one of us' and none of Max's encouraging smiles made her feel comfortable. It was easy sometimes, after the war, to think that these class divides, these comedies of manners, had been smashed down. But they were still there, sitting quietly in dark dining rooms in Surrey. Vivien hardly ate anything, just picked and moved the food around her plate (which, oddly, Max's mother, Edwina – a tall and painfully thin woman with a loud, posh, penetrating voice – did seem to approve of) and she drank too much wine in an attempt to calm her nerves so that when she stood from the dinner table, leaving Max and his father to drink their port, she felt dizzy.

'You look as though you could do with some fresh air,'

Edwina sniffed and pointed Vivien in the direction of the terrace before disappearing into the labyrinth of the biggest house Vivien had ever seen. She had no idea how she'd find her room later on or, indeed, how she'd ever find her way out again in the morning. The angry part of Vivien that she tried to keep hidden, deep down in her belly, fired up at the thought of a house this big for three people, a house with servants no less, when the people she grew up with, her own family in fact, had lost their houses in the Blitz and had lived on nothing but goodwill for years afterwards.

She didn't know how long she'd been out on the terrace when Max came to find her. She felt instantly calmer when she saw his smile. Max was different, after all; he wasn't like his parents or the people like them who'd complained so much about having to hand their huge houses over to the army during the war.

'There you are,' he said. 'Are you all right?'

She shook her head.

'What's the matter, sweetheart?' His voice was gentle; it was the first time he'd used any term of endearment towards her and she looked up at him, surprised. It was as though the evening had softened him somehow, as though he no longer held himself so tightly. Was there more affection there than she'd thought? He'd said, at the Royal Academy, that he couldn't stop thinking about her but she hadn't been sure how truthful he was being. She wasn't sure she was in love with him, in fact she thought she probably wasn't. But in that moment she was more sure than ever before that she could grow to love him very quickly.

'Vivien? What's wrong? Talk to me.'

She looked at him and leaned against the wall, turning

away from his earnest look. 'I don't fit in,' she said. 'That's clear. I didn't know what to say or where to put my arms or—'

'Shh...' He stepped towards her, and as he took her hand in his she shivered. 'I don't care about any of that,' he said quietly, his voice a whisper. 'Times are changing and I don't care about cutlery and wine glasses and what you wear to dinner.' He paused, letting go of her as he took something from the inside pocket of his jacket. He held out his hand to reveal a small velvet box. 'Open it,' he said.

Inside was the most beautiful ring Vivien had ever seen – a thing of beauty and fantasy, a diamond larger than she could ever imagine.

'What's this?' she asked, even though it was obvious what it was.

'It's your engagement ring,' Max replied. 'Do you like it?'

'It's beautiful.'

He took the box from her, dropping to one knee in front of her.

'Vivien Burke, will you do me the honour of becoming my wife?'

'Of course,' she said, pressing her hand to her lips. 'You already know that; it's why we're here!' Laughter bubbled up inside her. 'Of course I'll marry you.' She suddenly felt surer of that than she'd felt about anything in her life.

After Max had placed the ring on her finger he stood up and kissed her, his lips brushing gently against hers at first and then harder, kissing her in that way Vivien had only ever seen at the movies before, kisses she associated with America, not England, not rambling old family homes in Surrey. He pressed her against the wall and she wrapped her arms around his neck, burying her fingers in his hair as she felt his knee between her legs, pushing them apart.

And then he stepped away from her, leaving her breathless, adjusting himself. When he looked at her again, he smiled.

'Let's get married as soon as possible,' he said.

Vivien had visions of a big white wedding out in Surrey, of hundreds of guests she didn't know, of food and drink she had never heard of before. Max's mother had the same idea but it wasn't what Max wanted, and, in the end, Vivien was glad. She was nervous enough about standing in front of everyone and saying her vows, nervous of her first dance with her new husband, and of what would happen later that night behind closed bedroom doors.

Max had been more affectionate since that night on the terrace – stealing kisses whenever he had the chance, brushing his fingers against hers whenever they met – but she still had no idea what her wedding night would be like other than the stories she'd heard from her friend Merry who'd married the butcher's son and had made unflattering comparisons to pigs.

'There isn't time for a big wedding,' Max had told his mother. 'We want to be in Norfolk by March.'

Norfolk. Vivien had hugged herself. She was going to see the sea. She hadn't asked how long they were staying, or where they would be living when they returned – she presumed Max's flat in Kensington – she'd been too excited about the prospect of finally seeing the sea to care.

They'd married on a cold, bright morning on the first day of March at Kensington and Chelsea Register Office.

Before he walked her inside, her father told her that this was where Wallace Simpson had married her first husband, but Vivien didn't think that boded particularly well. There was a small crowd – their parents and a handful of other family members on both sides, a few of Vivien's neighbours and old friends from Bow, a few of Max's friends from the Slade – not Charlotte though, in her tight jumper. It was a short ceremony followed by lunch at The Savoy. Max wore a dark suit and Vivien a simple gown that had been made by her mother and her colleagues at the dressmaker's – all of them staying after hours to get it ready in time, wondering to themselves if it was a shotgun wedding.

The next morning – after a wedding night in the Kensington flat that bore no resemblance to pigs – the newlyweds climbed into Max's MG Midget, with the top down of course, and headed off on honeymoon.

'To the sea,' Max laughed, reaching over to kiss his new wife as they left.

Vivien was finally getting out of London.

She didn't even look back.

14

Norfolk – July 2019

The windows, as it turned out, were easier to secure than Isobel had thought they would be thanks to a product called, rather improbably, Wood Hardener. Kev waved the bottle at her explaining what it did while Isobel nodded, trying, and failing, not to snigger at the name. Nick, she noticed, had wandered into the garden.

'I'll drill away the rotten bits,' Kev said. 'And fill them up with this. It does exactly what it says on the bottle and will do the job until we can get your new frames made up and installed.'

'Right,' she replied, feeling as though she was going to burst with mirth. 'I'll…well…I'll leave you to it.' And with that she fled from the room.

She found Nick sitting on the patio steps in the back garden, his shoulders shaking.

'Are you all right?' she managed to ask.

He was pink with giggling. 'Your face when Kev showed you the wood hardener,' he said.

'Don't, you'll set me off again,' Isobel said, sitting next to him and joining in the giggles. It felt good to laugh over something so ridiculous. She couldn't remember when she'd last done that.

'You always did love a double entendre,' Nick said eventually.

'Queen of the filthy-minded, that's me.'

Nick turned to her then, holding her gaze and just for a moment it felt as though they were teenagers again, not a care in the world.

Except they'd had plenty of cares that summer, hadn't they? Nick especially. And it only took one look at the garden that spread out in front of them to see how much had changed, how overgrown and out of hand everything had become.

The garden felt like a metaphor for life.

'The garden is an absolute mess too,' Isobel said quietly, her laughter gone, dissolved on the summer breeze. 'It used to be such a pretty garden, do you remember? I'll have to do something with it too, I suppose.'

'House first, garden later,' Nick said. 'Number one rule of renovations.'

'Really?'

'Well, one of the rules anyway. To make this house beautiful again you'll need scaffolding up and there'll be contractors tramping about all over everything. The garden will look worse by the time it's over so save it for later.'

Isobel nodded. 'I feel a bit helpless,' she said. 'Like I don't know where to start or what to do.'

'How about a cup of tea?' Nick said, standing up. 'And we can go through some initial thoughts on the kitchen.'

'Is the kitchen a good place to start?'

'Always. Get the hub of the house up and running.'

Isobel wondered if there would be any hub to this house if she was living here alone with no friends to speak of other than Spencer, and she wondered again if this plan of hers to start her life again in Norfolk was lunacy. She should be looking for a job rather than sitting about drinking tea and talking about kitchens.

Not that she had any tea. 'I'm a bit low on supplies,' she said. 'I'd better…'

'You put the kettle on,' Nick said. 'And I'll pop to the shop and get some bits for you.'

'Nick, you don't have—'

'Let me help you settle in, Isobel. Moving to a new place is always hard, even when it's somewhere you used to live. Starting again is…' He looked away, sighed. 'Well I could do with tea so I'm going to the shop. Be back soon, get that kettle boiling.'

She watched him walk around the side of the house, the gravel crunching under his feet.

By the time Nick was back, Isobel had boiled her grandmother's old, slow kettle and washed three china cups she had found in a cupboard. The cups were probably older than she was.

'Tea, milk, sugar, bread, butter, jam, cereal,' Nick said, unpacking the bag onto the kitchen counter. 'And I got us some scones as well from the cafe opposite the pub. Have you been there yet?'

Isobel shook her head.

'It's nice, you should try it. Introduce yourself to the owner. She makes all her own cakes and stuff.' He started taking the scones out of the bag. 'Have you got a knife and a couple of plates?'

'I think so,' Isobel said, hunting through the cupboards and drawers, trying to remember where Vivien had kept everything. 'Here's a plate and…yes…cutlery. Are you having the scones now? It's only 10:30 in the morning.'

'Morning tea,' he said. 'Another important rule of house renovation.'

Nick had always had a sweet tooth. Isobel remembered how he used to go to the post office and fill a bag with penny sweets as though he was eight rather than eighteen.

'Do you not want one?' he'd ask when he offered her the bag and she'd refused.

'They'll rot your teeth,' she'd replied jokingly.

'Not today they won't.'

This house, this village, the very sea itself was so full of memories, all of which seemed to be coming back to her in waves. Snippets of the life she'd lived here that she couldn't quite sort out into any kind of timeframe.

'Does Kev take milk and sugar?' she asked, trying to push the memories away.

After Nick had given Kev his tea, and he'd slathered the scones with thick layers of butter and jam, eating his in nearly one bite, he started to tell Isobel his great vision for the kitchen.

'We can open it up,' he said, spreading his arms wide. 'Take out this wall here,' he tapped the wall between kitchen and dining room, 'to create an open-plan kitchen-diner – lots of light colours and wooden countertops – a range and butler's sink like I said before, and we can turn the French windows in the dining room into bi-fold doors so you can completely open up that side of the room on warm summer days…' He turned to her, grinning. 'I know you don't want to change things that much but this way I think we can keep the integrity of the house while giving it a modern feel. What do you think?'

His smile was infectious and Isobel grinned back. 'You don't have to do the sales pitch with me, Nick. I need your help desperately, you know that!'

'But what do you think?'

'Honestly, it sounds wonderful. I'll admit that part of me just wants to preserve this house exactly as Nana left it but I know that's not practical, particularly if I want to live in it. I want a home, not some sort of weird living museum where even the kettle takes an eternity to boil.'

'So, is that a yes?' He was as excited as a small boy, as excited as the eighteen-year-old version of him had been when he bought penny sweets, and Isobel realised that back in the summer before university he had never looked like that when he'd talked about medical school – he'd always looked drawn and worried as though it was the last thing he wanted to do. She remembered the mornings they'd spent sitting in the tree in her grandmother's garden, talking about the future. She remembered how unsure Nick had sometimes seemed. She looked out of the window towards the tree now – overgrown after years of neglect and looking as though it should probably be cut down.

Nick was clearly carrying something around with him, something dark that she recognised in herself, but when he talked about the kitchen, about the walls and the light and the butler sink, his face changed, his whole body changed. He loved doing this, she realised, he loved doing up houses in the same way that she loved to draw, to paint, to create.

Or at least in the way she used to love to create. It had been a long time since she'd felt as though her work lit her up. There was that brief moment of sketching in the hallway on Tuesday morning – and she felt her cheeks heat again at the thought of Spencer catching her sketching Nick – but it had been fleeting and the desire to draw hadn't returned since.

She wanted to feel again, but she was afraid she didn't know how.

'It's a yes,' she said to Nick now.

'I can knock the wall down?'

She nodded. 'But not right this minute.'

'No,' he said, draining his tea as the light drained from his eyes. 'Not right this minute. In fact, I must check on Kev and then we should leave you to it. You'll probably want to start moving your stuff in if you're staying here tonight.'

'Really?' she said, excitement curling in her stomach.

'Thanks to Kev and his Wood Hardener.' She giggled again and Nick winked at her. As he turned around, calling to Kev as he went, she felt a wave of warm satisfaction wash over her. For the first time since Mr Brecher had given her the key to the house and she'd finally understood the work it would need, she felt that this was actually possible. And if that were possible, perhaps other things were possible too.

It was late by the time Isobel had unpacked the car. She hadn't brought very much with her – Little Clarion was furnished, after all, even though she knew that much of the furniture would have to be sold or refurbished – but she took her time making sure that everything was in the right place, that the house felt as much like home as she could make it feel in its current state. She folded her clothes carefully, putting them away in the mahogany chest and hanging those that needed it in the little nook where the walls didn't quite form a right angle – a nook that had been her teenage wardrobe. She unwrapped the new sheets – a treat from Laura Ashley that she'd splashed too much of her savings on – and made up the bed, spraying the linen with lavender water to remind her of Vivien. Then back in the kitchen she replaced her grandmother's kettle with her own and found places for her microwave and her toaster – essentials for her limited cooking skills.

Finally, she was left with her art supplies, her easel, her sketchbooks, paper and canvases. She hadn't worked out which room she would use as a studio yet – how could she when she was barely drawing? When she'd been young, when everything she'd owned was in her room on the top floor, she had longed for more light. Now she had the whole house to herself she could pick and choose her rooms. She thought that she would try all of them once inspiration hit. If it ever did.

As the sun began to set and the light in the house grew

deep and golden, she made herself hot toast dripping with butter, and a mug of strong tea – breakfast for dinner – before sitting in the old wing-backed chair that had been Vivien's, settling into the places her grandmother's body had moulded over the years, and allowed herself to listen to the house, to the memories held within the walls. And her mind drifted back to the photograph of Vivien in the ballroom of Silverton Hall, of the midsummer party that took place in the summer of 1953, of her grandfather, who nobody ever talked about, and of Silverton Bay itself. Why here? Why did her grandparents choose the Bay to settle in?

Recently she'd tried to think about the Bay less and less in an attempt to stop herself from regretting everything. It was another reason – alongside her deep fear of Vivien getting old, of Vivien not being there anymore – that her visits to her grandmother had become less frequent and her time spent in the house reduced so dramatically. She had told herself over and over that she was a teacher in Cambridge now, a good teacher, a talented teacher – that it was enough, and she had to concentrate on the future, not what could have been.

But that hadn't been the truth, of course. It was all an avoidance tactic, and now sitting here, in her grandmother's chair, the memories that she'd been avoiding for so long hung thickly in the air around her. She remembered the childhood Christmases and summers she had spent here with her parents before they'd moved to New York – they'd always rented a cottage by the beach in the summer, her father telling her it was so they could be nearer the sea but she knew as she got older that it was so her mother and Vivien didn't spend the whole summer arguing. She remembered the day she'd moved into Little Clarion after her parents went to America, and her first day at the school in the next town along the coast, how happy she'd been to be living in Silverton Bay, so happy that she barely missed her parents and didn't miss her old life in London at all. She remembered the day she got her A level results, the day she left for London, the graduation party that Vivien had held in the garden here and invited the whole village to. The only people who hadn't been at the party were Isobel's parents; her father at work and her mother stranded in New York, unable to get on a plane. And Nick, of course; he hadn't been there either and Isobel had made a point of not asking Spencer about him.

Then, for the first time in over a decade, she allowed herself to remember properly the summer she'd spent here with Nick – the afternoons spent talking on the beach, her head in his lap; the evenings in The Two Bells and the slightly tipsy walks home, hand in hand; and the kiss against the tree near Silverton Hall. If she let herself, she could still feel the sensation of his lips on hers, of the tree bark against her back.

It was too much, oppressive even, to sit here and remember it all, to wonder where her potential had gone, to question what had happened. She was here to make a new start, not dwell on past failures. Nick was right when he said she needed to properly modernise the house. She needed to make it hers, dispel the sadness and regret.

She stood up slowly, taking the plate and cup into the kitchen. After two nights at Silverton Hall and another two at Spencer's, coupled with the nights of worry before moving here, she was exhausted. She was hoping to fall into her old bed tonight and sleep.

She woke suddenly, sitting up in bed, the duvet tangled around her legs. She wasn't sure what had woken her, but she'd been dreaming about Vivien, dreaming that she was still alive. Moonlight shone through the gap in the flimsy curtains and Isobel made a mental note to get new curtains, thicker ones. She looked up as the moonlight caught the portrait of Vivien that hung outside her bedroom door and her heart skipped for a moment as she thought her dreams had come true. And then her brain woke up properly and remembered that it was just a portrait, a portrait painted from a photograph she had never known about. She felt her brow furrow. Now was not the time to start thinking about family mysteries that probably had a perfectly rational explanation. Nick was right, she did need to call her mother.

Perhaps though she would move the portrait in the meantime, hang it somewhere else. Vivien's death was still too raw and she wanted to make this house her own, she was sure of that now she had spoken to Nick. The house deserved a new lease of life and so did she. So did Nick, it seemed. She wanted to ask him what had happened but she knew she couldn't until she was willing to tell him what had happened to her after she had won the portrait competition.

She picked her phone up from her bedside table – 02:11 and still no signal. There was never any signal here at the top of the house. She turned on the lamp and picked up her book, but the words just jumped about on the page refusing to be tied down enough to tell their story. She'd never been a great reader – not of fiction anyway; she had boxes and boxes of art books hidden away in storage – unlike her mother who devoured books and sent Isobel twice monthly emails containing lists of recommended reads. But then, Gina hardly left the house anymore according to Isobel's father, except for the summers spent at their beach house in Montauk, so she had plenty of time on her hands. Isobel felt a wave of guilt wash over her. She usually spent the early part of the summer vacation with her parents, had done for years, and it became yet another bone of contention between herself and Adam before he unceremoniously dumped her. Each summer Isobel and her parents would drive from New York to Long Island together to spend a few weeks by the coast. Gina would read, Isobel would paint (or, more recently, pretend to paint) and Tim would fish and drink beer with the locals. But she hadn't gone this year. She hoped her parents understood that she had to be here for the house. She could still hear the disappointment in her mother's voice when she'd told her that she couldn't make the trip this year.

Perhaps the house could have waited. Perhaps 'Isobel's new start' could have happened in the autumn.

It was pointless lying awake like this, her head full of fluttering thoughts. She was never going to get to sleep however many times she turned the pillow over. She felt confused and lonely – her parents so far away and no friends to speak of nearby. She missed Mattie, the warm, solid presence of her in the bedroom at the end of the corridor that she'd grown so used to. She couldn't think any longer about whether she'd made a terrible mistake moving to Norfolk, so she pulled herself out of bed and padded downstairs.

She found herself in the room that Vivien had always called 'the office', the room that had been Max's until he died. Years later, after Gina left home, Vivien had taken the room over for her own studies, and her teaching work. After Vivien had retired, the office became a sort of library of both books and memories. It was the memories that Isobel wanted to look at tonight, hard copies of the flickering images in her head

The photograph albums sat on a low shelf in a regimented row of white labelled spines. For a woman who talked about the past only reluctantly, Vivien had been very particular about her photo albums – uniform volumes spanning the years since she'd married Isobel's grandfather in 1953. Isobel crouched down so she could see the dates on the spines in the dim light and flicked past the early albums – pictures of Vivien and Max's rather low-key wedding.

'Nobody had big weddings at the time, Isobel. There was so much poverty and rationing still after the war and it would have been in bad taste,' Vivien had said as though Isobel was still too naïve to work out that Gina was born less than six months later, explaining clearly why the wedding was both small and speedy.

Isobel flicked past the albums that were dated through the 1960s and 70s and that she knew contained pictures of Gina as a child and, later, as a tall, sulky teenager in miniskirts and long socks. Then the pictures of Gina and Tim and their definitely not low-key wedding in London during the long, hot summer of 1976.

It was the albums after that Isobel was interested in tonight, the albums of her own memories.

She settled back into the brown leather office chair that had once been her grandfather's and slowly turned the thick pages of the album. She smiled at photos of her as a toddler digging holes on the beach right here in Silverton Bay. She turned the page to a row of pictures taken at Christmas – a six-year-old version of herself standing sandwiched between her parents, her father grinning indulgently at her whilst her mother stared at the camera as if challenging it. Despite the fact there was always an initial frostiness between Vivien and Gina when they first arrived, Christmases at her grandmother's house were some of Isobel's happiest childhood memories. Memories full of warmth and laughter and freedom and so much food. Far better than the stuffy seasonal parties at her paternal grandfather's house in Kent where everything had to look like the pages of a magazine and Tim's stepmother made sure Isobel was never allowed to touch anything.

Hit hard by a sudden unexpected wave of nostalgia, Isobel slammed the photo album shut. She was doing it again, wallowing in the past, a past she couldn't and shouldn't try to recreate. A past she definitely couldn't change. Those days were gone and if she wanted to make Silverton Bay her home now it had to be on her terms. But she needed to define those terms, work out what she wanted, meet some new people, earn some money. She needed to write a list of ideas, of pros and cons. She leaned across the desk towards the pot of pens that sat there, dusty with lack of use, and started searching around for a piece of paper or a notebook, anything she could begin writing on. She had to get this down before this burst of energy disappeared into the inertia she'd been feeling for so very long.

She needed more light than the dim bulb hanging from the ceiling was providing, but when she tried the desk lamp it hissed and popped and the bulb exploded onto the desk.

'Shit,' she whispered to herself, standing up, unravelling herself from the leather chair. As she did so she knocked the photo album on to the floor. 'Shit,' she said again, bending down to pick it up. She was clearly much more tired than her brain was telling her. Perhaps she should go back to bed. Try again in the morning.

As she turned to put the album back on the shelf, something fell out of the back of it. A black and white picture of Vivien standing on the beach at Silverton Bay, not far from where Isobel and Nick had eaten their fish and chips the night before. She was barefoot and wearing an old-fashioned swimsuit, her hair was wet from the sea and a towel was draped around her shoulders. She looked so beautiful and happy, laughing at whoever was taking the photograph. Isobel wondered when it had been taken and who was behind the camera. Was it Max? She turned the photograph over.

`July 1953` the faded inscription on the back read in what looked like Vivien's handwriting.

Something bothered her about the date and the photograph and she turned it over to look at the picture again. It took a while for Isobel's overtired brain to work it out, but eventually the cogs turned and her heart skipped.

Vivien may have hidden her pregnancy for quite some time before and after her wedding but by late July 1953, less than two months before Gina was born, there would have been no hiding it anymore.

And yet here she was, standing on the beach in a swimsuit, her stomach as flat as Isobel's own.

15

Norfolk – Spring 1953

Vivien got through the early months of her marriage in much the same way as she had got through the months of the Blitz as a child – by daydreaming. Her imagination had always been at its most fertile when she didn't really understand what was happening to her or what was expected of her. Those months of bombing, while so many of her schoolfriends were away in the countryside, had terrified and confused her at first. But after a while there was a routine to them – the sound of the air raid siren, the nightly trips to the communal bomb shelter that smelled of other people's sweat, stepping out into the daylight the next morning like so many moles wondering what destruction had happened overnight. But it was a routine with no meaning for Vivien, who didn't understand why the war was happening, or what on earth it had to do with her or her family.

She had always loved books, borrowing them from the school library and immersing herself in the imaginary worlds of *The Enchanted Wood, Mary Poppins*, and *Milly Molly Mandy*. But there were only so many books that the school could provide her with and no books at home – her parents couldn't afford such luxuries – and so, late at night, while the Luftwaffe dropped bombs on London, Vivien would snuggle under one of the scratchy blankets in the bomb shelter and make up stories of her own. Stories of a world without bombs, without wars and where her father was still at home, smoking his pipe and telling his own stories.

It had become a coping mechanism for Vivien, a way of dealing with the unknown, For a while, when she was young, she had harboured dreams of becoming a writer herself, but that was before she had to leave school to work in the dressmaker's with her mother.

Now, here in Silverton Bay, over a decade later, Vivien found herself turning to the stories in her head for comfort once again.

She wasn't sure what she'd expected from the early days of her marriage so she wasn't exactly disappointed – but she hadn't expected to be quite so bored. She'd thought she'd be living in Max's flat in Kensington by now, that she would be able to see her friends, her parents, able to wander around the London parks and gardens that she had always loved. She hadn't realised that the Norfolk Coast would become her home. She hadn't realised how separated she would feel from who she used to be.

Max had shown her the house on their first full day in Silverton Bay. They'd arrived late in the afternoon on the day before and, despite the excitement when they'd first set off on honeymoon, Vivien had felt tired and grubby after the long drive. They had gone straight to their hotel – if you could call it a hotel when it hadn't officially started trading yet. Silverton Hall had been privately owned by a family called the Harringtons until quite recently. Vivien had heard of their department stores, even if she had never been in one. The Hall had become one of the great country houses that had run out of money after the war and turned into a hotel by a rich entrepreneur eager to cash in on the rise of the middle classes, the end of rationing, the need to live a carefree life again.

They were greeted by a Mrs Castleton ('Call me Miriam,' she insisted to Vivien), who had been the Harringtons' housekeeper and now had the onerous task of helping prepare the Hall to welcome hotel guests in the early summer months. She showed them to a room, bigger than any bedroom Vivien had ever seen, decorated in the sort of colours that she had always associated with the sea, with fishermen, with sailing – blue-and-white stripes, soft, neutral walls. When she owned her own house, Vivien thought to herself, this was how she wanted it to look.

'When can we see the sea?' Vivien asked when Mrs Castleton had left them to settle in. She had glimpsed it from the car as it crested the brow of the hill into the village, but she wanted to stand near it, smell it, listen to it.

Max had smiled. 'How about right now? Before it gets dark.'

It had been even better than she'd imagined. Vivien stood, transfixed, at the bottom of the cliff listening to the roar of the waves, breathing in the salty air.

'Shall we get closer?' Max had asked as he sat down to take off his shoes and socks, and roll up his trouser legs.

'What are you doing?' It felt strange to see her always immaculate husband behave like this. It felt strange to call him her husband.

Max looked up at her, squinting against the watery spring sun that was low in the sky. 'Join me,' he said.

So she squatted down in the sand too, taking off her cream-coloured shoes, rolling down her silk stockings – she had never owned silk stockings before she met Max – giggling and embarrassed, shivering in the cold March breeze.

'There's nobody much around,' Max assured her, taking the hand that wasn't grasping tightly to her shoes and leading her towards the shore.

The tide was out and the sun glinted on the water as they walked across the sand, which slid between her toes and then became firmer, colder, damper as they neared the sea itself. Vivien stopped suddenly, pulling away from Max, afraid of the power of the sea. She watched as Max put down his shoes and stepped into the water.

'Come on,' he encouraged, holding out his hand to her again.

She placed her shoes and stockings next to Max's brogues, the Argyle socks tucked neatly into their toes, and tiptoed towards the water's edge. Her feet were already almost blue with cold and she wondered if her husband was mad, standing there in the sea on such a chilly afternoon. There was a reason nobody was about. Sensible people were all safely ensconced in their houses, warm by their fires.

But when the water washed over her feet, the gentle waves lapping at her toes, she realised that he wasn't mad and that this was the best feeling in the world. Vivien had never felt so free, so absolutely herself as she did that March afternoon standing ankle-deep in salt water, the briny breeze messing up her hair.

They waded through the water together, laughing and talking, until the hem of Vivien's dress was damp and they were both shivering with cold.

'We used to come to Silverton Bay when I was a child,' Max said. Vivien hadn't known that, but it made sense of course. 'My cousin George and I would stay in the sea until our lips were blue. There's truly nothing like it.' He smiled as though remembering, looking out towards the horizon.

'Is George still here?'

A silence.

'He died.' The words echoed across the bay, out to sea.

She squeezed his hand. 'I'm so sorry,' she said. 'When did—'

'Last December,' he interrupted. 'It's where I was when…'

When you disappeared during the smog, Vivien thought.

'I should have told you,' he said.

'You can tell me now.'

Max's eyes snapped back to her from the horizon and with that look the mood changed again. 'This is no conversation for the first day of our honeymoon,' he said. 'Besides, you look as though you're freezing.'

'A little.'

'Well let's get you back to the hotel then, before we get in trouble with Mrs Castleton.'

They ran back up the cliff path together, shoes pulled on hastily, stockings stuffed in Max's trouser pocket, and hurried back to the warmth of Silverton Hall.

Max wouldn't mention George again for months.

Later that evening they ate together in the huge dining room that would soon accommodate countless holiday makers.

'Splendid, isn't it?' Max said, looking about him as he drank his soup. 'Imagine how it will look when it's full. The English country house is giving way to the English country hotel. It's going to be a marvellous thing.'

Vivien nodded, unable to imagine any of it.

Later still they'd made love in the big blue-and-white bed and had fallen asleep curled up together in the sheets. The sea air lulled Vivien into a deep sleep the likes of which she hadn't slept since she was a small child, before the war. A sleep where there had never been bombs, or the Luftwaffe, or a hole in the street where her house used to be.

Max woke her early the next morning.

'I've got a surprise for you,' he said.

'Better than the sea?'

'Perhaps, but I'll let you be the judge of that.'

The surprise had been the house she now lived in, the house by the sea – a three-storey, redbrick Victorian. A house Max had insisted on calling Little Clarion and that was so much bigger than anything Vivien had lived in before or needed, but still a dolls' house in comparison to Clarions (or Big

Clarion as Vivien now thought of it), the house in Surrey that Max had grown up in.

It had been a surprise both good and bad. A house by the sea meant she never had to leave and Vivien was absolutely not ready to leave yet. That taste of what it felt like to have one's feet in the salt water had just left her wanting more – more than even a week-long honeymoon could give her. She'd wanted to go back to the beach straight after breakfast on that first day of their honeymoon, but Max had wanted to show her the surprise.

'I've bought you a house,' he said, and even as she looked around it, all she could think about was the sensation of the water on her skin. She wanted to feel that all over – was that possible? Did people swim in the sea? Men probably did, but what about women? Vivien had no idea.

But however much a house by the sea might appeal, she had been expecting to go back to London, to live in the flat in Kensington, to see her parents and to try to articulate to them somehow the wonders of a seaside holiday. She wasn't ready to leave London just yet, she wasn't ready for the 'settling down' that Max was talking about. Perhaps she wasn't ready after all for marriage or the responsibilities it held. Perhaps this had all been a terrible mistake.

They did go back to London though for a while, and they even lived in the flat in Kensington for a week or two whilst Max 'tied matters up' and Vivien said goodbye to her parents, telling them they could visit anytime ('we've so many bedrooms') and collected her belongings. She tried not to notice the tight smile her mother gave her or the way her father kept asking 'are you sure about this, love?'

By April she was installed in the house and surrounded by all the mod cons she could ask for, including one of the new-fangled twin tub washing machines that she had read about but had no idea how to operate, and an electric iron. It was a far cry from the tub and mangle that her mother had used when she was a child or the iron that was heated in front of the fire – not that her parents had a fire now in their flat, or even a mangle. Just a launderette at the end of the road that left everyone's clothes smelling a little bit musty. There was a launderette in Silverton Bay too, but it was over by the caravan park and used by holiday makers and Max had made it clear that it wasn't a part of the village he wanted Vivien to frequent, so she would just have to work out how to use the twin tub. Max wanted to pay for someone to come in to help with the cleaning and the laundry, but on that point Vivien had put her foot down. How could she sit around all day, a lady of leisure in her enormous house, while somebody else did the chores for her?

Max bought her books, magazines, clothes – filling the rooms and the cupboards and the wardrobes with things to make up for the fact that he was gone more than he was there. London and his father's bank called him away for most of the week. But no amount of things could make up for the emptiness Vivien felt when he was gone, the huge gulf that opened up between her life now and her life in London, a gulf that grew bigger every day. The only thing that helped was being near the sea, but without Max she never dared to dip her toes in.

Thank god for Mrs Castleton, the housekeeper from

Silverton Hall, who turned up on Vivien's doorstep late in April when Max was away, bearing a tin of fairy cakes.

'I thought you might like to see a friendly face,' she huffed as she pushed her way into the house without invitation. 'Mr Chambers told me he was away a lot and, to be honest, I'm happy to get away from the hotel from time to time. It's chaos down there – dust everywhere. How we're going to get everything ready for opening in June, I don't know.'

'You're opening in June?' Vivien felt a frisson of excitement at the thought of something new happening.

'Just after the coronation.'

Miriam Castleton became the friend Vivien hadn't known she'd needed. Not only did she come over on a regular basis armed with baked goods and village gossip, she was also the person who told Vivien that people did indeed swim in the sea, even women and she, Miriam Castleton, was one such woman.

'There is nothing like the sea to keep your strength up,' she said before asking Vivien if she would like to join her one morning. Did she have a bathing suit?

Vivien didn't even hesitate in her answer; she would love to join Miriam in the sea and so Miriam had arrived early the next morning with bread rolls to sustain them afterwards and a plain black bathing suit.

'This one should fit you,' she said, handing over the jersey and nylon costume. 'So much more comfortable than those awful things we had to wear before the war.'

Vivien went off to get changed, putting the bathing suit on under her dress before going down to the beach and giggling to herself at the thought of Lord and Lady

Harrington's housekeeper swimming in the sea on her days off. She wondered if they knew.

Miriam Castleton was standing thigh-deep in the water before she asked Vivien, still on the shoreline, whether she could actually swim. 'I probably should have asked that first,' she said.

Vivien had been so wrapped up in wondering what the water would feel like on her body that she hadn't stopped to think about the implications – the fact that she would have to swim in the sea, the wild, unpredictable sea that could flood the village in certain weather, that could wash houses away.

'I can swim,' Vivien said hesitantly as she remembered her teenage swimming lessons in the municipal pool, being bellowed at by a short, squat woman who had allegedly swum in the 1936 Olympic team ('the Nazi Olympics,' Vivien's father had muttered when she'd told him). The lessons had stopped when the pool had been closed after a polio outbreak. Vivien had been lucky enough not to contract the dreaded virus, but Merry, who later would marry the butcher's son, still walked with a limp. 'But this is a little bit different to the swimming baths in London.'

Miriam laughed and waded back towards the shore. 'It is that,' she said, taking Vivien's arm and leading her slowly into the cold water. 'But it's worth it.'

And it was. Once she was in the water, performing a slow breaststroke across the bay, following Miriam that first time, she felt free again, as though it was just her and the sea. Nothing else mattered and time itself stood still.

'Do you swim all year around?' Vivien asked later as she stood on the beach, towelling the salt water from her hair.

'I don't, but plenty of people do. There's a big Boxing Day swim every year that I always try to do though. Even Mr Castleton takes part in that.'

Boxing Day, Vivien thought. It seemed so far in the future, but she knew Christmas would come as it always did. Would she see her parents? Would she have to spend Christmas in Surrey with Max's family, wondering which knife to use? Would she be pregnant by then? The thought made her gasp, made her realise that she really wasn't ready for the implications of marriage. Should she say something to Max? How did one even bring that subject up?

'Are you all right?' Miriam asked.

'Just a bit cold.'

'Let's get back and have a nice hot cuppa then.'

Tea, yes. That was exactly what Vivien needed.

She swam every morning after that, even when Max was there in the Bay, joining Miriam most days. On Sundays though she went by herself because her friend was at church. Vivien had never been to church in her life – her father was not a believer, which got them some funny looks when she was growing up – but here in Silverton Bay in 1953 she was surprised to discover that missing the Sunday morning service wasn't completely frowned upon and that she wasn't the only one who had trouble believing in the existence of God. She supposed it was the war that had done that. It was hard to believe that a loving God would have let all that devastation happen.

Despite the lure of the sea and the gentle, pleasant pace of the village, Vivien missed London terribly; the busy dirty streets, the bright lights, the shops she couldn't afford to buy anything from. She even missed Mr Musgrove and the clack-clack-clack of the typewriter keys at the solicitor's office. Every time Max went back, she hoped he would invite her to join him.

'You'll be bored, sweetheart,' he said. 'I've got to work.'

'I could go to see my mother.'

'Maybe next time.'

But next time never came and with each rejection Vivien found it just a little bit harder to love her husband in the way that she knew she should do by now. She wondered too if he loved her, if he had ever loved her. She wondered what they were doing.

The only time Vivien didn't feel that umbilical pull back to London was when she was in the sea. When she lay on her back in the water, arms and legs spread like starfish, staring up at the sky, all she could feel was that moment – the breath in her body, the shape of her legs. It became her lifeline.

Morning swims started to become the only time she saw Miriam, who was increasingly busy at the Hall during the day and with her husband in the evening – mysterious Mr Castleton who Vivien had never met. The rest of Vivien's time passed slowly; she didn't really have any other friends in the village yet although she was starting to learn people's names, to say hello to them when she passed them on the High Street.

Give it time, Viv, she told herself. *It'll feel like home soon enough.*

She read a lot from the stacks of books and magazines that Max brought back from London with him, and at the end of May he came home with a very special surprise indeed.

A television.

Vivien stared at the wooden cabinet standing on its four spindly legs displaying its blank, curved, grey screen. Another thing she'd read about but had never seen before.

'Goodness,' she said.

'I thought we could watch the coronation on it,' Max replied. 'Together, but with the rest of the world who'll be watching on television too. Isn't that a strange thought?'

Vivien nodded, her feelings torn in two. She'd been hoping to go to London for the coronation of the new young queen, to join her parents at the street party they were organising with their neighbours ('It'll be as big as that street party we had for VE Day,' her mother had written to her. 'Do you remember?'). But on the other hand, the thought of being here with her husband, the thought of precious alone time with him, was tempting enough for her to comply with Max's wishes.

'How does it work?' she asked when Max set the television up.

He turned and smiled at her. 'Magic,' he said, and she laughed, knowing that he had as much idea as she did.

As it turned out, the day of the coronation was cold and wet and Vivien was happy to be at home, snuggled on the sofa with her husband's arm around her. The whole day had felt very emotional, as though they were finally seeing the beginning of a new and important era – the New Elizabethan Age. A time that would be glamourous and fun, that would help them move on from the war, help them forget. She and Max were part of a new generation – the disaffected post-war youth trying to change the world. Although mostly Vivien felt as though middle age had found her twenty years too soon.

The glamour and fun would start in just a few weeks at Silverton Hall, which was finally ready to open for business and to celebrate with the inaugural midsummer party to which Max and Vivien were guests of honour. Max had bought her a navy-blue silk gown in London. It was the most beautiful thing Vivien had ever seen, even more beautiful than her wedding gown.

'It must have cost a fortune,' she breathed as she held it up in front of herself in the mirror

'It's worth it for you,' Max replied as he stood behind her, his lips brushing her neck. 'I want to take advantage of these early days of our marriage, before children come along.'

Vivien looked away from her reflection, knowing that her feelings about that must have been very clear in her face.

'Do you not want to be a mother?' Max asked, as he turned her around to look at him. 'All women want to be mothers, don't they?'

Vivien didn't know where to begin. She knew, of course, that the things she and Max did in the bedroom – things that made her cry with pleasure and then blush with shame in the cold light of day – led to children, and she knew that producing an heir for Max was what was expected of her. But she wasn't sure she did want to be a mother. Was that all she was here for, tucked away on the Norfolk coast bearing Max's children while he lived his life in London? She felt momentarily angry until she saw her husband's face. He looked sad and dejected and Vivien remembered that she had wanted this, she had spent her days in London wishing to be somewhere other than the typing pool and longing to one day see the sea. Hadn't Max given her all of that? How could she possibly tell him that she didn't feel ready for children?

'Of course I want to be a mother,' she said.

Max stepped towards her, taking her in his arms. 'Good,' he said. And then he kissed her hard, his hands fumbling with the zip of her skirt.

16

Norfolk – July 2019

Isobel awoke with a start, a crick in her neck and an ache in her spine. It took her a moment to work out where she was, her legs sticking to leather, her head slumped. She sat up and stretched. She must have fallen asleep in the office last night. As she stood, something fell on to the floor in front of her – a photograph with a date on the back. She rubbed her eyes as it all came back to her. The memories, the sleeplessness, the lack of phone signal, the photograph albums and the mysterious photograph from a few weeks before her mother was born. Another mysterious photograph.

She bent to pick up the picture of her grandmother on the beach, taking it to the window where the early morning shone through the dusty glass. She looked at it closely and then turned it over to read the date again.

July 1953.

Obviously it was a mistake and the picture had been dated wrongly. It wasn't like Vivien to make mistakes; she was meticulous with the record-keeping of her photograph albums. But nobody, not even Vivien, was perfect. It must have been 1954, after Gina had been born, or perhaps even later. It was impossible to tell.

Isobel smiled to herself for thinking it was another mysterious photograph. She was clearly tired and looking for complications where there weren't any. A photograph with the date written incorrectly on the back. No mystery at all.

Unless…

She tapped the photograph against her chin for a moment and then went to sit back at the desk, picking up the album she had been looking at the night before. She turned to the photographs of family Christmases in the 1980s, pictures of herself in brightly coloured jumpers standing with her parents by a Christmas tree, looking for one specific picture.

Isobel hadn't seen many photographs of her mother and grandmother together. After Max died, she supposed, it was always Vivien behind the camera. This particular picture had been taken on Christmas Day 1989. She didn't need to take the photograph out of the album to check the date, she could remember because it was the Christmas that she lost one of her front teeth. Her father must have taken the photo because it was of three generations of women: Vivien, Gina and six-year-old Isobel grinning through the gap in her teeth.

But she hadn't looked for the photograph purely for nostalgic reasons. She'd looked at it to remind herself how unalike Vivien and Gina were. Vivien fair and blue-eyed, with a typically English rose completion, and Gina much darker – brown eyes, thick eyebrows, dark brown hair cut in a severe fringe.

Gina could, of course, look like her father. Isobel herself was much fairer than her mother and looked very much like Tim's side of the family, after all. But she was sure she could remember hearing people say how different Gina and Vivien were, and they wouldn't have said that if her mother had looked like Max, would they?

She slammed the photograph album shut and pushed it away. What nonsense! How ridiculous she was being. She was looking for stories where there were none to look for, and overthinking everything because she'd seen a few pictures at the Hall of a party she hadn't previously known about.

It didn't mean anything at all.

But why, then, did she feel so uneasy? Why was the photograph of Vivien on the beach tucked in the back of an album instead of carefully displayed on one of the album's pages? Vivien had always been so fussy about her photo albums – three photographs to a page, each one carefully tucked into the white cardboard corners that held it in place. She'd believed that photographs were to be looked at, but this one had been hidden away as though someone was trying to banish a secret and rewrite history. It had fallen out last night to be looked at for the first time in years, as though it was time for that secret to be revealed, time to face up to the truth of the past.

Now I really am being fanciful, Isobel thought, standing up and putting the album back on the shelf.

It would be easy enough to clear up, though. She would just call her mother, who would have a rational explanation and that would be that. The photograph could be forgotten all over again. She ignored the little voice in the back of her head that was trying to remind her how dismissive and obtuse her mother usually was whenever she was asked questions about her childhood.

Isobel wondered what time it was and as if on cue the antique mantel clock that sat above the fireplace chimed six. It was far too early to call New York, so she would just have to occupy herself until her mother was up and about and fit to be spoken to.

She stood up and stretched, turning her back on the shelf of photograph albums as though that would banish the peculiar anxious feeling she'd had since waking up. She hadn't felt like this for a long time, not since she was a teenager, and it must just be a side effect of being back in the house, of sleeping in her teenage bedroom again. Or not sleeping there as the case may be. Perhaps it was the wrong room to choose, perhaps she should rethink that.

As a teenager, whenever she'd woken up early in the morning feeling anxious, she had found there was only one thing that could put her back on her feet, something her grandmother had taught her.

A long soak in cold salt water.

A few years ago Isobel had read an article about one of the astronauts who had spent time on the space station. She had skimmed most of it, never really that interested in the cosmos, but one thing had stuck with her. The astronaut had said that the first time he had seen the earth from above, floating like a globe in the atmosphere, it had made him see how insignificant he was, how trivial the things he worried about were.

When Isobel floated on her back in the sea, looking at the watery sky above her, she felt a similar sensation.

'The sea always puts things in perspective,' her grandmother had told her. 'Makes you reassess your priorities. It's why I like living here.'

Isobel had been glad she'd unpacked so carefully the day before; finding a place for everything meant she had been able to change into her swimsuit quickly and be down at the beach before she could second guess herself, or talk herself out of it. The sea was colder than she remembered, but once she was submerged the sensation of the water, the bobbing of the tide, the way the brine supported her limbs was so familiar it was almost as though she had never been away. And after a few minutes of vigorous swimming she was able to lie on her back and think without that feeling of panicky tightness.

Vivien had loved the sea, and it was she who'd taught Isobel to love it too – first taking her to paddle as a toddler, never going further than her ankles, Vivien's skirt knotted at her knees, and then later whilst wearing a bright-blue costume with a frilled skirt, teaching Isobel to swim with the tides, to float on the waves, and to respect the sea. Isobel thought of the photograph again, Vivien in her old-fashioned suit, salt in her hair. By the look on her face in that photograph, it was clear that she had always felt better after a swim in the sea.

I miss you, Nana, Isobel whispered quietly to the sky. She thought about the photographs again – the ones at Silverton Hall and the one in the back of the album – and felt as though she was supposed to work something out or uncover something. Was that why Vivien had left her the house? Was that why the photograph had appeared when it did?

She shook her head, laughing at her overactive imagination again, and dived beneath the surface of the water once more.

She walked slowly back to Little Clarion from the beach after her swim, shorts pulled on hastily over her wet swimsuit, feet sandy in her flip-flops, hair damp and salty and draped over one shoulder. It was still too early for anybody much to be about and she stayed on the sunny side of the road, drying slowly as she made her way back home.

Home.

She really was home; she could feel it now that she had salt water on her skin once more. She felt revitalised, renewed, as though she could really do this. She could make her grandmother's old house into the home of her dreams, she could find work, she could draw again and she could live happily here for ever. And she thought of Nick, the joke they'd shared on the patio the previous day, the way the corners of his eyes crinkled when he smiled. She touched her lips remembering his kiss all those years ago. How could she remember something that had happened only once and almost half her life ago? She couldn't remember how Adam kissed. Clearly it had never been very memorable.

She shook the thought away. She didn't want to think about Adam. Or Nick, for that matter. She had to concentrate on herself, on her own fresh start.

She was distracted by the smell of baked goods and turned to see a cafe, painted white with pots of geraniums outside. This must be the place Nick had bought the scones. He'd recommended it to her, told her to introduce herself to the owner. Her stomach growled telling her it was high time for breakfast, encouraging her to go in and introduce herself.

She stepped inside and was greeted by the smell of French patisserie and freshly ground coffee. She was glad she'd tucked her bank card into the pocket of her shorts.

'Hello,' Isobel called into the empty cafe.

'Hello!' a woman replied as she popped up from behind the counter. She was wearing a pink-and-white-striped apron and her dark hair was pulled back into a neat ponytail. 'Sorry, I was just getting everything ready for the day. How can I help you?'

'I'm new around here,' Isobel began. 'Well, I used to live here when I was a younger but I've just moved back and my friend, Nick, he recommended I pop in and...' She was babbling, she only wanted a coffee and a pain aux raisin.

The woman nodded, smiled. 'I'm Sarah,' she replied. 'And you must be Isobel.'

She could feel herself blush. 'My reputation precedes me,' she said, hoping it sounded like the joke it was intended to be.

'Nick told me all about you,' Sarah said. Then she paused, her face changing expression, her head tilting slightly. 'I'm so sorry about Vivien.'

Isobel shrugged and looked away. 'Thank you,' she said.

'She used to come in at least once a week for tea and cake. She liked the Victoria sponge the best. She just used to buy a slice and said there was no point baking a whole cake for herself.'

Guilt sliced through Isobel like a knife. What had she been doing wasting all those years in a job she hated when she should have been here, looking after her grandmother? Vivien shouldn't have been by herself. They should have been together, baking Victoria sponges.

But then it occurred to her that perhaps Vivien hadn't needed looking after, perhaps she had been happy with her trips to the cafe and her walks with Spencer. Isobel didn't know which was worse – the guilt or the feeling that her grandmother hadn't needed her at all.

'We used to make Victoria sponge together,' she said to Sarah. 'Nana taught me to bake.' Another thing Isobel hadn't done for a long time. Vivien had been right when she'd said she had been drifting in her letter. The last few years seemed to have passed Isobel by and she felt as though she was only now catching up again. She felt anxious at the thought of what she might have missed and she desperately tried to cling on to the last vestiges of calm from being in the sea.

'What can I get you?' Sarah asked.

'A cappuccino and...' She hesitated, looking at the selection of pastries. She always chose pain aux raisins, but she was very tempted by the cinnamon swirl. 'One of those and one of those,' she said pointing at them both. She'd save the cinnamon swirl for later, she thought, but then her stomach growled again. Maybe. 'Swimming always gives me an appetite.'

Sarah turned away to prepare the coffee and Isobel looked around the shop. There were several tables with cloths made of the same material as Sarah's apron and each one had an old-fashioned sugar shaker on it. The whole place had a wonderful vintage feel that made Isobel happy. She loved cafes like this.

Then she noticed the paintings – watercolours and charcoal sketches of the sea, the beach huts, the cliff tops. They were beautiful.

'Nick says you're doing up Vivien's old house,' Sarah said over the noise of the milk foamer.

'Yes…well, I'm trying to. To be honest, I don't know what I'm doing. It'll be Nick doing up the house, I suspect.'

'You've known each other a long time, he said.'

Had he? What else had Nick been saying? 'Well we knew each other as teenagers, which was quite a long time ago now.'

'How serendipitous is that though, you both being back at the same time!'

Wrapped up in the pictures, Isobel only half heard her.

'These watercolours and drawings,' she said. 'Are they yours?'

'Oh no, I wish.' Sarah laughed. 'I can bake a passable Victoria sponge, but I can't draw to save my life. No, they're done by a local art group – they display their work here for sale.'

The cogs in Isobel's brain started to move against one another. 'There's a local art group?'

'Eat in or takeaway?' Sarah asked.

'Takeaway,' Isobel mumbled, turning back to the paintings.

'The art group meet in the village hall,' Sarah said, pouring the foamed milk into the takeaway cup. 'But they are missing a tutor at the moment.'

Now that's serendipitous, Isobel thought.

'Nick says you're an artist,' Sarah went on. 'If you wanted, I'd be happy to show some of your art for sale too.'

'I…' Isobel turned back to her. 'Well I'll bear it in mind,' she said. 'Thank you.'

She took her coffee and pastries.

'It's been lovely chatting,' Sarah said as Isobel paid. 'Pop in anytime.'

Isobel felt that sensation of softening again. This was home, this was her community, this was her opportunity to heal.

'Thank you,' she said. 'So much.'

Even before she'd got back to the house she'd decided that 'the office' – her grandfather's old dark mahogany study, later commandeered by Vivien when she started teaching – would be her new studio. The seeds that had been planted when she'd seen the paintings in Sarah's cafe and heard about the art group with no teacher had started to take root as she walked home, sipping her cappuccino. She would paint again, she would stop hiding, stop drifting. She would become a person who would make her grandmother proud.

The office had the biggest windows and the most light – she wondered if that was why her grandfather had chosen it – but the light was ruined by the heavy, dark furniture. So it would have to go and she'd need Spencer's help. Then she could sort out all the books – work out which ones to keep and which to donate – paint the bookcases a lighter shade, the walls white and she could have the studio space she'd always dreamed of. There would be no excuses then, no reasons not to paint and draw.

And then I guess we'll find out if I've still got it in me, she thought.

She wanted to get going straight away, as soon as she let herself into the house. She wanted to start moving the furniture, clearing out the books. But as she put her almost empty coffee cup down on the mahogany desk she thought of the photograph again and her mind slipped back to where it had been before she'd stepped inside the café, before she'd seen the watercolours of beach huts and charcoal drawings of the sea.

She dug the photograph out from the back of the album again. She'd tucked it back in there deciding it was, of course, merely dated incorrectly. But she couldn't stop thinking about it. If it had just been this photograph of her grandmother on the beach, then she may well have put it down to a mistake and forgotten about it. But there were the photographs at the Hall as well, and the stories that Vivien had apparently told Ella and the other staff up there. She held the photograph between her thumb and index finger and sat down at the desk. What was she missing?

She wasn't missing anything, of course. There was nothing to miss. But she phoned her mother, just the same.

'Mum, it's me.'

'How's the house?' Gina's voice sounded so distant. There were times Isobel hated living so far from her parents. The last three months had been hard on her own.

'The house is a mess, to be honest,' she said. 'We've already had to fix the windows, get rid of a mouse infestation and try to deal with a damp problem.'

'Who is this "we"?' Gina asked.

'Do you remember Nick Hargreaves? Spencer's grandson?'

'I remember you telling me about him.'

'Well he's back too, he's staying with Spencer at the shop and he does up houses for a living…'

'I thought he was going to be a doctor.'

'Yes, well, life doesn't always go quite the way we plan, does it?'

Gina didn't say anything so Isobel ploughed on with as much enthusiasm as she could muster. 'Nick's going to help me, we're going to…well we haven't decided on a final plan but we're going to renovate the house, modernise it. Nana left me some money to pay for it and Nick has got loads of contacts…'

She paused but Gina didn't fill in the silence like she usually did. She didn't want to talk about Vivien. Or maybe she simply couldn't.

'Mum, I found this photograph—'

'Oh, Isobel, you know I don't like talking about the past or my childhood. Leave those photo albums alone, for goodness' sake.'

'It's of Nana standing on the beach here, by the cliff, wearing a swimsuit. It looks like she's been in the sea.'

'Well she always enjoyed swimming,' Gina said.

'The thing is, well…the thing is that the date on the back of the photo is July 1953 and…' Isobel took a shaky breath. 'Well that can't be right because she isn't pregnant and—'

'Somebody has dated it incorrectly,' Gina snapped before Isobel had a chance to finish her sentence. 'Clearly it's dated wrong.' Gina laughed then – a hollow, empty sound.

'OK.' Isobel said. Her mother had said the words she'd been expecting to hear, that the date was wrong. But there had been something about Gina's tone that didn't quite ring true.

'I saw these other photographs, up at Silverton Hall...' she began.

'What are you reading?' Gina interrupted, very clearly changing the subject. Her mother may not want to talk about the past very much, but that just seemed rude. Isobel knew not to push it and played along, reeling off a couple of books from her mother's recent emails that she hadn't actually read, feigning enthusiasm.

'I'll send you some more recommendations,' Gina said. 'I've read some excellent ones recently.'

'I was thinking of using the old office as my art studio,' Isobel said.

'Dad's old office?'

'Yes, I'm going to clear it out and get Spencer to value the furniture unless...' She paused. 'Do you want any of it?'

'All that old mahogany? No thanks! But are the books all still there?'

'They're all here,' Isobel replied. 'I mean, I haven't checked them all yet – I'm going to paint the bookshelves so I'll go through the books then, catalogue them – but it doesn't look like anything has been moved for years, judging by the dust.'

Gina laughed, but it again didn't sound genuine. 'Well your grandmother was never big on housekeeping.' She paused for a moment. 'Isobel?' she said, the end of the word rising in a question.

'Yes, Mum.'

'You won't get rid of any of the books without asking me, will you? I learned to read in that room, learned to love books in that room. Some of those books are old friends.'

'You could always come and help me,' Isobel suggested, knowing it was almost certainly a futile request.

'You know I can't do that, Isobel.'

'No, Mum, I know,' she replied sadly

As she ended the call though, Isobel was suddenly sure that there was more to the photograph of Vivien on the beach than an incorrect date. She just needed to find out what.

17

Nick was falling in love with her all over again. He'd realised that it was happening as they'd giggled together on the patio of Vivien's house, but he knew it had started days before, when she walked into Odds & Ends on the verge of tears looking for his grandfather, totally lost as to what to do about this huge house she'd inherited. It had reminded him of the day he'd first set eyes on her and had felt as much like a punch in the guts as it had done all those years ago.

Perhaps he had always been in love with her, he thought as he walked along the High Street, hands deep in the pockets of this trousers, his thoughts lost in the summer of 2001. Perhaps he had never truly fallen out of love with her, he'd just stopped himself thinking about her, stopped himself wondering what might have been. His marriage had never stood a chance. Poor Jeannette.

But now he was back here, now he'd seen her again, it was impossible not to think about her or to wonder what the last eighteen years had brought her. There was something about her quietness and vulnerability that seemed to run deeper than just the grief she must be feeling at losing Vivien, and he wondered what that was and if she'd share it with him.

Was he willing to share the intervening years with her?

Perhaps.

He rubbed the back of his neck with his palm. It was still early but the sun was already warm and the walk was making him sweat. He realised that he was taking the route towards Silverton Hall that he'd used to take with his grandfather's dog, Brenda, all those years ago. He didn't know what was drawing him there – memory he supposed – but he went along with it, following his feet.

He had barely slept the night before. He'd tossed and turned and thought about Isobel and the secrets she was hiding; the house and what he could do to it; the slow, inevitable collapse of his marriage; and the story that Isobel had told him the day before of Vivien and the party at Silverton Hall.

The party had captured his attention the most – it didn't feel as though it directly affected him so he could think about it without upsetting the delicate equilibrium of his own anxieties. Too many thoughts about Isobel, or the house, or his erstwhile marriage might be more than he could handle right now.

It was hard to imagine Vivien at glamourous parties, but then it was always hard to imagine your parents and grandparents as young people. His own grandchildren, should he ever have any, would probably stare in disbelief if he ever told them the things he'd got up to as a medical student. What was odd was that Vivien had kept it all a secret from Isobel.

But Vivien did keep secrets if he'd understood what he'd overheard that afternoon two years ago in Odds & Ends. He was sure now he'd heard correctly, sure it wasn't a figment of his imagination, a side effect of his healing brain. And he was sure that Isobel didn't know.

If Vivien was the sort of person who could keep a secret like that, she could also be the sort of person who decided not to tell her granddaughter about other things – like going to glamorous parties at Silverton Hall.

'Do you know Silverton Bay?' Isobel had asked him that first morning they had met in his grandfather's shop.

'I haven't been back to England since I was eleven,' he'd replied. He'd been very aware of his accent and how dry his mouth had felt. He could remember that morning like it was yesterday.

Isobel had taken it upon herself to show him around, pointing out the cliff tops, the golf course, the pub, the rows of shops in the High Street. Then she'd taken him up to the top of the village and along the country lane towards Silverton Hall, a place he'd used to come with his mother when he was a little boy.

'It's Jacobean,' he could remember his mother telling him as they'd walked in the grounds. His mother had still taken an interest in him then, back before his father had had that affair and been advised to take the job in Singapore. 'Can you remember what that means?'

'Related to James I of England,' he'd parroted, and his mother had smiled and squeezed his hand.

'I used to come here when I was small,' he'd told Isobel. 'My mother used to like walking around the gardens and sometimes we'd have tea in the conservatory.' As they'd looked through the gate, they'd seen that the gardens seemed a bit run-down and untended. The Hall had been boarded up back then, one hotel closed waiting for another to eventually open.

'Don't you think there's something quite spooky about it?' Isobel had said. 'Now that it's all shut up?' Then she'd skipped ahead of him and spun around so that she was facing him, walking backwards away from the Hall, her huge blue eyes locked on his.

He'd smiled at her dumbly. He'd barely managed to string a sentence together that first morning. Although he got better as the summer wore on and was able to have conversations with her eventually, even some that were long and felt meaningful, he often found himself wanting to be the silent spectator, watching her energy, relishing being with her.

It had been the same when she'd walked into his grandfather's shop the other day. Time had stood still for a moment and he'd become that eighteen-year-old again – mouth dry, arms crossed across his chest.

His feelings for Isobel had grown so strong that summer that he'd had to get away from her sometimes, to be on his own. That's why he'd started taking Brenda for her afternoon walks up to Silverton Hall, circumnavigating the walls around the estate – just as he was today – staying out for longer and longer, staying away from Isobel for whole afternoons because he hadn't wanted to feel like that about her. Not when he'd known he'd be leaving at the end of the summer.

On their last day together, the day before his grandfather had been due to drive him to Peterborough so he could take the train to Sheffield, move into his halls of residence and start his medical career, he'd asked her to join him while he walked Brenda.

'I never thought you'd ask me to come on one of your afternoon walks,' she'd said. 'You're so secretive about them.' She'd been teasing, but he'd wondered if he had hurt her by not asking her, by disappearing on his own every day.

'You said you didn't like the Hall,' he'd replied. 'You said it spooked you.'

'I'd like it well enough if I was with you,' she'd said. Her voice had been quiet, tentative. She'd slipped her hand into his. 'I can't believe this is the last day I'll see you. The summer has gone too quickly.'

'We'll see each other again though, won't we?' he'd asked.

'I don't know.' He'd watched her tanned shoulders slump a little. 'Our lives are going to be very different from now on.'

Nick had felt the stone in his stomach and the lump in his throat that he'd always felt when he'd thought about medical school. This was his father's dream, not his. Wasn't he supposed to have a calling?

Instead of dwelling on the future, he'd told her that he wanted to kiss her, that he'd wanted to kiss her all summer.

And she'd smiled. 'I thought you'd never ask,' she'd said.

He ran a hand through his hair, realising he'd walked to almost the exact place where they'd shared that kiss – a kiss he'd never been able to forget. He stopped for a moment, leaning against a wall to catch his breath, to pull himself back into the present. So much had changed since that summer for both of them, but his feelings for Isobel had never gone away. Not really.

He kept walking around the Hall, wondering if he should go in and look at these photographs of Vivien at the Midsummer Party that she had told him about, wondering if seeing them for himself would help solve the mystery Isobel was clearly trying to work out. Was it a mystery, though? Vivien had gone to some parties when she was young. It didn't mean anything unless it was connected to what he thought he knew...

He turned on his heel to walk back to his grandfather's shop. He wasn't in the right clothes or headspace to go into the Hall. He was hot and sweaty and he could feel a sense of panic creeping up on him again as if from nowhere. Would that feeling ever go away completely? Would he ever be able to heal completely from the trauma?

One thing he did know was that he had to make a decision about what he was going to do with the rest of his life. That he needed to throw himself into the renovation business properly and stop treating it like a stopgap. He wasn't going back into medicine, he knew that well enough, but he needed to fill his time with meaningful work and stop spending so much of it alone, thinking. Thinking never did him any good. He already knew that.

'Excuse me,' a voice said, interrupting his thoughts.

He turned around to see a woman from the village – Laura, or maybe Lorna – smiling at him. He wasn't sure where he recognised her from. The pub? His grandfather's shop?

'Hi, Nick, it's Lauren, remember me? You did some work on our house just before Christmas.'

Lauren then. Nick nodded, he remembered now.

'I hear Isobel's back, we were at school together. A few

of us wondered…' She paused, smiled again. 'She's an art teacher, right?'

Nick nodded again. He wanted to get away from this woman who seemed to know both him and Isobel and a connection between them that he wasn't aware of.

'Could you ask her something for me?'

18

Isobel's head felt as though it was stuffed full of cotton wool and all the clarity she had gained from her swim had vanished. She couldn't stop thinking about the photographs. Whilst she'd been swimming, submerged in the salt water for the first time in years, the huge Norfolk sky above her, everything had felt still and insignificant. When Vivien had first taken her to swim in the sea as a child, she'd told her that there was nothing quite like it in the world.

'I didn't believe Mrs Castleton when she first told me that,' Vivien had said. 'But it's true.'

And it was true for Isobel as well. Just as Mrs Castleton – her grandmother's friend who had died before Isobel was born – had gone swimming every day with Vivien, so Vivien swam every day with Isobel. Being in the water this morning had made her feel close to her grandmother again and she'd almost forgotten about the photograph of her grandmother on the beach.

But back in her grandparents' office, after the stilted conversation with her mother, she wondered again about the significance of the photographs and their connection with the parties at Silverton Hall, which she realised she hadn't asked her mother about. It had been easy to believe, as she'd floated on the surface of the sea, that her grandmother would never have lied to her, that nobody could have kept such a secret, especially in a small village where everybody knew everybody else's business, but now she was convinced again that there was something neither Vivien nor Gina had ever told her.

But was it important in the grand scheme of things? Perhaps her instincts when she'd been in the sea were correct. She should leave it alone and concentrate on her own life, the house, earning some money. Vivien was still her grandmother, no matter what the DNA floating around in her body might tell her. She needed to concentrate on something else and the best thing to do was to concentrate on the closest thing to an opportunity she'd come across since she got here – displaying her art at the cafe and finding out some more about this art group.

Of course it matters though, said a small voice in her head. Were the parties at Silverton Hall connected to the photograph of Vivien in her bathing suit on the beach somehow? She wished she could ask her grandmother about it. She wanted to make a pot of tea and sit in the living room and talk to Vivien, ask her why she had never told her any of this before. She closed her eyes and took a breath. What she would give for just one more day.

She pushed the thoughts away. She had too much time to think, that was the trouble. Too much time to mull over the past and go through her grandmother's things. Perhaps her mother was right. Perhaps the past was something to leave well alone.

Instead of listening to the rather persistently curious voice in her head, she thought about the feeling she'd had as she'd walked back from Odds & Ends earlier that week – the itching feeling of needing to have a pencil in her hand, of needing to draw again. But she couldn't fill the cafe with pictures of Nick Hargreaves or people would talk. She had to find a way of feeling that itch about something else – the sea, the skies, the fields.

Portraiture had been her speciality at St Martin's, but she had also loved landscapes especially the wistful, Romantic and sometimes turbulent landscapes of Turner and Constable. Some of her peers thought it was a bit old fashioned and stuffy, thought she should be more interested in the brightly coloured acrylic landscapes of Hockney or Diebenkorn's *Ocean Park* paintings. But she believed it was easy to forget – so conditioned were we by the Impressionists, the Surrealists, the Cubists – how shocking Turner's shimmering landscapes had been to Victorian audiences. So Isobel continued to love her nineteenth-century landscape painters; their work spoke to a part of her that she'd always kept hidden, a part that perhaps nobody would ever really accept even at art college. Constable, in particular, held a big place in her heart. His pictures of Suffolk, the enormity of its skies, always reminded her of home. When she was back in Silverton Bay in the summers, she would try to recreate Constable's work, painting the Bay and the nearby lavender fields over and over again until Vivien reminded her to stop trying to be somebody else and paint from her own heart – and that was when it had clicked with her, when she had found the things she loved most about North Norfolk and translated them on to her canvases.

That was what she needed to do now, to get back out there with her easel and her watercolours, to paint the place she loved more than anything else in the world. And, perhaps, if any of those paintings were good enough, she could see what Sarah thought, whether she would display them on the whitewashed walls of her cafe.

Isobel felt the buzz of a new project, a feeling that had become so rare that it made her dizzy and she had to hold on to the desk for a moment. This was it, she thought to herself, the start of something. It wasn't much, she knew that, but it had been a long time since she'd felt anything. And it would certainly keep her mind off old photographs.

Whilst much of the initial work for the paintings would happen out and about, she wanted to get the office ready too because she sometimes liked to paint from photographs and make finishing touches indoors in an artificial light similar to that in which the painting would be displayed. She needed to get this room cleared out, the books sorted, and the dark built-in bookcases painted as soon as possible. She looked around at the furniture in the room – two desks, a selection of ancient chairs stacked in the corner as though forgotten, a couple of cabinets, probably full of out-of-date paperwork if she knew her grandmother. She didn't want any of it and, as this had been the room where her grandfather worked and then later where her grandmother marked history essays, it held no sentimental value to her. She could be ruthless, she could get rid of everything and, finally, for the first time since art school, she could have a studio space that was all her own.

Odds & Ends was dark and cool when she arrived, and it took a moment for her eyes to adjust from the bright, hot sunshine outside.

'Hello, love, how are you?' she heard Spencer ask from the back of the shop, and, as her eyes grew accustomed to the gloom, she saw him cloth in hand, polishing a chest of drawers.

'I'm OK,' she said, channelling the determination of her new project. She noticed Nick leaning against the wall behind the counter and her stomach flipped in a way she wished it wouldn't.

'I went to the cafe this morning and met Sarah,' she said to Nick. 'Fabulous pastries!'

'Tell me about it,' he replied, patting his stomach. 'It's just as well I've got a physical job.' He paused awkwardly then, his eyes flicking away, realising, Isobel supposed, that the subject of his job and the significant change of career was something they still hadn't talked about.

'She said I could display some of my art there.'

'That's great, Isobel,' Nick said.

'I mean, I need to actually paint something first…' And then it was her turn to look away from the awkward silence because it wasn't as though she'd told him much about her own disastrous career either.

'I met somebody this morning that you went to school with apparently,' Nick said, filling the silence. 'Lauren Guilder.'

'Cooke,' Spencer said from over by the cabinet. 'Lauren Cooke now she married that accountant.' Spencer had quite a low opinion of accountants for unknown reasons.

'Well she was telling me that she's part of this local art group,' Nick went on. 'They meet in the village hall every week.'

'Yeah, I saw some of their art in the cafe.'

'Their tutor has left and she'd heard you were back, wondered if you had time to take over the group after the summer holidays.' He smiled, shrugged. 'I don't think it pays much, but it's a start, right?'

Isobel smiled. She didn't want to tell him that she already knew that the art group was looking for a tutor, she didn't want to spoil the moment. 'It's a brilliant start,' she said instead. 'Thank you so much, I'll call her. It'll be nice to catch up after all these years.' She felt a wave of guilt at how she'd left the Bay without really keeping in touch with anyone, leaving for Adam and their artistic London life that never amounted to anything anyway.

After Nick had given her Lauren's number, Isobel forced herself to get on with things.

'The reason I came here was to ask for your help, Spencer,' she said. 'I need to make a space for my studio so I can draw and paint and wondered if you'd help me clear out the furniture in the old office at the house.'

Spencer's eyes lit up. 'Oh yes,' he said. 'There's some fantastic pieces there that I'd love…' He stopped and smiled apologetically. 'If you don't mind, of course, if you don't want to keep them. I'll pay, naturally.'

Isobel laughed. 'No, I don't want any of them,' she said.

'How about I come by tomorrow morning?'

'That would be great, I'll see you then.'

Nick walked back outside with her and they stood in the sunshine outside the shop.

'Are you OK?' he asked.

She smiled at him in that determined way again, trying very hard not to notice how close he was standing to her.

She just wanted to reach out and touch him. 'Of course,' she said. 'Why?'

'You just seemed a bit distant in there,' he replied. 'As though you're thinking about other things…' He paused awkwardly again. 'Which of course you're entitled to without having to tell me anything.'

Isobel looked away, wondering if she should tell him. She had to tell someone, she might burst if the only person she told was her unresponsive mother.

'I found an old photograph of Nana,' she began.

'Oh, Isobel.' She felt the warmth of Nick's hand on her shoulder. 'It's only been a few months; it's bound to still hurt.'

'No,' she said. 'I mean yes, of course it still hurts, it's just…' She paused. 'It was a picture of her on the beach in this old-fashioned bathing suit. It must have been just after she moved here.'

Nick didn't say anything, just waited for her to go on. He didn't move his hand from her shoulder either.

'It was taken in the summer of 1953, not long before my mother was born. The thing is…' She stopped again, unsure of herself. Was her mother right and it was just incorrectly dated?

'The thing is?' Nick said softly.

'Well, she's very clearly not pregnant in it.'

Nick's fingers tightened on her shoulder and then dropped away. She heard him suck air between his teeth.

'Have you spoken to your mother?' he asked after a moment.

'She said it must be the wrong date on the photograph,

but I just have this really weird feeling that there's more to it than that.'

Nick nodded. Did she imagine the look that passed briefly over his face as he looked back into the shop, towards his grandfather? A look that showed less surprise at the revelation and more acceptance.

'Shall I come over this afternoon?' he asked. 'I need to measure up the kitchen and perhaps you can show me then.'

She felt relieved that Nick believed her and hadn't just dismissed her misgivings.

'In the meantime, try not to overthink things.'

Isobel smiled at him. 'Why do I think that's advice that you should take as well?' she said.

19

Isobel was sitting on the beach later that afternoon when her phone rang – her father's number appeared on the screen. Her thumb hovered for a moment as she wondered whether to accept the call or not, wondered what he wanted. No doubt by now her mother would have spoken to him about the conversation they'd had that morning. She wondered what her father knew about Gina's past, about Vivien and Max. She accepted the call.

'Sweetheart, how are you?' the familiar voice boomed into her ear. 'I haven't spoken to you in a while.'

'I'm fine, Dad, really.' Her father didn't phone her very often and if he did answer the phone when she rang her mother, he quickly made his excuses and passed the call over. She wondered what he wanted and suspected that it must be connected to the conversation she'd had with her mother. It was too much of a coincidence otherwise.

Just like the photographs.

She'd meant to go straight home after leaving Odds & Ends, but instead had found herself back at Silverton Hall to look at the photographs again. Ella had been pleased to see her but had been busy with a party of American golfers and Isobel had walked to the ballroom herself this time, following the route that she and Ella had walked a few days before and wondering if her grandmother had walked these same corridors when she'd been here for the midsummer party. As she'd stood in front of the photograph of her grandmother in her ballgown smiling over her shoulder at the camera, exactly as she was in the portrait that Max had painted of her, she knew she was becoming obsessed with the idea of these photographs and with the connection they had to herself. One last connection back to her beloved grandmother who she missed so much.

She'd known she was being ridiculous and suddenly needed to get out of the hotel, away from the dark ballroom thick with history and memories. She'd needed sea air to blow away the feeling that had returned as soon as she'd seen the photographs again. If she looked at them for too long she felt as though she'd find something out that she didn't want to know.

She'd gone straight to the beach and sat at the bottom of the cliff path, her bare feet scrunching into the sand. That was where she'd been when her father called.

'Is everything all right?' Isobel asked him now.

She heard him take a breath. 'You spoke to your mother this morning,' he said. It wasn't a question. 'You asked her about a photograph.'

'I shouldn't have done, should I?' Isobel replied. 'I had a feeling I hit a nerve, it's just…' She paused. 'Did she tell you what the photograph was of? That she thought it must have the wrong date on the back of it? She's probably right and—'

'You're allowed to ask questions about your own family, sweetheart,' Tim interrupted. 'And I'm phoning in the hope that I can answer some of those questions. Your mom asked me to see if you were OK.'

'Of course I'm OK,' Isobel replied. 'I don't understand.' Neither of Isobel's parents talked very much about their childhoods. Her father had a difficult relationship with his own father who'd left when he was young and married someone else, and Gina and Vivien had never got along, certainly not since Max had died so far as Isobel could work out.

Her parents had met in London. It was one of the few stories of the past that both her mother and father were happy to talk about, telling it together over secret glances and entwined fingers.

'I fell in love with her the moment I saw her,' Tim had always said and Gina would bat him away as though he was talking rubbish whilst secretly knowing that not only was it true but the feeling was mutual.

Isobel's mother had been working as a receptionist at an architectural firm called Stephenson & Malone in London, near Tower Bridge. It had been the summer of 1974, just after she graduated, and Gina had loved it.

'I used to sit at this smooth white reception desk with a view to the river through plate-glass windows,' Gina would say when she told the story. 'I loved working there so much, it felt as though I was meant to be there.'

'And thank goodness you were,' Tim would reply.

Isobel had never thought much about the fact that her mother had stayed in London after graduation, living with Vivien's parents, other than the fact that she didn't get on with her mother and didn't like Silverton Bay very much.

'The world felt like a much bigger place when I lived in

London,' Gina had explained. 'As though anything could happen.'

It was while she was working at Stephenson & Malone that she became completely obsessed with the World Trade Centre – a pair of skyscrapers that stood nearly a quarter of a mile high. She'd started to wonder if English had been the right subject to study at university, and she had begun to realise that perhaps there might not be enough time to find out about all the fascinating things that were happening in the world. She read voraciously and saved what she could of her salary for the plane ticket that would one day take her to New York City so that she could stand on the viewing platform of The South Tower and look out over Manhattan from the second tallest building in the world.

And then one afternoon the Americans had arrived for a meeting. One of them – tall and blonde with an impossibly white smile – had flirted with her, had asked her to come for a drink with him after work.

'I'm Tim,' he'd said, but it hadn't been until after he'd walked away towards the lifts that she'd realised he was Tim Malone, her boss's son who had stayed in New York with his mother after the divorce. There was another Mrs Malone now and three more children.

She had almost chickened out of the date.

Almost.

'Gina knew you were going to inherit the house,' Tim said now, in a way that made Isobel feel as though he was beginning to tell her a story. 'Vivien told her a while ago and she's fine with it. It's not like she can do anything with a house on the other side of the pond anyway.' Isobel imagined her father's sigh, the way he rubbed his fingers over his forehead whenever he thought about Gina's refusal to fly. She knew how much it frustrated and worried him. 'But she knew you'd want to live there, she knew your heart lay in Silverton Bay, and she knew that you'd find out about her past once you started sorting through Vivien's things. I just don't think that she expected you to find out so quickly. She'd hoped you'd come out here and she'd be able to tell you herself first.'

'Tell me what?' Isobel asked, even though she had a feeling she knew exactly what it was that Gina had roped her father into telling her. 'And why are you telling me?'

'I'm here because your mom asked me to tell you, because she's upset and embarrassed about lying to you this morning.'

'So she was lying about the date on the photograph.'

'The date on the photograph is correct. Gina doesn't know when exactly that summer it was taken or who took it, although she says probably your grandfather. But as Vivien was never pregnant that year, the date is probably right.'

'I don't understand...' Isobel said again, but she understood completely. What she didn't understand was why she was only hearing about this now at the age of thirty-six whilst sitting on a beach thousands of miles away from her mother. She couldn't work out whether she was upset or angry or both.

'Max and Vivien adopted your mother a few days after she was born. She grew up believing that she was their biological child and from what I understand, although of course I never met him, it was Max who refused to tell her the truth, who wanted her to grow up ignorant of where she came from.'

'When did Mum find out?' Isobel asked. 'Is that why she fell out with Nana? Why didn't Max tell her? Who…?'

'Hey, slow down, sweetheart,' Tim said softly. 'I'm going to try to answer your questions as best I can but you will need to talk to your mom about the details, although she doesn't know that many.'

'Why?'

'Look, back in the 50s when your mom and I were growing up things were different, attitudes were different, especially over there in Britain, in your strange little villages.' Tim Malone was born with New York City running through his veins and he'd never really understood the British countryside or village life. 'I read Agatha Christie as a kid,' he'd always said. 'You've no idea what's going on behind closed doors.'

'What sort of attitudes?' Isobel asked.

'Attitudes towards unmarried mothers,' her father replied. 'You couldn't just get on with your life like you can now, there was a lot of guilt and shame and blame put upon women then and a lot of shame attached to the child too. From what we understand, there was a young woman in the village who got herself in trouble…' He paused. 'Even the phrase sounds horribly old fashioned, doesn't it?'

'And makes it sound like the woman is entirely to blame,' Isobel replied indignantly. 'Whereas I always thought it took two people to make a baby.'

'I know, honey, I know. But the fact remains that it was 1953 and this woman, she worked at that big hall by the sea, she was unmarried and pregnant, and your grandparents agreed to adopt the child.'

'Why?'

'All we know is they felt it was the right thing to do, to help this woman out so she could go back to her family and start again. They wanted a family and they loved Gina as though she was their own. They never had any other kids so Gina must have been a huge blessing to them.'

'Who was she, the biological mother?' Isobel asked. 'Has Mum ever met her?'

'All your mother knows is the name of her mother on the adoption certificate. She never wanted to meet her.' Tim paused, sighed. 'We'd been married nearly a year before she even told me. She hates talking about it, hates how it changed her relationship with Vivien and her memories of Max.'

'How did she find out?'

'Vivien told her in the end, right before she went to university. I guess she had to know then; she'd have needed her birth certificate for registration and so on I suppose. They fell out horribly over and it and for years they hardly spoke. Gina lived with Vivien's parents in London until we met and...well, you know that story.' Isobel heard the smile in her father's words – the love between her parents had always been so strong, a love she had based her own relationships on and all of them, even Adam – especially Adam – had come out severely lacking.

'That's a lot to take in, Dad, suddenly now... I don't ...'

'I know, sweetheart, I remember how I felt when Gina first told me.'

'But I'm her daughter, why did she never tell me that Vivien wasn't really my grandmother?'

'I think for that reason,' Tim replied. 'Because Vivien was your grandmother in everything except blood, and you loved her, didn't you?'

'Well, yes…'

'And your mom didn't want to spoil that. She saw how alike the two of you were, how well you got on and so she just left things as they were. In fact it was you that helped mend their relationship.'

'Really?'

Tim laughed. 'I know it seemed like they didn't get on, honey, but that was nothing compared to how it was before you came along.' He paused. 'And Vivien adored you, right from the first time she met you.'

Isobel didn't say anything, she just sat there, looking out to sea and pressing the phone against her ear.

'Perhaps it wasn't the right thing to do,' Tim went on. 'But your mom never meant to lie to you or hurt you. She loves you so much, Isobel.'

'And Mum has never wanted to find her real mother?' Isobel thought she'd be bursting to know if she'd been in Gina's position.

'Not so far as I know. Like I said, she hates talking about it and—'

'Dad,' Isobel interrupted, suddenly feeling as though the world was spinning too fast, the sounds of the other people on the beach growing loud and as though a ball of something unpleasant was stuck in her throat. 'I don't think I… I mean I think, I think I need to go.'

'OK,' Tim said hesitantly. 'Are you all right?'

'I...' She hesitated, unable to really put how she was feeling into words. 'I'm all right, of course I am. I'm just a bit shocked, you know. Surprised by it all. And...'

'Go on.'

'Well, I'm a bit annoyed, if I'm honest.' That was an understatement. 'I don't really understand why neither Mum nor Nana ever said anything.'

'I can understand those feelings,' Tim replied. He sounded rather stressed and embarrassed. This was the first personal conversation that Isobel could ever remember having with her father, and it was certainly the longest. 'But I can't answer that, you know.'

'Dad, it's OK, I know I need to talk to Mum but I don't think either of us are ready for that right now.'

'No, maybe not.'

'Will you tell her...will you tell her I love her?'

'Of course I will.'

Isobel ended the call then, putting the phone back in her bag and looking around the beach at the people there – families playing cricket, couples sunbathing, swimmers' heads bobbing in the sea. As she'd sat here listening to the news that changed everything, life had just been carrying on as normal all around her.

Her mother was adopted and hadn't known until she was eighteen. It made a lot of sense when Isobel thought about it – the underlying resentment between her mother and grandmother, the lack of any interest on her mother's part in the village she grew up in, the way nobody ever talked about Max – but she wished she'd known sooner, wished her mother had felt able to confide in her. She felt both angry and upset about it even though she knew she probably had no right to be. This was Gina and Vivien's story after all.

But if she'd known, would it have changed things? Would Isobel and her mother have got along better? She would never know, she supposed.

She wondered who else knew. Silverton Bay was a small village and, in her experience, one where everyone knew everyone else's business. It was things like that her father despised about the British countryside. People would have known that Gina was adopted, lots of people. They would have been discreet, but they would have known. Yet Gina herself hadn't found out for eighteen years, seven years after her father passed away. Was it really any wonder that Gina never wanted to talk about her childhood?

Isobel heard someone calling her name and it felt as though it came from far away, as though it came from another lifetime.

'Isobel, Isobel.'

And as she heard his voice, she remembered the way he'd looked back into the shop towards his grandfather when she had told him about the photograph of Vivien on the beach. She knew then that he knew and that Spencer knew. Was she the only person who didn't?

'There you are,' Nick said. 'I've been looking everywhere for you.' A pause then. 'Isobel, are you OK?'

'I've just had the strangest conversation with my father…' she began. As Nick sat on the beach next to her, she found, to her embarrassment, that she was crying and she felt Nick's arms around her as she buried her face in his t-shirt.

She had no idea what these tears were about, whether they were tears of anger, frustration or just simple shock. But she did know that she felt a lot better for Nick being there.

20

Norfolk – June 1953

'That dress looks wonderful on you,' Max said as Vivien stepped down the stairs. 'I knew it would.' He smiled and held his hand out to her. 'I could paint you in that dress,' he said.

Sometimes Vivien forgot about her husband's artistic background and his training at the Slade. He seemed so tired and stressed all the time now and it was hard to imagine him as an artist, sitting in coffee shops, discussing life and truth and beauty, like the group of his friends had been on the evening they first met. He'd been so kind to her, and she'd said yes to his proposal because of that kindness. Admittedly she'd also said yes because she wanted something more, because she'd wanted to escape the mundanity of her life – the daily journey from Newbury Park, the endless typing for a man who didn't seem to acknowledge her existence at all – but she wouldn't have given up that modicum of independence for just anyone. She'd thought Max understood her, she'd thought they were the same. She'd thought they would live together in London. She hadn't realised that taking her to see the sea had meant leaving her there.

He was still kind to her when they were together – it's just that wasn't very often these days – and she wondered sometimes, when she looked at his tired, worried face, if he regretted it all – the double life, the endless travelling between Norfolk and London, if he regretted marrying in the first place. She wondered if he thought about her at all when he was away, because she'd found that she thought about him less and less unless he was back in the Bay with her. Surely that wasn't what a marriage was all about? She'd wanted to ask Mrs Castleton about it, but hadn't been brave enough yet.

Tonight though, things felt different. As she stepped down the stairs and gave him her hand, he drew her towards him and kissed her gently. He looked so handsome in his evening suit that Vivien felt herself soften. Perhaps things weren't so bad after all.

'I'm sorry,' he said softly. 'I've been a beast, haven't I? Work has been rather stressful, I'm afraid.' The way he looked at her reminded her of the day they met, the day he took her for coffee in Soho and told her that he worked in his father's bank rather than doing the painting he so loved. And then his face changed and he told her again that he would paint her in her new dress. 'Will you forgive me if I do?' he asked. Suddenly he was the man who asked her to marry him, the man at the Royal Academy. How many versions of Max Chambers were there? Did she even know them all?

'I'll forgive you,' she said although she knew her forgiveness would make no difference and nothing would change. He'd still go to London and she'd still get on with her life on the Norfolk coast and the painting would never be done. She wondered if, eventually, they would live separately, if Max would stay in London and she would stay here. She wondered, just for a moment, if there was somebody else – another woman who Max wanted to keep her away from. She briefly remembered Charlotte, the woman in the tight jumper at the coffee shop who had been at the Slade with Max.

But she pushed all that out of her mind for the evening because tonight was the midsummer party at Silverton Hall and she was determined to enjoy herself. The new dress that Max had bought did look fantastic on her and she felt, for this evening at least, like the sort of person she had hoped to become by marrying Max.

They walked up the hill to the Hall, her hand tucked into the crook of his elbow. Max carried his camera with him in a leather case, the strap draped over his shoulder. The camera was another hangover from art school, an old Kodak – so Max had told her – really not up to much now and he should buy one of the new, small Box Brownies – much more suitable for snapshots he'd said, and without the need to develop them himself. He'd used the same old Kodak to take a photo of Vivien on her wedding day, and even though he'd tried to explain the process to her – the darkroom, the trays of chemicals, the special photographic paper – it still felt like magic that a likeness of her in her wedding dress could possibly come from that square metal box in its leather case.

The evening was warm and, as they got nearer to the Hall, Vivien started to notice the other people heading in the same direction dressed in black tie and exquisite gowns, white gloves and diamond necklaces. Some of them she recognised from the village but didn't yet know, and some – those who were getting out of big black cars in front of the Hall – she had never seen before. She was nervous about not knowing anybody – Mrs Castleton would be there but in her capacity as an employee of the Hall so Vivien wouldn't be able to talk to her – but excited nonetheless. She had never been to anything like this before.

As soon as they stepped into the Hall itself, people began to crowd them; people Max knew from London. He introduced her to each of them. 'My wife, Vivien,' he said fondly, his hand on her lower back. But she had no interest in their conversations and as he talked she looked around her at the grandeur of the Hall – or The Silverton Hall Hotel as it had now become – and tried to take in as many details as she possibly could so that she could write to her mother and tell her all about it. Her mother wouldn't believe it when she did tell her. This hotel was something else.

She felt a gentle tug as Max started to move away from the people he was talking to and Vivien smiled and followed.

'I just love what you've done with the place,' one woman called after them with a laugh.

'What did she mean by that?' Vivien whispered. 'You didn't have anything to do with the Hall becoming a hotel, did you?'

Max patted her hand distractedly. 'It was just a joke,' he said. 'I'll explain it to you later.' And then he stopped and turned towards her, his face sincere. 'I'll explain everything tomorrow.'

Vivien looked at her husband. 'What do you mean?' she asked. 'What's going on?'

'Tomorrow,' Max repeated, turning away from her again.

She didn't have much time to think about it though because soon they were swept along one of the beautifully lit passageways towards a huge dining room. It was like something out of Vivien's dreams – the sort of room she had imagined when she had read about dances at Netherfield in *Pride and Prejudice*. She felt as though she needed to pinch herself as she was shown to her seat, which turned out to be next to an MP and a man who was about to inherit a baronetcy. Max was sitting much further down the table and he leaned back to give her an encouraging smile. Even so, she felt out of place as though the evening was becoming unwieldy and she didn't know what to do about it.

And then, out of the corner of her eye, she saw Mrs Castleton, organising a group of waiting staff. When Mrs Castleton smiled at her, she told herself that everything was going to be all right.

21

Norfolk – July 2019

'Did you know?' Isobel asked Nick as he started to unpack his tools the next morning. He turned away from her when she asked, his attention seemingly consumed by a hammer. 'Did Spencer know?'

He nodded slowly, his back to her still. 'We both knew,' he said. 'Although I don't think I was supposed to know.'

'Tell me,' she said. 'Tell me how you knew.'

The night before, after she had finished crying, after she had pulled away from Nick, she hadn't wanted to talk about it. She was too tired and embarrassed to talk about who knew and who didn't and she felt mortified about the tear stains on Nick's t-shirt. When he'd asked, she simply told him that she had found out her mother had been adopted, that Gina didn't know who her biological parents were and seemingly had no interest in finding out.

He'd asked if she wanted to get something to eat but she'd refused.

'I just want to be on my own,' she'd said. 'Can you walk me home?'

They'd walked in silence and when they'd arrived at Little Clarion they'd stood outside awkwardly, each waiting for the other to say something.

'I'm going to start on the kitchen tomorrow,' Nick had said. 'I'll be around about eight o'clock if that's OK?'

'Oh god, you were going to measure up, weren't you? You were—'

'It's OK, Isobel,' he'd interrupted softly. 'It can all wait until tomorrow. Try and get some sleep.'

Isobel had watched him walk away, back towards the High Street, and she wished he could wrap his arms around her again. She wished he could kiss her like he had on that September afternoon eighteen years before.

She might not have wanted to talk about her mother's adoption, but she hadn't been able to think of anything else. She had tried to distract herself with cheese on toast and another attempt at reading her mother's latest book recommendation, but it had been useless, her mind had been whirling. Once she got into bed she had lain there staring at the ceiling, wishing that she had talked to Nick, shared dinner with him, asked him what he knew. She felt frustrated by how little she knew and curious for the truth whilst also very aware that it wasn't really her story, that her mother and grandmother were entitled to their own lives, their own privacy.

'It was a couple of years ago,' Nick said now, staring at the hammer he was holding. 'Not long after I left…' He hesitated. 'Well, I was staying with Grandad.' He paused and looked over at Isobel as she leaned against one of the kitchen units that was going to be ripped out this morning. 'Vivien came in,' he went on. 'She was upset about something, I don't know what. She and Grandad went into the back to talk and I was working on a piece of furniture at the time so I was concentrating, or at least trying to. When they came out Vivien said something, but I don't think she knew I was there.'

'What did she say?'

'She said "the problem with Gina is she has never been able to believe me when I tell her that just because she's adopted doesn't mean I love her any less".'

'That's it?' Isobel asked. 'That's all she said?'

'It's all I heard,' Nick replied. 'But it was enough. I remember wondering if you knew, if you'd known that summer when we…' He trailed off, shrugged and turned his attention back to the hammer.

'I never knew,' Isobel said quietly. 'Not until yesterday.'

They looked at each other for a moment and it felt as awkward as it had done outside the house the night before. Isobel desperately wanted to ask him about leaving the hospital, but she sensed now wasn't the time. Would there ever be a right time to talk to him, to ask him how he was, to apologise for never replying to his letter all those years ago? He'd written to her that autumn when he was in his first year of medical school but, despite keeping the letter, she'd never written back. She hadn't been able to, not after everything that had happened the day after he left.

'I'll let you get on,' she said instead. It was easier perhaps to just stay in the present, to ignore how she was feeling about him. It would pass and there was too much else going on.

'Isobel,' Nick said softly as she turned away and she looked over her shoulder at him. 'Grandad will know better than me. Why don't you talk to him?'

She nodded and turned away again.

Spencer was coming to have a look at some of Vivien's old furniture, pieces that Isobel knew she didn't want to keep because they wouldn't go with the aesthetic she had decided on for the house. She had tried, the night before when she couldn't sleep, to start sorting out the office – the room she wanted to work on first. But she hadn't even been able to concentrate on that. Instead she'd stared at the photograph of Vivien on the beach and made up all sorts of crazy scenarios in her head about who her mother's real parents were. It had crossed her mind that, while Vivien wasn't Gina's mother, Max could be her father. But surely Vivien would have told Gina that. Surely...

Her brain had started to feel fuzzy then and she'd dragged herself off to bed, sleeping fitfully until Nick had arrived to work on the kitchen.

Part of her empathised with her mother for not wanting to find out the truth. Perhaps it was easier to not know, to get on with your own life, to make your own family. And she knew that she really should speak to her mother properly before asking any more questions or opening any more cans of worms.

She'd wait, she told herself.

But as soon as Spencer arrived and Nick made everyone a last cup of tea before the electricity and water got turned off, curiosity got the better of her.

'I spoke to my father yesterday,' she began.

Spencer ran his hand over Max's old desk. 'You sure you don't want to keep this, love?' he said.

'No, it's too dark and heavy.' Isobel sighed. 'Spencer, did you hear what I said about Dad?'

'I heard,' Spencer replied softly. 'Nick told me last night. He also told me what he'd overheard in the shop a couple of years back.'

'So you knew?' Isobel asked. 'You knew that Mum was adopted?'

Spencer turned towards Isobel. 'Vivien took me into her confidence,' he said.

'When?'

'Not that long ago actually. It was around the time you and your fiancé broke up.'

'Adam? What's he got to do with anything?'

'Vivien was worried about you. She wanted you to come back to the Bay so she could help, but she also knew you were a grown woman and you had to make your own decisions.'

Isobel nodded. 'I get that. I remember. I couldn't come back to Silverton Bay then because I was still teaching in London and then I got the job in Cambridge...' She stopped for a moment. 'But what's this got to do with Nana telling you that Mum was adopted?'

'She was worried about you, like I said. You wouldn't talk to her and she knew you wouldn't want to talk to your mum. She told me that she blamed herself for the way you and Gina didn't get on and I asked her why. That's when she told me about the adoption.' He paused and ran a hand over his face. 'She asked me not to tell you,' he said. 'She asked me not to tell anyone.'

Isobel sat down on her grandfather's old leather chair. 'Do you know why?'

'All I know is what Vivien told me,' he replied, leaning against the desk and folding his arms in front of him. It felt almost defensive and very similar to the way Nick folded his arms when he didn't want to talk about something. He sighed and went on reluctantly. 'She and your grandfather adopted Gina when she was a baby but for some reason Max never wanted your mum to know the truth. After he died, Vivien struggled with Gina a lot – she had always been closer to her father apparently. She wanted to tell her the truth but said she never found the right time. In the end she had to tell her, when Gina left home to go to university.'

Isobel tried to imagine what that would have felt like for her mother. She would have been excited to move to London to study, just as Isobel had been at that age. She would have felt sophisticated and grown up in a way, but also still a child, still trying to find her place in the world. She was probably still grieving her father when she was hit by the devastating news that he wasn't, in fact, her father and Vivien wasn't her mother.

'I just don't understand why they would have done that,' Isobel said. She was still struggling to understand what it must have been like to know that your childhood had all been a lie. She'd had a friend at art college who'd been adopted and she'd always known. What Vivien and Max had done to Gina seemed so cruel.

'There were some things that just weren't spoken about back then,' Spencer said, echoing Isobel's father. 'Times have changed and mostly for the better if you ask me, although I know lots of folk my age don't agree.' He smiled weakly.

'Did Nana tell you anything else?'

Spencer shook his head. 'No, not really. I don't know the ins and outs of it, if that's what you're asking. I don't know who Gina's biological parents were.' He paused for a moment and stepped towards Isobel, reaching out to squeeze her shoulder. 'The way I see it though is that she was no less your grandmother than if it had been blood. She loved you with all her heart – Gina too, even though they never managed to reconcile their differences.'

Isobel knew that Spencer was right, that it didn't change anything about her relationship with her grandmother. But that didn't take away the strange empty feeling in her stomach.

'Do you think it has anything to do with those photographs of the parties up at the Hall?' Isobel asked.

Spencer shrugged. 'I know as much about those parties as you,' he said. 'Vivien never told me a thing about that.'

'People must have known,' Isobel said. 'At the time, I mean. It's a small village and everyone has always known everyone else's business. It wasn't just my grandparents who lied to Mum, half the village must have been lying by omission.'

'Well,' Spencer said slowly. 'It was before my time so I really can't comment. Nobody has ever said anything to me about it except Vivien herself. Like I said, some things just weren't spoken about.'

'But people must have known,' Isobel repeated.

'Yes, people must have known.'

A loud tearing noise echoed out of the kitchen then, making Isobel start from her chair.

'What on earth…' she began.

'Don't worry, it's just the kitchen cupboards coming out. It'll get worse before it gets better.

'Is Nick OK on his own?'

'He's fine, love, he'll shout if he needs us.'

'I'm sorry,' Isobel said after a while. 'Finding out about Mum is just... Well, it's been a bit of a shock really.'

'I know you know this, but it's probably your mother you should be talking to.'

'She doesn't want to talk to me.'

'Give her time,' Spencer said with a smile. 'You young people always want everything done yesterday. Sometimes you just have to wait.'

Isobel smiled back. 'I know,' she said, realising that was an analogy for the house as well as the situation with her mother. 'Shall we just get on with the furniture instead?'

They worked through the morning, moving the furniture out to Spencer's van and taking inventory of it all. Isobel was impressed by how strong and fit Spencer was – although she felt exhausted from it all herself. 'Keep all these invoices,' Spencer said. 'You'll need them for your tax return.'

'Will you be able to sell it all, do you think?' she asked.

He nodded. 'There's definitely a market for it, even though it's a bit old-fashioned. Now, what about all these books?'

'That's going to be a slower process, I'm afraid. I need to make a note of all of them as there's some Mum won't want me to get rid of. But after she's had first refusal you can have the rest.'

'If I were you, I'd box them up and get them out of this

room. You can go through them somewhere else but you want to get this space set up for your art as soon as you can. Going through those books looks like a big task.'

Isobel nodded.

'You'll need some help,' Spencer went on. 'But Nick has time on his hands. I'm sure he'd go through the books with you.'

'I'll be fine on my own.' She was asking enough of Nick as it was.

'I'm sure you will, but that doesn't mean you shouldn't ask for help. Besides, it'll do the two of you good to talk. I'd say you've got some catching up to do.'

'Oh I think—'

'Don't forget to eat lunch,' Spencer said as he turned away, walking back towards his van. It was only after he'd left that Isobel realised she should have asked him if he needed help to unload once he got back to Odds & Ends.

She spent the afternoon half-heartedly pulling books off the shelves and packing them into boxes, which she then dragged into the dining room and stacked messily next to the kettle and microwave that would be serving as her 'kitchen' for the rest of the week. She couldn't find much enthusiasm for the task at hand and certainly wasn't in the mood to even look at the books, let alone start the list that she knew her mother would want to see. She felt irrationally angry at her mother – why should she spend time going through the books when Gina couldn't even tell her daughter the truth?

Nick found her slumped on top of one of the boxes and

handed her a sandwich that he'd bought for her from the cafe.

'Cheese and tomato OK?' he asked. She nodded and thanked him, but barely looked at him. Eventually he took the hint and took his sandwich back to the kitchen. She'd managed to talk herself into a bad mood, but she shouldn't take it out on the people around her, people who were helping.

When the water and electricity were back on she stopped her half-hearted book-boxing project and flicked the switch of the kettle. The least she could do was to make Nick a cup of tea as an apology for being so surly earlier. As she took his mug towards the kitchen she heard laughter, female laughter, and she couldn't account for the stab of jealousy she felt when she heard Nick laughing along. How ridiculous she was being.

'Hi,' she said as she pushed the door open. 'I've made you a cup of tea.' She turned to the woman who Nick was talking to. 'Can I get you—' She stopped as the woman smiled at her, a smile Isobel recognised immediately. Lauren Guilder – or Lauren Cooke as she now was, according to Spencer – hadn't changed a bit.

'Hi, Isobel, I heard you were back,' Lauren said. 'I couldn't wait to see what you're going to do with the house. Sorry to be so nosey!'

Isobel handed Nick his tea and turned to Lauren. 'There's a lot of work to do. It's all been quite daunting, to be honest!'

'Well you're in very good hands. Nick did some work on our house last winter and we couldn't be happier.'

Isobel smiled but didn't really know what to say. She felt embarrassed, truth be told. Lauren had taken Isobel under her wing on Isobel's first day at school after her move to Norfolk and they became inseparable. Even once they were both at university they'd pick up where they left off in the holidays. But then, after graduation, Isobel had left, without looking back. She wondered how Lauren had felt about that. She wondered if there was a deeper meaning to the words *I heard you were back*.

'I'm pretty much done here for today,' Nick's voice cut into the awkward silence. 'So I'm going to head off and leave you ladies to it.' He turned to Isobel, catching her eye and holding her gaze. 'See you in the morning?' he said.

'It's Sunday. You don't have to come on a Sunday!'

'We need to get this done as soon as possible,' he replied as he got ready to leave.

'I told you that you were in good hands,' Lauren said.

With Nick gone things seemed even more awkward.

'Would you like a cup of tea?' Isobel asked, holding up her own mug.

Lauren shook her head, looked away.

'This is weird, isn't it?' Isobel said and Lauren smiled again, the smile that reminded Isobel of school, that made Lauren look eighteen.

'It really is,' she said. 'But it's also really good to see you again. Are you back for good?'

'That's the plan.' Isobel paused. 'It's good to see you too,' she said, because it was. Moving back to Silverton Bay had been top of her bucket list for a long time but she hadn't quite reckoned with feeling so very isolated here without Vivien. It was wonderful to see a friendly face. 'Shall we go and sit down in the living room and catch up? It's still pretty habitable in there!' She paused. 'If you've got time, that is?'

'I've got time.'

Isobel led the way across the hall into the living room and Lauren sat down in Vivien's old chair. For a moment Isobel wanted to ask her to get up, it felt too strange to see anyone else sitting there. But she caught herself, knowing she was being ridiculous again and, instead, sat down on the other wing-backed chair on the opposite side of the fireplace. The chair that she'd always sat in when she lived with Vivien.

'So you're married, Spencer tells me,' Isobel said, feeling awkward again.

'It's been ten years in September. We've got two kids as well, can you believe! You've met him actually, my husband.'

'I have?' Isobel couldn't remember meeting any accountants since she'd been back in the Bay.

'Yes,' Lauren smiled. 'That last summer we were both here, the summer we graduated. I brought him back with me for a few weeks. You were working in The Two Bells just before you left for London.'

And there it was, hanging over them again. The fact that Isobel had left without saying goodbye. There had been so many reasons, but mostly she'd been in such a hurry to get on with her life. She'd felt so behind after having to take that year out before she started at art college. The only reason she and Lauren had graduated during that same summer was because Lauren's course had been four years long. Isobel had always wondered if she hadn't taken that year, if she hadn't gone to America to be with her mother, would she and Nick have kept in touch? She didn't suppose it mattered now. And Nick must know, of course, what had happened in New York City the day after he left Silverton Bay – September 11, 2001. Isobel could still remember the horror she'd felt when she'd heard, the panic as she tried to get in touch with her parents, and the year she'd spent in America with them afterwards that was meant to help her but instead had just made her worry about the future and ignore Nick's letter. Now of course, when she looked back, she couldn't understand why she'd been in such a hurry or why she'd always felt on the back foot ever since.

And none of it had been an excuse for the way she'd left for London, suddenly, overnight, as soon as Adam clicked his fingers. She'd behaved badly to Vivien, to Lauren, to so many of the people she loved.

I heard you were back.

'I don't remember,' Isobel said. 'I don't really remember meeting him.'

'It doesn't matter—'

'No, Lauren, it does matter. I shouldn't have left like that without saying goodbye. I should have kept in touch. Walking away like that, it was…' She hesitated, rubbing her forehead.

'Oh, Isobel, it was understandable. We were young and foolish, you wanted to start your new life in London. You'd just won that award. Vivien was so proud of you for that.'

'The highlight of my career.'

'Don't say that.' Lauren leaned forward in her chair as though she was going to reach for Isobel and then thought better of it, letting her hand drop. 'Life never really works out how you think it will. Look at Nick. I mean, what's going on there?'

'Him not being a doctor, you mean? I have no idea. He hasn't talked about it.'

Lauren raised her eyebrows but said no more about it.

Clearly what went wrong with Nick's medical career was something he was keeping very close to his chest.

'But you're an art teacher now,' Lauren said brightly. 'That must be so rewarding.'

'It can be; rewarding and frustrating in equal measure.' Isobel hoped her expression didn't convey how utterly unrewarding she'd found her last job. How depressing it was trying to teach young people who had no desire to be taught.

'Nick says you're in between jobs right now.'

'Yes I…well…' She hesitated. 'Nana's death knocked me for six, really. I left my last job at the end of last term to move here and I haven't really worked out what to do next. I'm starting to think that resigning was a mistake, especially now I know how much work there is to do on the house.' The words of Vivien's letter came back to her then, her grandmother's voice in her head telling her she was drifting, asking her to find herself again.

'I'm so sorry about Vivien, Isobel,' Lauren's voice interrupted her thoughts. 'The whole village loved her, you know. I was at the funeral but I didn't say "hello" and I know I should have done. I didn't know what to say after all this time and—'

'It's OK,' Isobel said, trying not to cry at the reminder of her grandmother's funeral. 'Please don't…'

'Do you know what you'll do next?' Lauren asked, changing the subject slightly.

'I'll go back to teaching,' Isobel replied. After all, she didn't have much choice about that. 'But first I'm trying to set up a place to work in my grandparents' old office. I met Sarah at the cafe yesterday and she showed me the pictures she has for sale. It all looks great and I hear some of it might be yours!'

'Ah, Nick told you about the art group, did he?'

'Is some of the art in the cafe yours?' Isobel asked.

She saw Lauren blush a little. 'Yes, a couple of the watercolours are mine but I don't think I'll be winning any awards any time soon. I'd always wanted to learn to draw and paint.'

'Had you?' Isobel was surprised to learn this. Languages had always been Lauren's forte at school and her degree had been in French and German.

'Well I wasn't going to admit that to someone as talented as you, obviously! But yes, it was a dream of mine so when the art classes started up, I forced myself to go along.' She paused. 'I don't know if Nick mentioned, but—'

'He said you're looking for a new teacher.'

'Ours had to leave and I really want the classes to continue. I'd hate it if we had to—'

'I'll do it.'

'You will?'

'Of course.' She smiled. She'd always known she'd say yes.

'Surely you'll need to think about it. You don't even know when we meet or anything yet.'

'I've thought about it and it's not as though I've got a whole heap of other stuff going on right now.'

'Really, are you sure?'

Isobel laughed. 'I'm sure. I saw those pictures in the cafe, Lauren. They're really good and I'd hate for your group to fall apart. Besides, it'll be fun to teach people who are interested. It's got to be better than teenagers claiming they are bored to death all the time.'

'I swear we're better behaved than teenagers. Oh this is so exciting! I can't wait to tell everyone, I can't wait for you to meet everyone.' This time when Lauren leaned forward she did reach over to Isobel and squeeze her arm. 'Thank you,' she said. 'This means a lot. It's not much money I'm afraid, but...'

'Lauren, it's fine, I know what adult education classes pay. I really want to do this.'

'I can get you up to speed on what we've been doing before September and so on and...' She paused and looked at Isobel, her head tilted to one side.

'What's the matter?' Isobel asked.

'Are you OK? I mean, I know you're probably not. I know Vivien's death must have been a terrible blow for you and you must miss her. And now this house is in the throes of renovation, which I promise will be worth it in the end but...' She paused again. 'I know we haven't seen each other for a long time, Isobel, but is there something else?'

Isobel looked away for a moment, considering. Should she ask the question that had been buzzing around her head. Lauren's family had been living in Silverton Bay for generations, there was a chance she or her mother, or even her grandmother if she were still alive, might know something.

'I've found something out,' she began. 'Something about my family that I never knew.' She stopped, thinking about what she would say next and Lauren sat quietly giving her the space she needed. She turned to look at her old friend. 'I found out that my mother was adopted, that Nana wasn't her biological mother, which means that...' She trailed off again, swallowing.

'…that Vivien wasn't your biological grandmother,' Lauren finished softly.

Isobel nodded.

'She still loved you, Isobel, just the same.'

'I know and apparently one of the reasons Mum never told me was because of that, because of how close Nana and I were. But Mum has never spoken about it – it was my father who told me everything after I found an old photograph of Nana.' She went on to tell Lauren about finding the photograph, the phone call to her mother, her father's explanation.

'Wow,' Lauren whispered. 'That's a lot to take on after Vivien's death and moving here and everything else. Of course you're not OK.'

'No, I really don't think I am. I'm not sure how I feel if I'm honest. Mum has no interest in finding out who her biological parents were, but I just can't stop thinking about it, even though I know it's not my business.'

'It's understandable that you're curious though.' Lauren sat back in her chair. 'I wonder if my grandmother knows anything.'

'Your grandmother?' So she was still alive. Isobel's memories of Lauren's grandmother were vague – a house on the edge of the village, homemade scones and jam, blackberrying in the early autumn.

'She would have lived here when your mum was born. It's a small village and everyone knows everyone else's business. Somebody must know something.'

'It's so long ago though and I don't want to bother your grandmother.'

'Nonsense.' Lauren waved Isobel's concerns away. 'Gran loves talking about the past.'

'Is she well?'

'She had a fall a year or so ago and needed a hip replacement. She had to move into sheltered accommodation after that as she's not as mobile as she used to be and needs help with some things, but she's still sharp as a tack. I'll ask her what she knows and don't worry...' Lauren went on, clearly seeing that Isobel's face was a mass of worry. 'I'll be very discreet.'

'I feel bad going behind Mum's back like this, but...' Isobel shrugged. 'Perhaps I shouldn't.'

'Look,' Lauren said, getting up to go. 'Why don't I see when Gran is free and you can come over and talk to her. I've already told her that you're back and she remembers you.'

'Does she?'

'Of course she does – you remember making blackberry jam with her, don't you?'

Isobel nodded, even though the memory was so faint.

'It's up to you what you talk about with Gran that way. You decide.'

Isobel found herself agreeing. Even if she didn't talk about the adoption, it would be nice to talk about Vivien with somebody who had known her for years. And perhaps Lauren's grandmother would know something about the parties at Silverton Hall. Maybe she'd even been to one.

As Lauren was leaving, Isobel reached out and touched her wrist. Lauren turned towards her.

'It has been so nice to see you,' she said. 'You'll come over again, won't you?'

'Of course,' Lauren replied. 'And if you need a home-cooked meal while Nick is destroying your kitchen, you just let me know.'

22

Spencer's van was parked in the driveway when Nick got back to Odds & Ends and he was relieved to see the furniture was all still in the back of it, relieved that his grandfather hadn't tried to shift it himself.

The doors of the van were unlocked, so Nick got to work straightaway taking the furniture inside, into Spencer's workshop – he'd want to check everything over first, see if anything needed mending, give everything a polish. It all looked in fairly good order to Nick – although he was no expert, not like his grandfather. He'd been surprised that Isobel had let it all go so easily. At first she'd seemed so determined not to let things change, to keep the house exactly as it always had been but he'd noticed a shift in her. It made him smile to think that she had listened to what he'd said, had agreed with his ideas, and he tried not to read too much into it. He was the experienced house renovator after all, she was just taking his advice.

As he struggled with the last piece of furniture – the mysterious Max Chambers' huge mahogany desk – he heard somebody call from across the street. He turned to see Brandon Lyons, the landlord of The Two Bells, walking towards him.

'Do you need a hand with that, mate?' Brandon asked.

Nick could have done with a hand of course – the furniture had been heavy, and it was stupid really trying to move it by himself but shook his head, manoeuvring the desk on to the driveway. 'It's all good,' he said. He'd lost his ability to engage in small talk years ago, and where once he could make people relax, get them to open up to him, now he could barely make eye contact. 'Isobel's having a clear out,' he managed, nodding towards the furniture. 'Turning one of the rooms into an art studio.'

'I should pop over and see her,' Brandon said. 'See how she is, see if she needs anything. I've been meaning to but I thought I'd let her settle in.'

'She'd like that,' Nick said, although he had no idea if she would like it and he wasn't keen on the strange jealous feeling that dug like a clamp into his stomach. Nick wanted to tell Brandon that he was already making sure Isobel was all right, that she had everything she needed.

He was glad when Brandon wandered off again, back towards the pub. Some days he hated who he had become, the way he could barely talk to anyone now, barely look at them. He leaned against the desk and looked down at his hands, splayed on the polished surface. They should have been surgeon's hands, but that hadn't been their fate, and Nick was happier now even if he couldn't always manage small talk and preferred to be on his own. Why was he so ashamed then to tell Isobel what had happened? Everyone made mistakes. There couldn't be many people in their late thirties who hadn't made a few wrong turns, who didn't carry a little bit of baggage and a few regrets. He wasn't someone who judged other people for their screw-ups, so why did he judge himself so harshly?

'Thanks for bringing everything in, Nick,' Spencer said. Nick looked up, only then noticing his grandfather standing in the doorway of the shop.

'I'm just glad you didn't try and bring it in on your own.'

Spencer smile sadly. 'I know my limits these days,' he said. 'But do you want a hand with that desk?'

Nick shook his head, just as he had at Brandon. 'I'm fine,' he said. 'I'm just enjoying the sun.' He hadn't been, of course, he'd been lost in thought, but now he'd looked up he noticed that it was that point in the afternoon when the light was perfect and everything looked beautiful. He felt the sun's warmth on the back of his neck and took a breath. 'I'm amazed you and Isobel got this into the van in the first place.'

'I'm off to the pub for a while,' Spencer said. 'I might eat there this evening. Do you fancy it?'

'Not really. I'll fend for myself.'

'Are you sure? You shouldn't spend so much time on your own.' Spencer worried about him, Nick could see that in his eyes. But then he worried about Spencer, so it was a fair trade.

'Honestly, I'm fine,' he said with a tight smile. Even the conversation with his own grandfather felt stilted this afternoon and he had a feeling Spencer wanted to say something to him.

'Look, Nick,' Spencer began.

Here we go, Nick thought. 'Don't…' he said out loud.

'You need to talk to Isobel,' Spencer ploughed on. 'You need to tell her.'

'I don't see how it will help.'

'She's not happy. She wasn't happy when she got here, even before she found out about her mother's adoption, and I doubt that's much helped her state of mind.'

'But none of that's got anything to do with—'

'She needs to talk to someone, to open up, and I think she'll do that with you if you, well…' Spencer hesitated. 'Got the ball rolling, as it were.'

Nick looked away.

'Go and see her this evening, make sure she has something to eat, help her with those damn books.' Spencer paused, squeezed his grandson's shoulder. 'Take it from there.'

Nick turned back towards his grandfather and nodded. 'OK,' he said.

'The night is young after all,' Spencer said with a mischievous wink.

23

Norfolk – June 1953

Hours later, Vivien was breathless and hot from dancing the night away in the ballroom of Silverton Hall. She had never felt so happy nor so beautiful. She had made it through dinner without making a fool of herself, she had eaten food that she wasn't sure she could pronounce and she thought she had managed to use all the correct cutlery in the correct order by remembering what Max had discreetly told her when they had dined with his parents. Dinner had been a much more relaxing experience than that night had been and the dancing afterwards had been out of this world.

She'd danced with Max at first, but then other men, people Max seemed to know, asked her while Max danced with their wives. More than one of the men commented on her dress and she felt quite the belle of the ball, even though she knew that was ridiculous – there were far more important people here than her after all.

Although, she thought as she leaned against the wall to catch her breath, occasionally it had felt that people may have mistaken her for someone else. There was that woman who had said how proud she must be to see the transformation that had taken place at the Hall and then that man that she danced with, an American called Joe somebody-or-other, who had made comments about how much money her husband must have made from 'the deal on the Hall'. He'd laughed as he'd said it but there was something sinister about him that made Vivien wonder if he thought she was married to somebody other than Max. It was so hard to hear properly in the crowded ballroom with the band playing.

But then she remembered the comments she had overheard at the beginning of the evening. The comments Max said he would explain to her later.

'Vivien!'

She heard her name called from behind her and she moved away from the wall, turning her head to look over her shoulder. It was Max with his camera – he must have got some fantastic shots tonight in the ballroom.

'Beautiful,' he said softly as he took the picture. He took her hand then and asked her to dance with him again, his camera stowed away safely, and she closed the most wonderful evening of her life by dancing with her husband. She wondered, as they danced, how one man could have so many faces – how he could be so stressed and tired, so driven in a job he self-admittedly didn't like, and then be so gentle and soft on other occasions. His camera, in particular, had seemed to bring him so much joy tonight. That must be what painting does to him too, Vivien thought. Why then did he not do it anymore?

'This is what our wedding should have been like,' Max

said as the inaugural midsummer party came to a close. 'I'm sorry it had to be so small and quiet.' Vivien still didn't understand why their wedding had been so rushed. It hadn't been as though she'd been pregnant or anything. The question must have shown on her face because Max looked at her, bent to whisper in her ear. 'I'll explain everything,' he said. 'Tomorrow.'

That word again. What was going on? Could she wait until tomorrow? Wasn't it tomorrow already, officially?

As they walked home together in the early morning light, Vivien realised that for the first time in a long time she hadn't thought about London all night, hadn't thought about her parents or her friends, nor about the 'clack-clack-clack' of the typewriters at Musgrove & Mortimer.

'You're very quiet,' Max said into the dawn air.

'I'm just taking it all in,' she replied. 'Tonight was like nothing I've experienced before. I used to daydream about this sort of thing and now I get to wear these beautiful clothes and go to these glamourous parties. Who'd have ever thought it?'

Max didn't reply, just smiled rather sadly and looked down at his feet as he walked. It was then that Vivien realised that all lives have sacrifices – some big, some small. Her father's generation had sacrificed so much for the freedom of the country, Max had sacrificed his love of art for his career at his father's bank – not that the two were comparable really. And her own small sacrifice was nothing at all. Because a quiet life in Silverton Bay with the sea and Mrs Castleton was a small price to pay for the wonderful night she'd had and the wonderful nights she knew that she and Max would have in the future.

But if that was the case, if that was going to be her sacrifice, then she had to know the truth and she wasn't going to let Max wait until 'tomorrow' to tell her his connection to Silverton Hall.

24

Norfolk – July 2019

Nick arrived just as the sun was setting behind the tree in the garden. Isobel had been standing by the window where her grandfather's desk had stood until Spencer had taken it away that morning. She'd promised herself she'd at least finish boxing up the books before she stopped to think about something to eat but she had been less than halfway through and transfixed by the golden light in the garden. She'd been wondering how she could paint that light, how she could do it justice, when she heard his knock on the door.

'I thought you might like a hand with those books,' he said as he'd leaned against the door frame. 'And something to eat.' He held out two packets of fish and chips. 'I know it's not very original and we had it the other night, but—'

'Thank you,' Isobel replied, falling on the food as her stomach rumbled. She hadn't realised how hungry she was. 'Although I really do need to eat something that isn't fried at some point.'

They ate off their knees in the garden, sitting on the edge of the patio where they'd laughed together just two days earlier. Had it really only been two days since she'd found the photograph of Vivien on the beach? Life could change so quickly.

After they'd eaten they started to work through the remaining books in companionable silence until Nick began to ask questions Isobel wasn't comfortable answering. Like why things hadn't worked out for her, and why she had given up after the portrait competition.

'Nick, are you asking me why I'm a teacher and not the next Tracy Emin? Because, honestly, life doesn't work that way.'

'You had such big plans though.'

'So did you.'

He turned to look at her then, but he didn't say anything and they stood staring at each other, both holding a pile of Max Chambers' old books. Nick turned away first.

'Touché,' he said, turning back to the box.

'I think things started to go wrong before I even got to art college,' Isobel said to Nick's back. 'I had to take a year out.'

Nick stopped packing, his body still.

'The day after you left for Sheffield, well, you know what happened.'

She heard him take a breath as though he'd only just realised the timing, the implications of what happened on that bright September morning in New York.

'The World Trade Centre attack,' he said as though to himself.

'Nana and I spent all day trying to contact Mum and

Dad. It was awful, one of the worst days of my life. I was so sure something had happened to them and then, once we'd got in touch, I had to be with them. It was strange really, after years of living here with Nana, of being happier here than I had been with my parents, I suddenly needed to be with them more than anything.'

Nick turned around again. He put the books down and leaned against the bookshelves. 'It's understandable,' he said.

'It took days to get a flight out, everything was such a mess and so frightening. And once I got a flight, I had a panic attack on board. The flight attendants were amazing, so I don't think I was the only one.'

'What was it like?' Nick asked. 'Being back in New York afterwards.'

'Awful. It was like a different city. But it changed Mum completely. More so than it changed Dad, which I've always found strange seeing as New York is his city, the place he grew up.'

She was still standing, clutching the pile of books to her chest as though her life depended on it, her knuckles whitening under her grip. Slowly she allowed herself to put them down and sank to the floor, crossing her legs. After a minute Nick came to sit next to her, close but not close enough to touch.

'Mum fell apart.' Isobel rested her elbows on her knees and her chin in her hands. 'She saw it, you see, I think that's the difference. Dad had left early to go to a client site visit but Mum, she was eating breakfast and...well. You could see the towers from their apartment building and...' Isobel had never had the words to describe what had happened to her father's home city that morning, or the effect it had had on her relationship with her mother. Already strained, it had felt, after that September morning, as though they would dance around each other forever.

'I took a year off,' Isobel continued. 'Once I was in New York I didn't want to leave, so I stayed with them for a while. Things settled down and Dad got me some work at his office and…' She paused, remembering. 'It got harder and harder to go back. It took a lot for me to return to London. Mum is completely terrified of flying now and refuses to go anywhere other than the beach house in Montauk and, I guess, maybe some of that fear rubbed off on me.'

'I wrote to you,' Nick said quietly. 'I didn't have an address so I wrote to Vivien's house and…'

'She sent the letter to me. I'm sorry I didn't reply.' She didn't tell him that she still had the letter, tucked inside one of her art books.

Nick rubbed a hand across his brow. 'I'm not surprised you didn't reply. I hadn't even thought about how that day would have affected you, hadn't even considered your New York connection. I was so self-centred.'

'That wasn't the reason I didn't write back,' Isobel said. 'I tried to write to you, but…' She stopped, shook her head. 'I felt as though I was a failure by not going to art school.'

'Anyone would have taken a year off in those circumstances though.'

'Logically I knew that, but it wasn't how it felt at the time. And your letter was so full of all the things I should have been doing – meeting new people, learning new things, settling into a new city…' She watched Nick pick at an invisible crumb on the carpet and wondered if he'd been unhappy even then. Had there ever been a time when medicine had made him happy?

'So your mum has never been back to England since?' Nick asked, skilfully turning the conversation as though he knew what she was thinking, what she was almost about to ask.

Isobel shook her head. 'And Nana never went to New York either. They never saw each other again.' She rubbed her eyes. 'I was angry when she didn't even try to come to Nana's funeral, but I suppose now I know there was more to it than just a fear of flying.'

Isobel stared down at the dark-red carpet, at the threadbare patches, the reminders of the lives lived in this house. Everything felt so different now, as though the grandmother she had loved so much had become a stranger.

'But you went back to London, didn't you,' Nick said after a moment. 'You went to art college?'

She pushed herself up to standing then, picked up the pile of books. 'Mum wants me to catalogue these.' Nick wasn't the only one who could change the conversation at will, but it did turn out that he was more stubborn about keeping the conversation going than she was.

'Tell me about art college, Isobel,' he said, standing up too, moving away from her a little, giving her some space.

'What's to tell? I went to London, I studied portraiture and landscapes. I wrote my dissertation on Turner, I got a first – although that was more good luck than talent. I won the portrait competition and I got engaged and then…' She stopped again, turned away, shrugged.

'Then?'

'And then nothing. I don't know what happened. After winning that competition I got lost somehow. I couldn't paint, or at least I couldn't paint anything of that calibre again. So I did my teacher training and, meanwhile, Adam, my fiancé, was going from strength to strength.'

'He was an artist too?'

She nodded. 'We met at St Martin's. He had so many commissions that he could hardly keep on top of them. He opened a studio and had staff and everything and me…well I was just a teacher.'

'Don't say it like that,' Nick said. 'Teachers are important. Neither you nor this Adam would have got into art college without teachers.' She noticed the way he said 'this Adam' with a touch of scorn. 'You didn't get married, I take it?'

'No. Adam didn't want to marry a teacher apparently.'

She heard Nick take a breath as though he was about to launch into a tirade about 'this Adam'.

'And what about you, Nick?' she said before he could start. 'Are you going to tell me why you fix houses for a living rather than people?'

'Well I did get married,' he said.

She hadn't expected that, it hadn't been the question she'd asked, and she turned to him.

'Really?'

'Is that so unbelievable?' he asked, a hint of a smile playing on his lips.

'No, I… That's not what I meant. I just didn't know, but then why would I?' She looked at his left hand. 'You're not married now?'

'I'm in the process of being not married,' he replied. 'Divorce is long and complicated.'

'Nick, I'm so sorry. What happened? Is that the reason you changed career?'

He shook his head. 'No, I'd already moved away from medicine when we separated.' Isobel heard him inhale. 'I think, much like your fiancé, my wife wasn't happy with my career decisions. She wanted to be a doctor's wife, not married to a glorified builder.'

'Ah.'

'Yeah.'

The awkwardness that Isobel had thought she and Nick had managed to transcend filled the room again. She didn't know what to say now he'd told her that he'd been married, that he was going through a divorce. It felt like a proper grown-up problem, so separate to whatever it was that had been holding her back for years – whatever it was that had made Vivien think she was 'drifting'. Drifting was exactly how it felt though. It hadn't been until she'd read her grandmother's letter that Isobel had been able to pinpoint what was wrong. Not that it had helped her plan a way out or anything, but that was what she was doing here in Silverton Bay – starting again, planning a new life. Not going over old hurts.

'Look, Nick,' she said into the silence. 'You don't have to tell me this. You don't have to tell me what happened. I love that you're helping me with the house and I'm so grateful for the fish and chips, but you must have things you'd rather be doing on a Saturday night.'

'Not really,' Nick replied.

'You don't have to spend the evening here with me because Spencer told you to.'

'How did you…?'

Isobel smiled. 'I know what Spencer's like,' she said.

'He did suggest I come over,' Nick confessed. 'But I didn't come because he told me to.' He paused, took a step closer to Isobel. 'I came because I wanted to spend time with you, wanted to get to know you again.'

'Really?'

'I left medicine because I was diagnosed with PTSD,' he said suddenly, the words tumbling out into the room in a rush.

Isobel felt something inside her tighten. 'Nick,' she said softly, closing the gap between them slowly and gently touching his arm. He placed his hand over hers. 'Are you OK?'

He nodded. 'Most of the time these days I'm fine.'

But he didn't look fine. He looked pale and very tired all of a sudden.

Isobel scanned the room for somewhere to sit but of course all the furniture had headed off to Odds & Ends with Spencer earlier that morning. 'Come into the living room,' she said, leading him out of the office. 'Sit down and let me get you something to drink.' She stopped. 'Although I don't really have anything except tea. We could go to the pub?'

'Tea's fine, Isobel, and I'm OK, really. I don't need to sit down.'

'Shall we take a break anyway?'

Nick nodded, heading for the living room while Isobel went to make the tea in her makeshift kitchen in the corner of the dining room. Nick was sitting in the chair that wasn't Vivien's when she took the tea to him. She sat opposite with her own mug and tucked her feet underneath her.

'I ended up specialising in emergency medicine,' he said. 'I don't really know how it happened as I'd always thought I'd be a surgeon but I was good at it. I had a way with people that calmed them down, or so I was told.'

Isobel nodded, encouraging him to go on. She could imagine him being good in an emergency – he had always been calm and solid and she could still see that now when he was talking to contractors. He was quick to put people at their ease.

'It didn't feel like enough though,' Nick went on. 'I didn't feel like I was doing enough. I worked endlessly and yet day after day I saw the results of people's bad judgements and awful behaviour – the drunken fights, the overdoses, the drivers who were well over the limit…' He paused for a moment. 'The women with the black eyes and broken ribs who blamed anyone but the man who'd done it to them. I got screamed at and vomited on, I smiled and I stayed calm but inside it never felt like I was making a difference. Isn't that what I was meant to be doing? Making a difference?'

Isobel thought about what Spencer had said to her in the pub over his scampi and chips.

I think perhaps it was his father's dream.

She realised that Nick hadn't spoken for a while, that he was sitting quietly, staring into his teacup.

'What happened, Nick?' she asked.

'I decided to join Médicins Sans Frontières,' he replied. 'The senior registrar of the emergency room put me on to it. He'd worked with them for a while in the Balkans back when he was a junior doctor. He said it helped him put his life in perspective, which felt exactly like what I needed at the time. I was sent to Afghanistan. I expect you can guess the rest.'

Isobel could guess the rest, but she didn't want to guess. She wanted him to confide in her, even though she knew that would be hard for him to do and she didn't want to push him.

'You don't have to tell me, Nick, not if it's too hard.'

'I do want to tell you though. I've wanted to tell you all week but it's hard sometimes to find the right words and I didn't want you to think...' He stopped again and she didn't push him. She knew how that sentence ended because she had felt the same.

I didn't want you to think any less of me.

As if she ever could.

'Was this before or after you'd got married?' she asked.

'After. I met Jeanette at the hospital. She's a physiotherapist, although she works in private practice now.'

'And was she OK with you going overseas?'

Nick laughed in a hollow sort of way. 'Not really,' he said. 'She wasn't really OK with me working in emergency medicine in general. She wanted me to pursue surgical.'

'But that's not what you wanted?'

'I never really knew what I wanted. Hindsight is a wonderful thing, but now I have it I realise that I probably didn't want to be a doctor at all.' Just as Spencer had said. Just as Isobel had suspected. 'Jeannette, my wife, she didn't want me to go to Afghanistan. She didn't understand why I needed to do something else, be somewhere else. I'm not really sure that I understood it at the time either, to be honest. I just knew I had to try. I think it was probably the beginning of the end. Anyway,' Nick went on, his voice barely more than a sigh now. 'Afghanistan didn't help either unless…well, it helped me make up my mind to leave medicine, I suppose.'

Isobel didn't say anything. She left him to tell her in his own time.

'I don't think I could put what I saw out there into words if I tried,' Nick went on eventually. 'It was the worst possible side of human beings, worse than anything I'd seen in a Sheffield emergency room on a Saturday night. The things that people are capable of doing to each other are…' He stopped again, rubbing his hand across his eyes. 'When I came home I thought I could pick up where I left off, that everything would be put in perspective just like my colleague had told me it would be.'

'I'm guessing it didn't work out like that?'

'No, not really. Whenever I was alone I could still hear the bombs and whenever I slept I dreamed that I was back there. I'd wake up in the night with this tightness around my chest, completely unable to breathe. I decided the best thing to do was not to sleep. I signed up for all the shifts available, I hardly ever went home, which obviously made me even more popular with Jeannette. I was in complete denial about everything.'

'Well I know that feeling,' Isobel said and for the first time since he'd started telling her, Nick looked up and held her gaze for a moment.

'I knew you'd understand,' he said.

'It's not the same though, is it? Nowhere near.'

'You lost your way and it broke you a little bit.'

'Yes,' she said, realising nobody had ever put how she felt so succinctly to her before. 'But…'

'My therapist once told me that everybody's problems are valid, regardless of how trivial they seem. Life affects people differently – some people are more able to cope than others.'

'Your therapist?' Isobel said. Adam had suggested to her several times that she needed to talk to somebody – a career counsellor, a therapist, her GP, anyone to help her 'get out of this funk' as he used to say. She never had, of course. She'd just kept drifting and suddenly she was angry with herself about that. There were so many other people with so many more serious problems in the world who were picking up the pieces and getting on with their lives.

Like Nick.

'I hadn't really wanted to start seeing a therapist,' he said. 'But one night at work I had what I suppose can only be described as a breakdown. All I can remember is that one minute I was treating a patient and the next I was lying on a gurney. Apparently it was quite dramatic though.' He smiled sadly. 'I've been seeing a therapist ever since. Not as often these days, just when I need to.'

'And your marriage?' Isobel asked, because she needed to know.

'My marriage is well and truly over,' he replied, as though he knew that Isobel needed that confirming. 'It had been over since I decided to join Médicins Sans Frontières, to be honest, although we kept trying after I came back, even though all we were doing was making each other miserable. Working with my therapist helped me understand that I'd never really wanted to be a doctor, that my father had pushed me into it for reasons that were to do with how he measured success. When I was first signed off sick from work I think Jeannette kidded herself that I'd go back eventually. Even when I bought that first house and flipped it, I think she thought I was just filling time until I was ready to go back to the hospital, but that first house changed everything.'

'You'd finally found something you loved to do.'

'I've never really talked about this with anyone before, but I remember after I'd finished that first house, I felt elated. I remembered how you used to look when you were sketching – that sensation of complete focus and delight. I'd never felt like that when I was working as a doctor but that's exactly how I felt when I was working on that house. It felt like coming home.'

'You thought about me?' Isobel asked, her voice a whisper.

Nick didn't reply at first and as the sun had long since set, the room was shrouded in darkness. She couldn't see his face anymore, couldn't work out how he was feeling or if he was even looking at her. The air in the room felt very still, and Isobel remembered the feeling of Nick's kiss from all those years ago. She tried to speak, but her mouth felt dry.

She watched Nick stand then, and step towards her. He hovered by her chair for just a moment before crouching down beside her, taking her hand.

'I never stopped thinking about you,' he said.

Isobel's heart flipped over. She hadn't realised how much she'd wanted to hear that. Had that kiss all those years ago meant as much to him as it had to her? Had…

Before she could finish that sentence in her head she felt his fingers brush against her cheek and his lips gently touch hers. For a moment she pulled away – a reflex action, a momentary concern. They had both been back for such a short time, they had only just told each other their stories…

But then a voice in her head – Nick's voice – soothed all her concerns.

It felt like coming home.

'Isobel, I'm sorry, I shouldn't…'

Before he could move away she touched him gently, her hand on his shoulder.

'Wait,' she whispered, her lips so close to his. 'Let's try that again.'

And when he kissed her she was eighteen years old again, her hopes and dreams still in front of her. It felt like coming home and it felt like starting again, like a clean slate.

And when he picked her up, lifting her out of the chair and carrying her upstairs to the room he'd never been allowed to go into before, she knew there was nowhere else she wanted to be and nobody else she wanted to be with.

25

Norfolk – June 1953

Three days after midsummer, Vivien met Evelyn Pugh for the first time. Max had arranged everything.

'I'll be in London, I'm afraid,' he'd said. 'But Miriam Castleton will go with you. She's known Evelyn for a while – they worked together at the Hall before it was sold.'

Vivien had nodded. She and Max had barely spoken since the morning after the party. What he had told her had changed everything about her life and about their marriage. Everything she'd believed had been a lie and everything she'd wanted had been an empty promise. On top of that, he had driven a wedge between her and Mrs Castleton.

Everything felt so final now, as though the whole of the rest of her life was mapped out. And the party, the wonderful, awe-inspiring party at Silverton Hall felt as though it would be the last party she would ever attend. The last party where she could ever be the version of Vivien that she wanted to be.

She couldn't help thinking that he should have told her much of this before the wedding, especially as it seemed as though he'd married her for one specific reason.

To become a mother to Evelyn Pugh's baby.

'Of course that's not the only reason I married you,' Max had objected, but it hadn't sounded sincere to Vivien. She wondered why it was that Max had chosen her, of all the women he must have met.

Probably because she was stupid enough to fall for his charms. She'd thought she was in control, that she was using him to help her escape her parents' flat and her monotonous job. She'd had no idea of course. He was the one who had been doing the using, right from the start. Max had insisted otherwise and had tried to tell Vivien that she was special, but Vivien knew that she was just stupid. She could kick herself.

Evelyn Pugh, who had worked at Silverton Hall with Mrs Castleton, was pregnant and the father of her baby had passed away. Of this Max had been adamant. Whilst Vivien hadn't accused him outright of being the father, the accusation must have shown in her face. He had been quick to knock it down, to tell her who the father was, to plead with her and explain that he was trying to keep a promise he had made months before.

Not that any of it meant very much to Vivien, and none of it changed anything.

Evelyn's baby was due in August, and Max and Vivien would adopt the baby straight away – the paperwork, Max said, had already been drawn up. In less than two months' time Vivien would be a mother to a child she had, until this week, never even known existed.

'How could you just spring it on me like this?' Vivien had asked. 'Why did you not tell me before?'

'I had to be sure everything was in order,' Max had replied calmly, as though they were buying a new kitchen appliance, not bringing somebody else's child into their lives. 'You said you wanted to be a mother.'

I lied, Vivien had thought to herself.

'How will I know what to do?' she'd said out loud.

'Nobody knows what to do with the first baby, surely,' Max had replied, looking flustered.

'But they usually have nine months to work it out. I've got less than two. And what about my parents? What am I supposed to tell them? My mother said, ages ago, before we were engaged that you were too good to be true and it looks like she was right.'

Max had sighed and touched Vivien's arm gently. 'Your parents,' he'd said quietly as though to himself and Vivien had wondered then if perhaps Max had not thought this crazy plan through as carefully as he'd thought he had. 'I'll tell them this week while I'm in London,' he'd gone on. 'Perhaps your mother will have some tips.' He'd smiled then, but it was tight and didn't reach his eyes.

And now Max was in London, presumably telling her parents along with whatever else it was he did in London all the time, and Vivien and Mrs Castleton were due to meet Evelyn Pugh.

They went to the beach for their daily swim very early, not long after sunrise and before anyone else was about.

'I suppose there won't be many more early morning swims in my life now,' Vivien said, trying to keep the sadness from her voice. 'I imagine I'll have my hands full for a good few years.'

'Don't think of it as the end of something,' Mrs Castleton replied quietly. 'See it as a beginning. Life is full of new beginnings none of us were expecting.'

Vivien nodded and turned away. Her feelings towards Mrs Castleton had changed since she'd found out that Max had been in contact with her for months about adopting Evelyn Pugh's baby, that he hadn't met Miriam Castleton for the first time at Silverton Hall on the first night of their honeymoon. She felt as though she'd been duped from the very beginning by everyone, as though the whole village had been in on this adoption plan except her. People must be laughing behind her back.

'Why did you never say anything?' Vivien had asked Mrs Castleton on the morning after the party at Silverton Hall.

'Mr Chambers asked me not to. Trust me when I tell you I wasn't very comfortable about it.'

'How long have you known?' she asked her friend now. There was still an awkwardness between the two women, but Vivien was trying to overcome it. She had a feeling that she needed as many friends around her as possible. She had questions and she wanted answers.

Miriam sighed and sat down on the sand. 'I've known about Evelyn's pregnancy since the beginning. We were practically the only two members of staff left at the Hall by then and it was fairly obvious she'd got herself in trouble. The rest of it, the plan for you and Max to adopt, well, that took a while to come together. Max was here just before Christmas last year. You know that, don't you?'

Vivien nodded slowly, putting the missing pieces from the story that Max had told her back together. He'd mentioned, on the first day of their honeymoon, that he had been here when his cousin had died the previous December. That must have been when all of this had been organised. Had he known then that Vivien, the woman he'd bumped into by chance, would be part of the plan or had that been a later addition? Was this the only reason Max had proposed? Why had she not asked more questions at the time? Why had she not asked more questions in general?

The truth was that the last several months had been a whirlwind and Vivien hadn't thought to stop for a moment to question what was going on. She had waited so long for something to happen to her, something interesting, that when Max had come along she had just accepted her new destiny blindly without giving any thought at all to what she actually wanted from life. It was only now as she sat on the beach with Miriam after her swim that she realised this was her life now and would be for ever, that she was never going back to her parents' flat in London. Her parents should perhaps have issued stronger warnings. Her father should have asked more questions when Max first proposed, but she supposed he was just relieved that his daughter had made a good match and he didn't have to worry about her anymore. She wondered what he would say when Max told him about Evelyn Pugh's baby.

'I've been so naïve,' she whispered to herself.

'Nonsense,' Miriam replied. 'How could you possibly have seen this coming?' She paused for a moment, looking out toward the horizon. 'For what it's worth I think Max was wrong not to tell you. Springing it on you like this is ridiculous. Of course,' she went on, lowering her voice a little as though the seagulls could hear what they were talking about. 'You don't have to go through with it, you could just leave.'

'And do what? Go back to my parents' flat with my tail between my legs?' Vivien shook her head. 'No, this is my destiny. I might have walked into it blindly but I'm going to do the best I can.' What else could she do after all? She thought of her mother trying to make ends meet during the war, not knowing where her husband was other than somewhere in France. And she remembered the look on her mother's face on the morning they emerged from the bomb shelter to discover the house had gone for ever.

This was nothing compared to what her mother had been through. Of course she could do it.

'Well in that case,' Miriam said, standing up. 'We'd best get ourselves ready.'

Evelyn Pugh sat in a faded armchair by an empty hearth in her room in the boarding house that Max was paying for. She would stay here until the baby was born and then she would go back to her family in Nottingham. Vivien wondered if the baby would ever be mentioned again once Evelyn went home or if she would have to pretend it had never been born.

She sat with her hands resting on her baby bump, her long dark hair in a loose plait over one shoulder. Vivien thought she looked very young, too young to be having a baby, although she was only a few months younger than

Vivien herself. Evelyn also looked extremely sad, which was no surprise given everything that she had been through.

'We don't have to do this,' Vivien said to her quietly once initial introductions had been made and Mrs Castleton had gone to rustle up a tea tray from somewhere. 'We don't have to adopt your baby.'

'Yes,' Evelyn replied quietly. 'Yes, you do.'

'But—'

'Listen to me, Vivien,' Evelyn said, taking Vivien's hand in hers. 'This is what I want. It's the right thing to do.'

'But you seem so sad, so—'

'My baby's father...' Evelyn paused, took a breath. 'He died. I thought he was going to look after us but things don't always work out the way you think they will.'

Vivien nodded. She understood that at least.

'I need to know that my baby is being looked after well. This is for the best, for both me and my baby. This way I have some hope of a normal life again one day. And my baby, well, I hope my baby will always be happy.'

'I'll do whatever I can to make it so,' Vivien replied, more determined now than ever to make this work, despite her own fears and reservations.

'Good,' Evelyn said with a small smile. 'Now, tell me all about yourself.'

And so Vivien did. She told her about the little house in Bow and the morning when it wasn't there anymore, about her father going to war and her friends being evacuated.

Evelyn nodded. 'Some evacuees stayed at Silverton Hall,' she said. 'That was before I worked there of course, but it's hard to imagine being taken from your parents like that.' She stopped and bit her lower lip, looking down at her bump. 'I've never been to London,' she said, changing the subject. 'I don't suppose I ever will. My family have moved to Nottingham now and that's where I'll go when…' She trailed off, looked away.

Vivien decided to talk more about London, telling Evelyn about VE Day and the bonfire they'd had on the street to celebrate, how she and her friends had danced around it in their dressing gowns. She told her about the day a few months later when her father finally came home. And then she told her about the dressmaker and how terrible her sewing was. That made Evelyn smile properly for the first time.

'I was always good at sewing,' she said.

'That's why I jumped at the chance when I heard about the vacancy at the solicitor's office,' Vivien replied. 'Anything to get away from sewing all day. And of course that's where I met Max.'

'At the solicitors' offices?'

'Well just up the road,' Vivien said and told her about the awful smog the previous autumn and how she'd walked straight into Max and lost her hat.

'Lost your heart as well by the sound of it,' Evelyn said. 'How terribly romantic.'

Vivien smiled and nodded. It did sound romantic, but she knew that had never been the case. She knew now that she didn't love Max, even though she'd tried so hard to, and she was sure he didn't love her. And the more she thought about it, the more she thought about everything that Max had told her on the day after the party, the more she began to wonder if even that first meeting in the smog was somehow contrived.

She was just about to ask Evelyn when she first met Max in an attempt to try to catch her husband out, or at the very least check up on him to make sure the stories aligned, but Mrs Castleton came in then with the tea tray and talk turned to Silverton Hall and how much money the nameless American hotelier had spent on its transformation.

Perhaps it is better not to know after all, Vivien thought.

Vivien didn't seen Evelyn Pugh again. When Max came back from London he barely asked about her, but instead started to make arrangements for when they brought the baby home. He'd ordered all sorts of baby furniture and equipment from London, which was delivered in big vans that blocked up the High Street and caused chaos on the cliff road.

He also brought back from London the photographs that he'd taken at the ball and developed in a friend's darkroom. They were beautiful. Even Vivien had to admit that the photograph of her looking over her shoulder at Max in the ballroom did make her look almost as beautiful as she had felt that night.

Max stayed in the Bay for weeks at a time that summer as they waited for the arrival of Evelyn's baby. They were both nervous and jumpy, neither of them really knowing what to do with themselves, neither of them sleeping well as though their bodies were already preparing themselves for the third person who would be coming into their lives any day. Max even started getting up early to swim with Vivien each morning, taking his new Box Brownie camera that he had finally bought himself under the excuse that it would be good for taking 'family snaps'. Vivien felt nauseous every time he mentioned the family they were about to become, almost as though she were pregnant herself. She wasn't, of course, which was perhaps just as well considering, and she wondered if Max had been doing something that stopped her becoming pregnant, knowing as he had done that Evelyn's baby would become theirs. How would she know if he had been?

Max took photographs of the beach in the early mornings, empty but for a few swimmers, and candid shots of Vivien as she swam, as she walked out of the sea, as she dried herself. It was the only time she felt like herself, the only time she felt relaxed. She wondered again if she'd ever be able to swim after the baby came to live with them.

He only went back to London once that summer, a few days before they were called to the hospital to collect the baby that Evelyn had given birth to. When he returned he brought with him a huge canvas wrapped in brown paper.

'Open it,' he said.

When Vivien tore the package open she found a portrait of herself staring back at her. A portrait of her wearing a midnight-blue ballgown and looking over her shoulder at the viewer.

'My god,' she whispered. It was almost like looking in the mirror.

'Do you like it?' Max asked. 'I've been working on it in a friend's studio in London and I only had the photograph to work from really.'

'I love it,' she interrupted. But she didn't turn to him, she didn't hold him or kiss him. She just kept looking at the painting and wondering why he'd done it.

'I never want us to forget that night,' he said. 'And I promise there will be more wonderful nights like that. This isn't the end of something, Vivien, it's just the beginning.'

But Vivien found that very difficult to believe.

26

Norfolk – July 2019

Isobel woke from a dream in which her grandmother was still alive, sitting in her armchair by the hearth. The Vivien in the dream was talking but Isobel couldn't make out what she was trying to say. As she blinked her eyes open she felt disorientated and then, when she remembered that her grandmother would never sit in her armchair again, she was floored by yet another wave of unbearable grief.

After a moment she realised that she was alone in the single bed on the top floor of Little Clarion and that when she had gone to sleep she hadn't been alone. At some point during the night Nick had left.

The evening hadn't gone how she'd imagined at all. It had been a surprise when Nick had come over with food but she had been so pleased to see him, so glad of his company, his laughter, somebody to voice her theories to – theories that involved her mother's adoption being directly linked to the photographs of Vivien that hung in the ballroom of Silverton Hall. But they hadn't talked about that and the curiosity and discomfort that Isobel felt when she thought about the photographs, about her mother's adoption, lay thick and heavy in her stomach still.

Instead she had surprised herself by telling him about that terrible year in New York before she went to art school, about what happened after she won the portrait competition, about Adam. And then he had surprised her with his own revelations, a past she would never have guessed and a darkness that he would carry with him for ever.

They had shared so much more than words, but apparently he couldn't stick around to face her in the morning. Did he regret telling her the truth? Did he regret spending the night with her?

She sat up in bed. How dare he just disappear like that? Where the hell was he?

Angrily, Isobel got out of bed and pulled on her still-damp swimsuit – she really must buy another if she was going to get into the habit of daily swimming – and stomped down the stairs. She didn't want to feel angry with Nick on top of everything else. Right now she didn't want to feel anything for Nick and she certainly didn't want to think about his kiss, or the way his body had felt against hers. She wanted to put Nick Hargreaves out of her mind, at least for the time being, and the best way of doing that was to float in salt water for half an hour.

She saw nobody as she walked to the beach. It was early on a Sunday morning and even the shop and cafe were closed. As she walked down the cliff path towards the sea, she pushed all thoughts of Nick aside, which was easier said than done. She could think of a dozen reasons why he'd left while she was still sleeping, but she remembered the voice in her head the night before warning her that it was too soon, that they had only just started to get to know each other again, that it was easier if they were just friends.

As if that was going to be possible now.

She walked towards the sea, dropping her towel and shorts at the shoreline, desperate to submerge herself in the water and wash her feelings away. She felt raw and open and she wanted the protection of the water around her.

There were only two other swimmers this morning, along with a few dog walkers on the sand, so after ten minutes of vigorous swimming to warm her, up Isobel floated on her back once again. The sun was breaking through the clouds and she could feel its warmth already. It was going to be another beautiful day.

Whilst her swim had relaxed her body, her brain was not playing along this morning, jumping from thought to thought, from problem to problem. Should she find Nick and talk to him? Should she keep digging through Vivien's things to see if she could find out more about her biological grandmother or should she leave that well alone as her own mother seemed to want her to? Would Lauren's grandmother know anything? When would the kitchen be finished? Would Nick turn up to finish it?

Trying to calm herself down was pointless so she paddled back to the shore and dried herself off, pulling her clothes on over her wet bathing suit. She tried to think about more mundane matters, like which pastry she could have for breakfast this morning.

The church bells started ringing as Isobel walked back along the High Street, reminding her of Vivien's funeral and that raw, open feeling that she thought she'd left in the sea started to creep back. She smelled the welcome aroma of breakfast pastries and was glad to see the cafe open. She took a breath, remembering how much her grandmother had loved the cafe too, how Sarah had told her about Vivien's penchant for Victoria sponge and walked towards her breakfast. As she was about to go in she felt a touch on her shoulder, which made her jump.

'Oh I'm sorry, Isobel.' It was Lauren, dressed in a long summer dress with her hair in a complicated up-do, sunglasses perched on her head. She made Isobel feel bedraggled. 'I've been trying to call you.'

'I've been for a swim, obviously.' Isobel smiled, gesturing to her damp clothes and the towel around her neck. 'I left my phone behind.'

'Oh that's OK, it's just...' She hesitated for a moment. 'Well I spoke to my grandmother last night and she'd like to see you.'

Isobel's stomach fizzed. 'She would? Does she know something?'

'I didn't mention your mother or...well, you know,' Lauren replied. 'But, like I said, she knows you're back and when I mentioned you she said she'd like to see you. She says she wants to see you today.'

'Today?' Isobel wasn't sure she was ready to hear anything Lauren's grandmother had to tell her. She wasn't sure she should be hearing it at all, not without speaking to her mother first. And she had to find Nick as well.

'I did say you might not be able to see her at such short

notice.' Lauren laughed. 'But she says that at her age one can't afford to wait.'

'Do you know what she meant?'

Lauren shrugged. 'Not really. It's up to you though. Would you like to talk to her or are you going to let sleeping dogs lie?'

I should talk to Mum, Isobel thought. *I should try to find Nick*.

'I'd like to see her,' she said out loud.

'OK.' Lauren smiled gently. 'I can come with you. We're just going to church...'

'We?' Isobel half expected Lauren's grandmother (whose name she couldn't remember for the life of her) to pop up from somewhere.

'My husband and kids are just over there.' Lauren pointed across the street where a tall blond man was trying to get two small children – a boy and a girl – to wait quietly. When he spotted Lauren and Isobel, he raised a hand in greeting. 'I can pick you up in an hour and a half?'

Isobel nodded. 'I'll see you then, I guess.'

Suddenly she didn't feel hungry after all.

Lauren's maternal grandmother, Bee Burnage, lived in sheltered accommodation at the end of a cul-de-sac just off the King's Lynn Road. It was a small apartment – living room, bedroom, kitchen and bathroom – and in each room there was a red alarm button to call the warden if Bee fell again or was taken ill.

'I've got one around my neck too,' Bee said when she saw Isobel looking at the emergency button in the living room, smiling as she pulled the panic button out of her dress. 'Now, Isobel Malone, let's have a look at you – I haven't seen you since you were a teenager.'

The little flat smelled of lavender, which made Isobel almost dizzy with the memory of her own grandmother, but she turned to Bee and smiled. 'I'll always remember making scones in your kitchen,' she said.

'I've made some this morning actually,' Bee replied. 'Lauren, can you be a love and go and put the kettle on so Isobel and I can have a natter?'

Lauren caught Isobel's eye and raised her eyebrows before going into the kitchen to make tea. Isobel followed Bee into the living room – the older lady used a stick to walk and had a noticeable limp.

After Lauren had left her outside the cafe to go to church, Isobel had walked home slowly, feeling a strange pressure in her head. At first she'd thought it was a migraine coming on. Part of her longed for the excuse to go back to bed, draw the curtains on the day and stop thinking about everything. But by the time she'd arrived at Little Clarion she knew that she couldn't do that, even if it was a migraine. She wanted to talk to Lauren's grandmother. She wanted to know.

She had showered and dressed thoughtfully, remembering how smart Lauren had looked. She wore a yellow flowery sundress and a cream cardigan and put her hair up carefully, rather than in its trademark messy bun. Finally she had looked at herself in the mirror properly for the first time in a week. She'd been surprised by what she'd seen. Already she was looking better than when she'd arrived – her skin sun kissed, her face more relaxed. She'd reminded herself that this was why she'd come back – to start again, to have a better life, not to meddle in the past.

Her head had been feeling better as Lauren had driven them to Bee's flat and she'd tried not to think about how she should have spoken to her mother first or made finding Nick more of a priority. Was he OK? What if he'd had another panic attack somewhere? But if she thought too much about any of that, the feeling of pressure in her head returned.

'Sit down and make yourself comfortable,' Bee said now as she carefully lowered herself into her chair in the living room.

'Are you OK?' Isobel asked. 'Lauren told me about your fall.'

'Oh I'm fine.' Bee waved her hand. 'It'll take more than a silly fall to finish me off. But are you OK, Isobel? You and Vivien were always so close. I am truly sorry. I did so want to come to the funeral but Lauren talked me out of it what with my hip and everything.'

'I am OK,' Isobel said, realising perhaps for the first time that she really was. Seeing her reflection in the mirror had made her new life in the Bay seem more real, more tangible somehow. Despite everything that was going on in her head – her mother's adoption, Nick's disappearance – she was feeling more like herself than she had in a long time. 'I miss Nana all the time, of course, but being back in Silverton Bay is all I ever wanted.'

Bee nodded. 'I do miss the Bay but dear old Spencer comes out to see me now and then and Lauren brings the great-grandchildren after school and there's a lot going on here too – dances and quiz nights and so on. I'm not lonely.'

'Spencer comes to see you?'

'Yes, he drives that old van of his up here once a week or so. He keeps me updated on village gossip. He used to bring Vivien every now and then before—'

'He did?' Isobel interrupted, surprised.

'And sometimes he'd drive me back to Silverton Bay to have tea with Vivien at that little cafe opposite the pub. Have you tried it yet?'

Isobel said she had and then she broached the subject of Silverton Hall, telling Bee that she'd stayed there before she met up with Vivien's solicitor.

'Oh, you lucky thing. I've heard it's absolutely gorgeous.'

'It really is. Haven't you seen inside since they reopened?'

Bee shook her head and looked away as though she was hiding something.

'Nana would never go to the Hall for some reason so that was the first time I'd seen it,' Isobel went on but her comment was met with an awkward silence.

'It was Spencer who told me you were coming back to the Bay,' Bee said eventually, changing the subject. 'And then, when Lauren said she'd been talking to you, I knew I had to see you again myself.' She gave Isobel a long, appraising look as Isobel listened to the sound of Lauren making tea in the kitchen. She seemed to be taking an inordinately long time.

'Please don't take this the wrong way,' Isobel began. 'But why did you want to see me? As you said, you haven't seen me in a long time. I'm surprised you remember me.'

'Oh it was impossible to forget you. Vivien talked about you all the time. She was very proud of you, Isobel.'

'Was she? Even after I became a teacher? I always felt I'd let her down.'

'Nonsense!' Bee waved her hand in the air dramatically again. 'She was a teacher herself after all. She was proud you'd followed in her footsteps.'

Isobel had never thought about it like that. She'd allowed Adam's prejudices to colour her own self-esteem.

'Listen to me,' Bee said, leaning forward in her chair. 'Life never works out the way we think it will when we're young. But that doesn't mean we shouldn't be proud of what we achieve. Just because things turn out differently doesn't mean they aren't worthwhile. Besides, you've still got a lifetime ahead of you to do all sorts of wonderful things. And make sure you do because when you're old and your hip doesn't let you get much further than the door those memories will be priceless.'

'I'm sorry. I'm being rather self-absorbed. I'm trying to see where my new life takes me. I'm going to start teaching Lauren's art class in September.' She nodded towards the kitchen, wondering how much longer Lauren would be. She suspected Lauren wouldn't return until Bee summoned her.

'It must be hard with all your grandmother's things around you, all those memories.'

'Spencer is helping me clear out a lot of that stuff and Nick is helping with the renovation.'

Bee nodded, but she didn't say anything for a moment. It felt as though she was waiting for Isobel to ask a question. But Isobel didn't really know how to bring the subject back around to Silverton Hall.

'I saw some photographs,' she began, quietly.

'Of your grandmother at Silverton Hall,' Bee said quietly. That was quick. Silverton Bay gossip really did fly around at the speed of sound. How on earth had anyone kept the truth from Gina for so long when she was growing up?

'Um yes, how did you...?'

Bee chuckled. 'Don't look at me like that,' she replied. 'Vivien told me she'd given them to one of the managers there for some display or other. Not that I ever saw the display of course because Vivien would never go to Silverton Hall, would she?' She gave Isobel a little wink.

'So you know about the parties in the 1950s.'

Bee nodded. 'I know she went to the first midsummer party at Silverton Hall. The first and last party she used to call it. She and Max went to other parties after that, of course, but it was that inaugural ball where everything changed.' Bee turned to Isobel then and narrowed her eyes a little.

'Is that when she found out about my mother?' Isobel asked. 'I found another photograph, you see.' She went on to explain about the picture of Vivien on the beach, of the suspicions that she'd dismissed at first, and of the telephone call she'd had with her father.

'Did your parents tell you anything else?' Bee asked.

'They didn't seem to know anything else. My mother hadn't wanted to find anything out.'

'She's still in New York, I assume.'

Isobel nodded. 'Still unable to get on a plane.'

'And you want to know more than your mother can tell you,' Bee went on. 'You want to know who her biological parents are.'

'I do,' Isobel confessed. 'But it feels wrong when Mum doesn't want to know. Perhaps I should talk to her first.'

'Well I don't know any more than she does about her parentage,' Bee said. 'So I'm not going to betray any secrets there. But I can tell you a little about what happened, if you like.'

Isobel thought for a moment. Should she pursue this conversation? She looked away from Bee for a moment. She thought about the sensation of pressure in her head, that feeling of having drifted through her life. She tried not to think about Nick.

'I'd like to know,' she said.

Bee took a deep breath and settled back in her chair, crossing her hands on her lap in front of her. She looked, just for a moment, as though she was about to read a bedtime story.

'I remember when they brought Gina home,' she began. 'Such a lovely baby and she grew into a beautiful young woman.'

'How well did you know her?' Isobel asked.

'Fairly well. She was good friends with my Susan, that's Lauren's mother,' Bee nodded towards the kitchen where Lauren was doing whatever it was she was doing to keep out of the way. 'Susan lives in France now.'

'And did Susan know that Mum was adopted?'

Bee shook her head vigorously and pursed her lips. 'No. Plenty of people in the village did know, of course. You can't keep a secret like that in Silverton Bay, but it was never spoken of.' She paused and looked as though she was casting around for the right words. In the end, she shrugged. 'I don't know,' she said. 'They were just different times. We didn't talk about certain things and in hindsight I'd say that wasn't such a good thing really.'

Isobel remembered that Spencer had said something similar about time being different but not necessarily better.

'But the next generation, Susan's generation,' Bee went on. 'Or the baby boomers as we call them now, the baby boomers of Silverton Bay.' She giggled. 'We never told them. None of Gina's contemporaries knew she was adopted. If Max and Vivien didn't want to tell her then it was nobody else's business. We might be a bunch of old gossips in the Bay, but we can keep a secret when we have to.'

'Do you know why Nana didn't tell Mum for so long?'

Again Bee shook her head. 'No idea at all. I remember thinking, after Max died, that it would come out, that Vivien would tell her then. But she left it until the last possible moment and then all hell broke loose.'

'In what way?' Isobel couldn't really imagine 'hell breaking loose' in Silverton Bay.

'It was a huge shock to Gina, of course. She was terribly upset and felt very betrayed I think, although I never really spoke to her after she found out. She was off to London and didn't come back very often. But it was a shock to all her friends too, to everyone she was at school with.' Bee paused for a moment, remembering. 'Susan was dreadfully upset about it all, particularly about Gina leaving, although she understood why she did. She and Gina were never really friends again afterwards. I don't really know why – I suspect Gina just felt like a different person who needed a new start but you'll have to ask your mother about that, I suppose.'

There was a lot Isobel needed to ask her mother about.

'We should all have seen it coming really,' Bee said sadly.

'My mother never told me about it at all. She says that's because she didn't want it to come between me and Nana, which I suppose I understand but…' Isobel paused and looked at Bee. 'Do you know anything about where Mum came from?'

'Well, her birth mother's name was Evelyn Pugh,' Bee replied. 'That's no big secret and your mother already knows that because the name will be on the adoption certificate. She worked up at Silverton Hall for the last Lord Harrington before the Hall was sold.'

'The one who died young?' Isobel asked, thinking of the photograph of the man in plus fours on the wall of the ballroom that Ella had showed her.

'That's him. She was one of the few remaining staff up there, along with Vivien's friend Mrs Castleton. Do you remember her?'

'She died before I was born, but I've heard all about her. She taught Nana to swim in the sea.'

'That's right.' Bee smiled to herself. 'Your grandmother did love the sea. Anyway, this Evelyn Pugh, she got herself in the family way…' She giggled. 'I'm sorry, that's a terribly old-fashioned thing to say. You'll have to forgive me. Evelyn found she was pregnant and she never would say who the father was.'

Isobel took a breath. 'And Nana found all of this out after that first midsummer party?'

Bee nodded slowly. 'That's what she told me,' she said. 'Years later, mind, but that's what she said.'

'Well it's no wonder she never wanted to go up to Silverton Hall with me.' But Vivien had gone up to the Hall, hadn't she, to drink coffee and talk to Ella? Isobel couldn't help feeling hurt by that, even though she knew they were probably memories that Vivien couldn't share with her. Memories that were easier to share with a stranger. 'And nobody knows who Mum's father is?'

'After Max and Vivien had adopted her, a lot of folk in the village thought perhaps Max was the father,' Bee said.

'No!' Isobel replied, feeling shocked at the thought. 'Surely not.' She did some quick maths in her head. 'He'd already met Nana by then, fallen in love with her back in London, hadn't he?'

'Well I don't know about the falling in love bit,' Bee said. 'I know the story of them meeting during the smog seems terribly romantic, but romance and a good marriage are two very different things.' Isobel couldn't help but think of Adam as she heard those words. He was always terribly good at the romance, less so at the whole commitment thing.

'Even so,' she said. 'He was in London.'

'Some of the time he was but he was here in Norfolk quite a bit around that time. He had something to do with the Hall, if I remember correctly. Some sort of cousin or something? Oh I don't know, I don't remember things as well as I used to.'

Isobel remembered that there had been no heir after the last Lord Harrington died, that the Hall had gone to a cousin. She felt a strange tingling feeling on the back of her neck and the pressure in her head returned.

'But if you want my opinion,' Bee went on, interrupting Isobel's thoughts. 'Max wasn't the father. Vivien knew who the father was, I'm sure of that. And if it had been Max, she wouldn't have been so blasé about all those rumours.'

'But who could it have been?' Isobel asked, even though she had her own suspicions.

As soon as she asked the question she knew she'd lost Bee. The older woman's face closed down and Isobel knew that she either didn't know any more or, if she did, wasn't going to tell her.

'Be a love,' Bee said. 'And see where Lauren's got to with that tea.'

27

Lauren dropped Isobel off at the bottom of the hill near the High Street. 'I can walk from here,' she said as she got out of the car.

'I can take you home if you like.'

'No, I need a walk,' Isobel replied. 'I need some time to think.'

Lauren nodded. 'I'm sorry. I hadn't expected her to know so much. It must be—'

'It's OK.'

'Call me if you need me,' Lauren said as Isobel quietly shut the car door.

Lauren had heard a lot of the conversation from her hiding-place in the kitchen. She hadn't really been eavesdropping she'd insisted in the car home, she'd just been waiting for a good time to bring the tea in, but there hadn't been one. She'd thrown away two pots of tea when they'd over brewed. It didn't matter to Isobel that Lauren had overheard. After all, it saved her having to repeat everything.

'I can't believe an entire village, especially this gossipy one, managed to keep that a secret for so long,' Lauren had said. 'And I had no idea our mothers were friends either.'

'Me neither,' Isobel had replied. 'But Mum hardly ever talks about Silverton Bay or her childhood at all really.' She hadn't shared with Lauren the creeping feeling she'd had about her grandfather since the conversation with Bee – that Max Chambers might be the distant cousin who had inherited Silverton Hall in 1952.

But that couldn't be right, could it? Isobel thought to herself as she trudged up the hill towards her house – deliberately taking the long way around so that she didn't pass by Odds & Ends. The last thing she needed was to see Nick right now.

If her grandfather had inherited Silverton Hall, why didn't anybody talk about it? The Hall should be part of family legend, if not legacy anymore. And if it was true, how did all of that tie in with her mother's adoption? Bee had seemed sure that Max hadn't been Gina's biological father, so who had been?

She was still thinking about it and about who Evelyn Pugh was and whether or not she was still alive, when she turned the bend in the road that led to her house and saw a car that was very much welcome.

'Mattie,' Isobel called to the woman who was leaning against the car door scrolling on her mobile phone. 'What on earth are you doing here? You never called!'

'Surprise!' Mattie said, opening her arms to hug Isobel. 'The phone signal around here is terrible, by the way. I'm assuming that's why you haven't kept me updated on all things Nick.'

'I'm sorry,' Isobel said, remembering their last conversation by the tree in the back garden. 'It's been...

there's been... Oh god...' Before she knew it, Isobel was crying and back in Mattie's arms.

'What's the matter, Izzy?' Mattie said. 'Is it me? Have I done something or said—'

'No, it's not you.' Isobel sniffed and pulled away. 'I've never been more pleased to see you in my life.'

'Well that's nice!' Mattie grinned. 'But whatever is the matter. Is it Nick?'

'No, yes...sort of. So much has happened.'

'Well perhaps you'd better tell me. Preferably over something to eat as I'm starving. Let's go in and you can show me this amazing house and make me something to eat.' She grinned and Isobel realised how much she'd missed her bossy friend. She also realised how hungry she was. She'd hardly been able to swallow the scones at Bee's flat; they'd tasted like ashes in her mouth.

'There's no food in the house,' Isobel said. 'I don't even have a kitchen.' She ran a hand across her forehead remembering the state of the inside of the house – the rubble in the kitchen, the unboxed books all over the office, the rumpled sheets in her bedroom where her bed was still unmade from the night before.

Nick. Just the thought of him made her breath hitch.

Mattie looked at her with concern, but didn't say anything. 'How about that pub then? Are they still serving food?'

'I need to talk to you in private. Away from prying ears. I can't do that in the pub.'

In the end they bought sandwiches from Sarah at the cafe just as she was closing up for the afternoon ('You just caught me,' she said. 'You can have them half price.') and took them back to the house. They ate sitting cross-legged on the living room floor. Mattie talked about Cambridge for a while, about the new clerk at her barristers' chambers ('utterly useless') and the latest case she'd just won for her client ('He's guilty of all sorts,' she said. 'But not that particular crime.') and Isobel smiled in all the right places, nodding whenever she thought she was supposed to.

When she'd finished talking, Mattie wiped her hands on a paper napkin and leaned back against the side of one of the wing-backed chairs.

'You haven't really heard a word I've said, have you?' she asked. 'Are you going to tell me what's up?'

Isobel looked up and exhaled. 'I don't know where to start.'

'How about where we left off? Nick was getting rid of rats and looking extremely handsome, if I remember correctly.'

'Mice,' Isobel corrected.

'Rodents are rodents, Izzy. Now, spill.'

And Isobel spilled. She told her friend everything – the photographs in the ballroom, the visit to Mr Brecher and the letter and money that Vivien had left for her, the fish and chips on the beach with Nick and their tentative truce, the renovations they'd decided to make on the house and the picture of Vivien on the beach.

'Your mum's adopted?' Mattie asked softly.

Isobel told her about the conversation she'd had with her mother and the later telephone call with her father and how Nick had found her on the beach. And then she told her about wanting to turn the office into a studio, about Nick and Spencer helping her, and while she didn't go into any detail about what had happened to Nick in Afghanistan, that wasn't her story to tell after all, she did tell her about the kiss and how he'd carried her to bed, about how right it had felt until she'd woken that morning to an empty bed.

'He left in the middle of the night?' Mattie asked. 'But why? I thought—'

'And I haven't had a chance to think about any of it because today I was invited to morning tea with the grandmother of an old school friend who told me about the summer that my mother was adopted and how the whole village knew but there was some sort of unspoken agreement to cover it up. My biological grandmother's name was Evelyn Pugh, by the way, but we don't seem to have any sort of confirmation on my biological grandfather.' Isobel didn't tell Mattie about her suspicions or about the connections with Silverton Hall. She'd already told her too much, she could tell by the slightly dazed look on Mattie's face.

'And all of this has happened since Wednesday?' Mattie asked. Isobel had never seen her friend so lost for words.

'Yup.'

'Wow, it's… Well, it's a lot, isn't it?'

'It's a lot.' Isobel suddenly felt extraordinarily tired. She wanted to go upstairs and curl into bed, to sleep in the sheets that would still smell of Nick.

'Where's Nick now?' Mattie asked.

'No idea. Back at his grandfather's shop, I should think.'

Mattie nodded and sat quietly for a while. Isobel lay down on her side on the floor and wondered if Mattie would notice if she fell asleep.

She didn't know how much time passed but she was just on the point of dozing off when Mattie's voice woke her.

'What?' Isobel said, sitting up again.

'I said, go and talk to him. Get up, go and find Nick and talk to him.'

'After everything I've told you that's what you think my priority should be?' Isobel felt sleepy and confused.

'Absolutely I think that's what your priority should be,' Mattie replied. 'You've been in love with Nick half your life.' When Isobel opened her mouth to protest, Mattie just held up her hand. 'You know it's true, Izzy, and you also know if you don't try and make it work you'll spend the next eighteen years regretting it. All of this other stuff – the photographs, the adoption, the guessing game as to who your mother's father is – none of that is really about you.'

Isobel stared at her friend. How could she possibly think that the revelations of the last few days weren't about her? They had upended everything. 'They are about me though…' she began.

'They're about your history, yes,' Mattie conceded. 'They're about the past, but they're not about you now. They're not about making yourself happy and starting again. Nick, on the other hand, is about your present. If you walk away from him again now, if you don't find out if there's a future in this, you will regret it.'

Isobel opened her mouth to argue, but closed it again. Mattie was right. She had to find out why Nick had left.

'What if he regrets last night though?'

'Then at least you'll know,' Mattie replied. 'Now go upstairs, spruce yourself up and then find him.'

'Now?'

'Now.'

She did as Mattie told her, not even stopping to spruce

herself up but leaving the house straight away and heading to Odds & Ends before she lost her nerve. Mattie offered to wait at the house for her, for which Isobel had been grateful. If all this went wrong a friendly face back at home would be just what she needed. As she walked back up to the High Street she tried to rekindle the anger she had woken up with. By the time she was almost at Spencer's shop she was ready to ask Nick how he even dared walk away from her again after all these years.

But when she got to Odds & Ends there was an ambulance outside, it's blue lights flashing and a very pale-looking Spencer was being stretchered towards it.

'Nick,' she said as soon as she saw him following the paramedics towards the ambulance. He turned to look at her; he looked relieved. 'What can I do?' she asked.

He hesitated for a moment, his eyes shifting between the ambulance and his truck that was parked around the side of Spencer's shop.

'Can you go with Grandad?' he asked. 'I'll follow in the truck.'

She nodded and turned away towards the ambulance, everything forgotten except Spencer's wellbeing.

28

Nick sat in the hard plastic chair in the hospital corridor, Isobel next to him, fingers entwined with his. He squeezed her hand.

'I'm glad you're here,' he said.

'I'm not going anywhere. I can stay as long as you and Spencer need me.'

And he did need her, more than she knew.

When she'd arrived at Odds & Ends that afternoon, Nick had felt the most indescribable sense of relief that she was there, that she could help him. He knew he didn't deserve her help or kindness, not after what he'd done. And he knew he had to explain to her somehow why he'd done it. Why he'd left her alone in the early hours of the morning.

'Did you phone your friend?' he asked. She'd had somebody staying with her, a friend from Cambridge.

'Yeah, I said I'd be a while so they've gone back home.'

'You didn't have to do that, Isobel.'

'Yes, I did. Mattie and I can catch up anytime.' She paused and Nick wondered if Mattie was male or female. He felt a stab of jealousy and hated himself for feeling that when his grandfather was lying unconscious in a hospital room.

After Nick had left Isobel's bed – and how he still cringed at himself for doing that in the first place – he'd walked to the beach. The sun was just beginning to peek out over the horizon and he'd sat on the bench on the cliff near the lighthouse and watched its ascent. A new day, he'd thought to himself. He should have felt cheered by the previous night with Isobel – he'd wanted that to happen for half his life – but instead he felt as though he wasn't ready, as though he might have blown it.

That wasn't how he felt now though, as he sat here holding her hand. Finding his grandfather in a crumpled heap at the bottom of the stairs had changed everything.

'Were you there?' Isobel asked. 'When he fell?'

'Yes, thank god. He was upstairs prepping for this evening. He wanted to make me a roast dinner. I was working on some of the furniture we brought from Little Clarion and I called him to ask a question…' He stopped, rubbed his eyes. 'He must have lost his footing. I've been telling him for ages he needs to move, that the stairs are too much.' He turned to look at Isobel. 'Imagine if I hadn't been there, if it had been last night when…' He stopped and shook his head gently. 'I'm sorry,' he said. He hadn't meant it to sound like that, as though he hadn't wanted to be with her.

'It's OK, Nick,' she replied calmly. 'But Spencer was fit and healthy for his age – he could get up and downstairs easily enough. You can't blame yourself.'

Nick looked down at their interlocked hands. 'I can blame myself for leaving you last night though,' he said quietly.

'You don't have to explain, Nick, not now. Not here.'

'But I want to...'

'Mr Hargreaves?' a doctor interrupted. He looked exhausted. Nick suddenly remembered that feeling of hours and hours on duty, nobody to relieve you, no time for a break, a glass of water or even a pee half the time. He didn't miss it. Not even a little.

'Yes, that's me,' he said. 'How's Grandad? Is he going to be OK?'

'He's conscious again,' the doctor said. 'Which is a very good sign at his age. Unfortunately, he's broken his ankle. He's incredibly lucky though.'

Nick didn't say anything, his mind blank. He felt as though that old medical part of him should kick in and he should know what to do, what questions to ask, but instead all he could think about was how long broken bones took to heal in the elderly, how there would undoubtedly be osteoporosis and how, with a broken ankle, Spencer wouldn't be able to come back to live at the shop for a long time.

'It could have been so much worse,' the doctor went on. 'Do you know how it happened?'

'I think he just missed his footing on the stairs,' Nick said. 'I'm sorry, I don't really know. I was in a different room when it happened.' Just as he thought he was going to cry he felt Isobel's hand slip back into his.

'How is Spencer feeling?' Isobel asked the doctor, filling the silence.

'And you are?' The doctor's voice was flat, almost bored. Nick knew it was because of tiredness rather than rudeness or any sign he didn't care.

'Isobel Malone,' she replied.

'She's a close friend of the family,' Nick managed.

'Well he's awake and surprisingly bright.'

'How much pain is he in?'

'He's on strong pain relief now but it's going to be quite a painful recovery for him. We'll need to keep him in for a few days and then…' The doctor hesitated.

'Then what?' Isobel pressed.

'Well, he's going to need care after he's discharged, but we can talk about that later.'

Where could Spencer go once he was discharged? Nick couldn't bear to put him in a nursing home, he wasn't going to let that happen.

'Would you like to see him?' the doctor asked, his voice gentler now.

'Is that OK?' Nick replied.

'Follow me.'

As Nick turned to follow the doctor, he felt Isobel pull gently on his arm. 'I'll go back home,' she said. 'Leave you to it.'

'Don't be silly. He'll want to see you. Come with me.'

'Are you sure?'

In response Nick pulled her against him and they followed the doctor hand in hand down the corridor towards Spencer's room.

'I'm a daft old man,' Spencer said as they came into the room. He looked small and frail under the harsh hospital lights.

Nick swallowed, mouth dry. This was the first time he'd been in a hospital since he'd left medicine. He could feel the familiar shaking in his hands, the knots in his stomach.

'Anyone can fall down the stairs,' Isobel said from behind him. She was still holding his hand and when he turned to her she looked almost as pale as Spencer. 'Accidents happen.'

'Come and sit here, Isobel,' Spencer said, indicating the chair next to the bed. Nick felt her move away, her hand slipping out of his. He heard her trying to make Spencer more comfortable on the scratchy-looking hospital pillows and he walked to the end of the bed to look at his grandfather's medical charts. He used to be able to read these things but today the figures and lines just seemed to be jumping around.

'Put that down, Nick,' his grandfather's voice interrupted him. 'And come here.' He gestured towards the second chair by his bed. 'I don't want to talk about my broken ankle or my blood pressure or what will become of me now I'm just a doddery old man. Tell me something more interesting than that. How's the house coming along?'

'Not much progress since you saw it yesterday,' Nick replied, smiling at his grandfather and sitting down on the opposite side of the bed to Isobel. 'But we did pack up a lot more books. Those bookshelves are almost ready to paint now.'

Spencer chuckled to himself. 'Packing up books,' he said. 'Is that what they call it these days?'

Nick saw Isobel blush and look away.

'I went to see Bee Burnage this morning,' she said, changing the subject.

'Who?' Nick asked.

'She's Lauren Cook's grandmother.'

'And what did she have to say for herself?' Spencer asked.

'A lot as it happens, including that you go visiting her quite often.' There was a teasing quality to her voice and Nick loved her for that, for sitting here in this hospital and staying positive, talking to Spencer like she always did.

Spencer chuckled again, his eyes closing slightly. 'A man's allowed friends,' he said.

'And she told me about when Mum was adopted,' Isobel went on, telling Nick and Spencer what Bee had said that morning. When she'd finished speaking Spencer seemed to be asleep but Nick didn't move. He knew they should go, that visiting hours must be over, but he couldn't bring himself to do anything right now.

'The whole village must have known that your mum was adopted,' Nick mused, thinking about what Isobel had said. 'How on earth did they keep it so quiet?'

Isobel shrugged and Spencer moved his head on his pillow, turning to Nick and opening his eyes.

'Because Max Chambers paid them off in exchange for them keeping their mouths shut,' he said.

Nick frowned at his grandfather. Was this the morphine talking?

'What?' Isobel asked. 'How do you know that?'

Spencer closed his eyes again and seemed to fall back to sleep. Nick was just concluding that what he'd said must be meaningless nonsense brought on by the pain relief and was just about to suggest that he and Isobel make a move when his grandfather spoke again.

'Isobel, listen to me,' he said, his voice quiet. Nick watched Isobel lean closer so she could hear what Spencer was saying. Her hair had escaped its clip and was lying in soft tendrils around her face. He wanted to reach over and tuck them behind her ears, but he kept his hands to himself.

'There was a diary,' Spencer said. 'Inside the other desk, the roll-top, from the office at Vivien's house. I found it when I was getting it ready to polish up yesterday. I shouldn't have read it. I didn't read it all but I shouldn't have read any of it. It's still at the shop, just tucked inside the desk. I meant to put it in a safe place for you but then I fell.'

'But that desk was empty,' Isobel said. 'We checked.'

'Secret drawer,' Spencer smiled. 'Those sort of desks often have them. Easy to find if you know where to look.' By the sound of his voice he was really fading into sleep now. 'You need to go and collect it, Isobel, love. It'll help fill in some blanks.'

Isobel looked stunned. Nick was casting around for something to say to fill the suddenly uncomfortable silence when a nurse popped her head around the door.

'Time to go, I think,' she said kindly. 'You can come back in the morning.'

Nick pulled the truck into the driveway of Odds & Ends. They'd driven home in silence, both he and Isobel lost in their own thoughts. He put the handbrake on.

'Isobel,' he said softly. She turned to him. She looked exhausted. 'Thank you for being there today.'

'That's OK,' she replied, undoing her seatbelt and turning to get out of the truck.

'Wait,' Nick said. 'Before you go I want to talk about last night. I'm so sorry I left you. I didn't mean—'

'It's OK. It's a very small bed,' she interrupted, trying to make light of it. 'And you'd spent a whole summer being told you couldn't go up to my room so I'm not surprised you freaked out.' She tried to laugh but couldn't.

'I didn't freak out. At least, I didn't freak out about that.'

'Then what was it?' she asked quietly. 'Was it me? Did I do something wrong? Say something?'

He reached for her, finding her hand, squeezing her fingers.

'Of course it wasn't you, Isobel. This is all me.'

'Because of your wife, your divorce?'

'No.' He stopped for a moment, looking out of the windscreen towards his grandfather's shop. He wondered for a moment if his grandfather would ever come back here. 'I still get panic attacks,' he said eventually. 'Particularly at night. I dream sometimes that I'm back there.'

'In Afghanistan?'

He nodded. Even talking about it was almost too much. 'I didn't want to frighten you if that happened so I tried to stay awake, but trying to stay awake was making me panic and... Well, in the end I decided to walk down to the beach.' He stopped again. 'I'm so sorry, Isobel, last night meant so much to me and I ruined it.' That was such an understatement. He'd been waiting eighteen years for last night. When he'd told her that he'd never stopped thinking about her, it hadn't been a line to get her into bed. It had been the truth.

He felt her shift in the seat next to him. 'Nick,' she said quietly. 'Look at me.'

He turned to her, his eyes locking on hers. God, she was beautiful. This Adam who had split up with her must be an even bigger idiot than him.

'You haven't ruined anything,' she said. 'We can work through this.'

'We can?' He couldn't believe she was going to give him another chance.

'We can, but not right now.' He felt his stomach drop and simultaneously felt selfish about his own disappointment. She had so much to deal with herself at the moment. 'I think we both need some time,' she went on. 'There's a lot to think about, and now there's this diary too. I need to work through some of this first. You understand, don't you?'

He lifted her hand to his lips and kissed her knuckles gently. 'Of course I understand.'

'And you could probably do with some time as well – to finalise your divorce and look after Spencer.'

He nodded. He knew she was right. 'Shall we see if we can find this diary before you go?' he asked, knowing that he was delaying the inevitable.

She followed him into the shop, walking over to the roll-top desk as soon as he'd turned the lights on. He watched her as she opened the desk and took out a thick leather-bound book. She flicked through the pages and then closed it again, hugging it to her chest.

'Is that it?' he asked.

'It's Nana's writing, but...' She hesitated. 'I feel as though Mum should read it first.'

He stepped a little closer to her. 'It's your story too, though,' he said.

'It isn't, not really,' she replied, remembering what Mattie had said to her that afternoon. It was Vivien's story. 'Maybe neither of us should read it. It's not really ours to read, is it?' She looked down at the diary in her hands, thinking about Mattie again. This was the past. It was her history, it was important, but not as important as right now. 'I don't know,' she said. 'I probably need to get some sleep. It's been a long day.'

Nick wanted to ask her to stay, to take her upstairs and try again, but he knew it wasn't the right time.

'Maybe you should go and see your mum,' he said instead. He couldn't believe he was saying it, advocating for her to leave the Bay, but he wondered if it was exactly what she needed.

'I usually spend a few weeks of the summer in America with Mum and Dad,' she said. 'But this year, with the house and everything, I haven't been.'

'I can work on the house while you're away. I'll get it done even quicker if it's empty.'

She smiled. 'Are you trying to get rid of me?'

'Of course not. I just think perhaps it would be the right thing to do and then, when you're back, we can talk.'

She stepped towards him then and her hand threaded itself around his neck. She stood on tiptoe and brushed her lips against his. When she stepped away from him she held his gaze for a moment.

'Let me walk you home,' he said, but she shook her head and started to walk away from him. Just before she got to the door she turned to him again.

'I've always loved you, Nick,' she said.

As she left, he thought his heart might burst.

29

Norfolk – October 1964

'We have to tell her, Max, she deserves to know the truth,' Vivien said quietly, calmly. Remaining quiet and calm seemed to be the best way to deal with Max these days. The only way she could get him to listen. But today she could tell that it was already too late. He was tired and distant, as though half of him was already in London. She'd picked the wrong moment.

'She doesn't need to know. She's still too young.' Max's voice sounded resigned. They'd had this conversation before and he was adamant that Gina didn't need to be told that she was adopted yet. Vivien could see his hands – spread on the mahogany of the desk – twitching as though he would rather be anywhere else than here, having this conversation again.

'She's eleven, Max,' Vivien pressed on valiantly. 'She's old enough to know the truth, to learn who she really is.'

Max sighed, closed his eyes. 'She is my daughter,' he said slowly, and she watched him pinch the bridge of his nose.

'I will decide when or even if she is ready to know,' Max went on. 'I don't want to talk about this now, Vivien. I'm very busy.'

Vivien took a breath to steady herself. She was used to her husband being distant, used to the amount of time he spent away from home, his tired, resigned attitude, and even the smell of another woman's perfume on his shirts whenever he came back from London. If it hadn't been for Gina, Vivien would have left long ago.

If she could bear to leave the sea behind.

'One day she'll need to know,' she said quietly. 'One day she'll want to travel, or go to university, or get married. We have to prepare her—'

'No,' Max said, and there was a finality to the single syllable, as though the conversation was over before it had even begun.

Vivien reached out a hand towards her husband as though to squeeze his shoulder, but when he glanced at her she thought better of it, snatching the hand back and putting it in her apron pocket. She stood for a moment wondering if there was anything else to say. She watched as Max picked up his pen and went back to the pages of figures on the desk in front of him. No, she decided, there was nothing left to say. Not today at least.

She turned away and walked out of the office and back into the hall, leaning against the William Morris wallpaper she had wanted so much and that Max had bought for her. It seemed so silly now, the things that he had provided that had made her think that their marriage meant something to him – the wallpaper, the television, the dresses, the parties at Silverton Hall. They were just tokens, things that meant very little to him – she had learned that anything that could be purchased meant very little to him as the Chambers family seemed to have almost inexhaustible funds. Nothing Vivien could do or say would ever mean anything to him. He only came back from London for one reason these days.

Gina.

Max adored his daughter. There was nothing he wouldn't do for her, nothing he wouldn't buy for her, nothing she could ask for that he would refuse. Vivien worried that she would begin to grow spoiled, that she would expect the world to always give her what she wanted. She tried to keep her daughter's feet on the ground. It often felt like fighting a losing battle, especially as most of the village treated her like a princess too.

That was why Vivien had wondered if telling Gina the truth might help. She was old enough and certainly mature enough to understand and, Vivien felt, the sooner she knew perhaps the sooner she could begin to live a more authentic life. Part of the problem, Vivien believed, was that half the village knew and were covering up a truth that Max was determined Gina would never discover. How could any of them go on like this?

When she and Max had first brought Gina home from the hospital things had changed in their marriage. Max had stayed at home more, doting on his new baby daughter. Vivien had felt that this life that had been thrown at her without any consultation could, after all, be a life of contentment, a life even of happiness.

But then she found it much harder than Max to bond with Gina. All she could think about when she held her daughter was Evelyn Pugh, sitting by the empty hearth in the rented room, her hair loose and her hands on her swollen belly. How would Evelyn feel now? Did she think about her baby all the time? Did she miss her? She must do, of course, she must miss her with every ounce of her being, and even though Evelyn had assured Vivien that adoption was what she wanted, the only way she could get on with her life and avoid the shame of being an unmarried mother, Vivien felt guilty every time she held Gina, as though she had taken something that wasn't hers to take.

And so the secret of Gina's birth felt harder and harder to keep as the years went by, as she grew from baby to toddler to child, looking less and less like either of her parents. Vivien wondered some days if she imagined the glances she and Gina got when they were out and about in the village, the nudges, the whispers. She knew people assumed that Max was Gina's biological father and there was nothing she could do to stop them thinking that. She couldn't tell them the truth; she'd promised Max that it would remain a secret from everyone.

Everyone except Miriam Castleton, of course, who knew everything. Even though the two women never spoke about the adoption or Evelyn Pugh again after Gina was brought back to Silverton Bay, Vivien was able to forgive her friend for the part she'd played in the deceit because she found a solace in being with somebody who knew the truth, somebody who wasn't judging her. All she could hope was that the village would keep its promises to Max and none of the nudges and whispers would find their way past the school gates and into Gina's classroom.

While Vivien knew that Max wasn't Gina's real father, she also knew that, as the years went by, he was by no means a faithful husband. She had fulfilled the role he had married her for – to be a mother to the baby he wanted to adopt. After those initial few months when Gina first came home, things reverted once again to how they had been. Max spent most of his time in London whilst Vivien stayed in Norfolk. When Max did come back to the Bay he only had eyes for his daughter, only wanted to spend time with her. There were more parties at Silverton Hall, which was getting busier and busier as word spread about the new country house hotel on the Norfolk coast, and while Vivien had a lot of fun at them, they never felt as magical as that first midsummer party. Everything had changed after that. She had to stop pretending once she knew the truth.

The parties became business events for Max, and Vivien spent those nights drinking too much and flirting wildly with other men and waking up the next day with a bad taste in her mouth and an overwhelming feeling of ennui, wishing she could go back to the innocence of that midsummer night in 1953. Her first and last party.

She tried to remember what her mother had told her on her wedding day.

Marriages are all about compromise, Vivien, love, remember that. Life may not work out exactly how you imagine it, but, if you and Max just keep talking, everything will be all right.

Good advice, but useless when it came to a man like Max. A man incapable of compromise, a man used to getting his own way no matter what. A man who had only married her as someone to stay at home with the baby he had felt dutybound to adopt.

But that last wasn't really fair, was it? He did seem devoted to his daughter; the two of them had a bond that Vivien seemed incapable of recreating with either her husband or Gina. Was she perhaps a little jealous of that?

She had felt more jealousy towards the ease with which Max and Gina bonded than she felt the first time she smelled another woman's perfume on his clothes, or the time, when Gina was six or seven, she found lipstick on his collar. She didn't know if it was one woman or several different women, but it hadn't surprised her. She'd known, deep down, that there must be somebody else when he started sleeping in the spare bedroom. She'd looked at that lipstick in the laundry pile and, instead of wondering whose lipstick it was, she found herself wondering if it was worth even trying to get it out. It would probably be easier to buy new.

An hour after Vivien walked out of Max's study, leaving the disagreement about whether or not Gina should know the truth unresolved, Max found her in the kitchen. He was wearing his coat and hat and had a small suitcase with him.

'I have to go back to London,' he said, his voice stiff. 'Something has come up.'

Vivien shrugged and didn't turn around. She couldn't bear to look at him. Let him go to London. At that moment she didn't care if he never came back.

Max had had a telephone installed several years before. It sat on the desk in his office and he was the only person who used it. What use did Vivien have for it, after all? Her parents didn't have a telephone and everyone else she knew she saw daily in the village. It never rang when Max was away.

So when it started ringing two days after Max left for London, Vivien walked into the office and stared at it, wondering what to do. She hoped it would just stop ringing but it didn't. The only way to make it stop was to answer it.

'H-hello,' she said nervously into the mouthpiece.

And she listened as a doctor told her what had happened – the fall on the escalator at King's Cross underground station that had knocked him out, how he hadn't regained consciousness, how he'd been dead before they got to the hospital.

'But he just banged his head, didn't he?' she said, unable to comprehend what had happened.

'Sometimes head wounds can be fatal,' the doctor replied.

Fatal.

She hadn't said goodbye because she was so used to him leaving, because he'd refused once again to talk to her.

And now he was gone.

30

Norfolk – July 2019

Isobel woke up on Monday morning to the sound of a phone ringing. It took her a moment to work out where she was, to slowly remember everything that had happened the day before, to remember that the last time she had woken up in this bed she'd realised that Nick had gone in the night. Looking at how small the single bed was, she wasn't surprised he'd left. There was barely space for two people in this room, let alone the bed.

The phone rang on and it was a ringtone she didn't recognise. Where was it coming from? She looked at her mobile, lying on the nightstand next to her, but it had no signal as usual up here at the top of the house.

After a moment she realised that it was, of course, Vivien's landline. The old telephone was pretty much the only thing left in the office.

By the time Isobel had made her way downstairs, the phone had long since stopped ringing so she walked into the kitchen to make a cup of tea. As soon as she opened the kitchen door to be greeted by bare plaster walls with holes in and a great deal of dust, she remembered the kitchen was, for now, out of bounds. She retraced her steps into the dining room and put the kettle on. She poured hot water over a teabag and took her mug into the living room where she saw the notebook, rescued from her grandmother's desk the night before, sitting on Vivien's old chair by the hearth where Isobel must have left it. She hadn't opened it since she'd flicked through the pages at Odds & Ends. It hadn't felt right. As she sat down with her cup of tea and looked at the diary, wondering what to do, the landline started to ring again.

She managed to get to it before the caller rang off this time.

'Hello, Isobel speaking.'

'Hello, this is Mr Brecher's office.'

Isobel's heart contracted for a moment. 'Is there a problem with Nana's will or her estate?' she asked, immediately thinking the worst – that there must have been a mistake and Little Clarion wasn't hers at all and yet she'd already ripped the kitchen apart. Why did she always think the worst about everything?

'Not at all,' the woman on the end of the phone replied. 'My name's Philippa and I'm Mr Brecher's assistant. I understand you were interested in the paperwork from when your grandfather bought the house you have just inherited.'

'Oh yes, of course,' Isobel said, feeling relief as she remembered the conversation she'd had with Mr Brecher the previous week. It felt like a lifetime ago – a time when she still thought of Max Chambers as her biological grandfather.

'Well I was in the basement where we store all the deeds,' Philippa went on. 'And I found some things I think you may be interested in. Would you like to come in or shall we talk over the phone?'

Isobel hesitated, not sure what to do. 'Can you tell me over the phone?' she asked. She didn't want to wait to hear what had been found.

'Of course,' Philippa replied and Isobel heard papers being shuffled. 'Your grandfather bought the house in Silverton Bay in February 1953, just before he and your grandmother married but what I think you might be interested in is where the money to purchase it came from. It is quite a special house, as you know.'

'Well his parents were quite rich, weren't they,' Isobel said. She knew so very little about Max Chambers' family. 'He grew up in one of those huge houses in Surrey with servants and everything – at least that's what Nana told me.' Isobel wondered what had happened to that house after her grandfather and his parents died. 'It was called Clarions and that's why this house is called Little Clarion.'

'That's right,' Phillipa went on. 'But that's not where the money came from.' She paused for a moment. 'He bought Little Clarion, although of course it didn't have a name then, with the proceeds that were left over after he sold Silverton Hall to an American hotelier and paid off the various debts and taxes.'

Isobel felt that familiar tingle in the back of her neck again that she'd felt when she'd been talking to Bee the previous day. Bee had said that Max was some sort of cousin to the Harrington family. If this was true it explained his continuing connection to the Hall after it became a hotel in 1953. It even explained, perhaps, why Vivien had always refused to go up there and then, in the last months of her life, finally returned to reminisce with Ella. She was remembering the husband that she outlived by so many years.

'Are you saying that my grandfather inherited the Hall after the last Lord Harrington died?'

'That's right. Apparently, your grandfather was the second cousin of George Edward Harrington – or the last Lord Harrington as you put it. George died when he was twenty-five; he seemed to have some sort of heart condition.'

The tingling in Isobel's neck got stronger and she felt as though she was on the verge of finding something very important out. She realised she had been looking at the two mysteries as separate stories – one about her mother's adoption and another about her grandmother's life before Max died. What if they were part of the same story?

'Second cousin,' she said, thinking out loud. 'Was there no closer relative to inherit the Hall?' She was trying to keep her voice as calm as possible because she didn't want to give anything away or start talking about her mother's adoption when it might not be connected at all.

She was sure it was though. Bee had told her that Evelyn Pugh had been working at the Hall when she had fallen pregnant.

'Well your grandfather's mother was a Harrington before she married and she would have been a slightly closer relative, but there was an entail on the estate that meant the Hall could only pass down the male line.'

'When did the last Lord Harrington die?' Isobel asked.

More papers shuffled on the other end of the phone. 'December 1952,' Philippa replied.

Just a couple of months after Max and Vivien met. Just before Max proposed, if the story that Isobel knew was true. And Max was apparently with George when he died. She remembered what Bee had said.

He was here in Norfolk quite a bit around that time. He had something to do with the Hall, if I remember correctly. Some sort of cousin or something...

She took a breath.

'My grandfather must have sold the Hall quickly after his cousin's death if he bought this house in the February.'

'It looks that way, doesn't it? It looks as though the American hotelier was waiting in the wings to snap it up. Your grandfather wouldn't have had much choice other than to sell, of course – the finances of the Hall were in dire straits; lots of debts and taxes to pay off.'

'They had to sell the department stores, didn't they?' Isobel asked.

'They did, although that happened before George's death, I believe. Obviously we weren't the lawyers for the Harringtons so we don't have any of their paperwork. Just your grandfather's.'

'And nobody else knew about this?' Isobel wondered out loud. 'About my grandfather inheriting the Hall?'

'Well plenty of people must have done at the time – the previous partners of this firm of course, Max's parents...'

'What about my grandmother? Would Vivien have known?'

'There's no way to tell. Things were different then and women had very little idea about finances unless their husbands chose to share the information with them. Whether Max would have told her, I can't say. Little Clarion was in his sole name but, later, when Vivien inherited it, well...' Philippa paused. 'If she hadn't known there would have been a paper trail for her to follow if she'd wanted to. Whether she did or not I suppose we'll never know.'

Another question that Isobel would never be able to ask her grandmother.

'You can come in and take a look at these deeds anytime,' Philippa said. 'It's your house now so you can also take them away if you want to.'

'No,' Isobel said, thinking about the journal that Spencer had found and wondering if the stories that linked all these clues together lay within its pages. 'Can you just look after everything for me for a little while? I'm going to be going away for a few weeks.'

'Lovely,' Philippa said. Her voice sounded strangely distant now. 'Anywhere nice?'

'America,' Isobel replied. Nick had been right about that; she did need to go. 'I need to see my mother.'

Nick phoned later that morning just as she'd finished booking her flights to New York and then her train tickets to Montauk. Her parents would be at their beach house by the time she got there and Isobel was quite pleased. Her mother was always more relaxed at the beach house and it felt somehow serendipitous to talk about Silverton Bay and everything that might have happened as they sat by the sea themselves. Her father had offered to drive back to New York to pick her up, but she'd refused. She loved the train journey from Penn Station out to Long Island.

'How are you feeling?' Nick asked.

'I've just booked flights to go and see my parents.' She paused. 'You were right, I do need to talk to them.'

'Have you read the diary?' Isobel knew that Nick cared about her but she also knew he must be quite invested in all this mystery by now and must want to know what was in the notebook that Spencer had found.

'Not yet, Nick. How's Spencer?'

'He's having some tests this morning, but I'm going to go and see him later. Would you like to come with me?'

'I would, but there's something I have to do first. I had a phone call this morning from Nana's lawyer. Well, from his assistant actually. She told me something...' Isobel hesitated. 'I want to go and look at the photographs in the ballroom at Silverton Hall again. Will you come with me?'

'Of course I will, Isobel, but are you sure you're OK?'

'I'll tell you everything when I see you.'

'I'll walk up to yours now.'

She met him outside the front door of Little Clarion and they walked slowly to the Hall together. She threaded her fingers through his as she told him about the phone call and the papers Philippa had found in the basement of Mr Brecher's office. He gently squeezed her hand as he listened intently.

'Your grandfather was the cousin who inherited Silverton Hall and sold it to the American hotelier?' Nick said, his voice a whisper of amazement.

'Unbelievable, right? How on earth did he keep that quiet for so long?'

'Nobody knew?'

'A few people must have known, but from what I understand nobody in the village knew. Nana must have known eventually, after Max died and she inherited the house, but Philippa couldn't tell me if she knew anything before that and the lawyer she used before Mr Brecher took over the firm is dead now.'

'But you still don't know who your mum's biological father is?' Nick asked.

Isobel shook her head. 'Bee told me that some people at the time speculated that maybe it was Max, but she didn't seem to believe that.'

'But she didn't know who it could be?'

'No. This Evelyn Pugh – my biological grandmother I suppose – worked at the Hall when she fell pregnant, but that's all I know.'

'And you think the photographs will give you a clue?'

'I don't know, I just wanted to look at them again.'

'I want to tell you that the answer is probably in the diary,' Nick went on. 'But that makes me sound mercenary, as though all I care about is the answer to the puzzle.'

Isobel smiled up at him. 'I don't think you're mercenary. You're bound to be curious, but I just don't know if I can read it without telling Mum about it. On the other hand, I don't know if I can stop my own curiosity long enough either.'

'When are you leaving?' Nick asked.

'The day after tomorrow. There's something I want to talk to you about before I go, but shall we go and look at these photographs first?'

Ella was serving coffee in the lounge when they walked in.

'Hello again,' she said. 'What can I get you?'

'Nothing really,' Isobel replied, introducing Ella and Nick. 'I was just wondering if I could take another look at those photographs in the ballroom. I'm off to see my mum in a few days and I wanted to see them again before I left so I could tell her about them properly. I was in a bit of a daze last time I was here.' All she had been able to focus on then had been the photograph of Vivien in the dark-blue dress.

'Of course, no problem, but you'll have to take yourselves down to the ballroom if that's OK. We're short staffed this morning.'

'That's fine.' Isobel smiled.

As she and Nick started to walk away, Ella called them back.

'Will you be back for the garden party?' she asked. 'It's on the second Saturday of September.'

'I'll be back for that,' Isobel replied and for a moment she wondered what it would be like if she could bring her mum back to Silverton Bay for a while to go to the garden party and show her the photographs. It was never going to happen, of course, but it was nice to imagine.

'You don't have to come back for the garden party if you don't want,' Nick said as they walked towards the ballroom. 'You should stay with your parents for as long as you need.'

'I'll be back by September to teach the art class and I suppose I'd better get registered for supply teaching too.'

It wasn't the photograph of Vivien looking over her shoulder at the camera that captured Isobel's attention this time, but rather the picture of the staff standing on the steps of the Hall. She didn't know how long she stood there staring at it, but after a while she heard Nick stand behind her, ask her if she was all right.

'I was just wondering if one of these servants is her,' Isobel replied. 'Evelyn Pugh.'

'I guess we'll never know.'

Isobel knew he was right. 'I don't know why I came here really. I'm sorry to waste your morning.'

'Spending time with you is never a waste, Isobel.'

She turned to him then and took his hand again. 'I'll be back by the garden party,' she said. 'Will you wait for me?'

'Of course I will.'

'And I was thinking that while I'm away—'

'I'll finish your house,' Nick interrupted with a grin.

'Well, yes and no. How long do you think it will take to get the kitchen and the downstairs bathroom up and running?'

'A few days depending on contractors and holidays. I've not got much else on at the moment.'

'I know Spencer won't be able to live above the shop for a while and I know that you don't want him to go into a nursing home. I could see it in your face last night.'

'Those places are so depressing,' Nick replied. 'I know it's what I'll have to do, but I'm worried it will kill him.'

'You might not have to, not if you think you could get

the ground floor of my house sorted in time for him being discharged.'

'What are you saying?'

'That you use the house while I'm away. That you and Spencer move in and Spencer can heal in a place that's familiar to him. Do you think it would work? Do you think you could get it ready in time?'

Nick hesitated, looking away. 'There'd be a lot to do and I'd have to ask his doctors and the social worker that will have been assigned to him but...' He turned back to Isobel and grinned. 'Yes, I think I could do it. But are you sure? What will you do when you come back if he's still not well enough...'

Isobel reached up and gently placed her finger on Nick's lips. 'We'll worry about that when I'm back. All I care about is that Spencer gets better and you're happy.'

Nick took a step closer to her. 'How can I ever thank you?' he said as he pulled her towards him.

'Oh I'll think of something while I'm away,' Isobel replied as she felt his strong arms wrapping around her.

31

Norfolk – Autumn 1964

Vivien assumed that she would be able to gently break the truth to Gina after Max's death, once the funeral was over and the two of them had established a new routine, a new way of life. She rather naively thought that she'd grow closer to her daughter and together they could talk about Max, about his life before he met Vivien, about his childhood holidays on the Norfolk coast and about Gina's real parents.

But then something happened at the funeral that made Vivien realise that discovering the truth about things wasn't always easy, or palatable, and that sometimes allowing people to believe a different version of events for a little longer wasn't such a bad thing. Afterwards, as the years went by and Gina grew older, it seemed harder and harder to say anything at all as she and Gina tried to find a way of getting along, of loving one another.

*

The village church was packed for Max's funeral. Vivien had thought that Max's parents would want him to be buried in Surrey and was surprised when they insisted that his body be laid to rest in the small graveyard behind the church that looked out over the sea.

'This way Gina can visit her father's grave should she want to,' Max's father had said, without meeting Vivien's eyes. It was only then that she realised Max's parents hadn't approved of the plan to adopt Gina.

Perhaps because of the number of people crowding the church pews, Vivien hadn't noticed the woman in the broad-brimmed black hat during the funeral service. It was only later as the family – Max's parents, her own mum and dad, Mrs Castleton of course, holding Gina's hand – gathered around the grave, that Vivien saw her, standing a little away from them, watching.

There was something about her that Vivien recognised, as though she had seen her somewhere before, and as the vicar droned on she kept finding her attention drifting away from his words, away from her husband's grave and over towards the woman in the black hat. Who was she?

The vicar finally stopped talking and the family began to disperse. Vivien's parents came up to her and tried to talk her into coming back to London with them. Vivien shook her head and pointed them in the direction of Silverton Hall where a small room had been put aside for the wake. 'I'll meet you there,' she said. 'We can talk later.'

Her parents walked away and Vivien touched Miriam's arm.

'Can you take Gina home?' she asked. 'I'm going to speak to a few people and follow you myself. I won't stay long at the wake.' Vivien had already decided that Gina could go to the funeral but the wake would be too much for her.

She turned to her daughter. 'I'll be home as soon as I can,' she said and Gina nodded, looking at her briefly with big, sad eyes, moist with tears. How on earth were they going to get through this?

When Vivien turned back towards the churchyard, the woman in the black hat had moved closer to Max's grave.

'Can I help you?' she asked as she approached and the woman turned to look at here. There it was again, that feeling of recognition.

'You don't remember me, do you?' the woman asked, her eyes still on the grave.

'I'm sorry, but no, I—'

'We met in a coffee house in Soho around twelve years ago. I'm Charlotte. You were with my Max.'

My Max.

The way she said it was purposely proprietorial, Vivien knew, and then of course, everything fell into place. The familiarity in the coffee house – a friend from art school he had said – the way Max had never wanted to take Vivien back to London, the smell of perfume, the lipstick on his collar.

'Charlotte,' Vivien said softly. 'Yes, I remember you.'

'Is there somewhere we could go to talk?'

'I really don't have anything to say to you,' Vivien replied, hooking her handbag firmly over her arm and beginning to step away. 'But you would be most welcome to come to the wake if you wanted. It's up at the Hall.' She started to give Charlotte directions but Charlotte shook her head.

'I was with Max when he fell,' she said. Her words made Vivien look up.

'You were?'

Charlotte nodded.

Vivien hesitated then, by the side of her husband's grave, and wondered if this conversation with the woman who was almost certainly her husband's mistress would help her or just open up another can of worms. Did she want to know what Charlotte had to say? Or should she walk away and forget about this, concentrate on her daughter, on their lives together without Max?

'We can sit in the church,' she said after a moment. 'It'll be empty now, we can talk there.'

Vivien led the way back towards the church and Charlotte followed, picking her way across the muddy churchyard. They went in by the side door, the unoiled hinges creaking as Vivien pushed it open. She headed towards one of the pews at the back and the heels of her shoes clacked on the stone slabs beneath her feet. She was suddenly reminded of the typing pool at Musgrove & Mortimer and, inexplicably, wished she was back there, wished she'd never left.

'I'm a photographer,' Charlotte said as she sat down. 'Of people mostly – musicians, actors, fashion models, that kind of thing. I sell a lot of pictures to *Vogue*.'

Vivien took a breath. She didn't care a jot about Charlotte's photographs or *Vogue*. Where was this going?

'Max used to use my darkroom,' Charlotte went on.

'And that's the only reason you and my husband stayed in touch, is it?'

'I...well...' Charlotte spluttered. It was the first time that Vivien felt she had got the upper hand.

'Were you having an affair with my husband?' she asked. Her voice was soft and far less accusatory than it should have been. Vivien might not believe in God anymore but a church was hardly the place for a showdown.

'What makes you think that?' Charlotte asked.

'Somebody was and there must be a reason why you are here at his funeral.'

Vivien felt Charlotte wilt slightly as she let out a breath. 'Max and I go way back, you know that. We met at art school.'

Vivien did know and could still remember the group of friends in the corner of the coffee shop, drinking from those tiny cups and enveloped in a cloud of cigarette smoke. They had made her feel stupid and insignificant.

'He asked me to marry him, you know.'

Vivien managed to stop herself from turning to Charlotte and shaking her, demanding to know when he'd asked and why. She pressed her lips together to stop the words spilling out.

'He wanted me to move to this backwater with him,' Charlotte went on, and Vivien could hear the disgust in her voice at the thought of having to live in Silverton Bay. 'He told me all about the Hall and his cousin, all that business with the baby. That's when he asked me. I said no of course, I wasn't getting involved in all of that.'

'I thought,' Vivien said tightly, 'that you were going to tell me how my husband died.' She paused for a moment. 'Perhaps I should go.'

'Don't go.' Charlotte touched Vivien's arm for a moment as though to make her stay. 'I just thought you might want to know the truth. Do you?'

'The truth about what?'

'About Max.'

Vivien sighed. 'I think I worked that out some years ago,' she said. But had she? Max had always been a mystery to her, coming and going at will and never really telling her in advance where he'd be. Springing all the business about Silverton Hall and Evelyn Pugh on her after the wedding when it was too late for her to walk away. At least he seemed to have given Charlotte fair warning, and Charlotte had had the good sense to turn him down.

'He didn't tell you, did he?' Charlotte asked, her voice echoing in the empty church. 'About the Hall and his cousin and that baby and all that?'

'No, not until we'd been married and had moved here.'

'Thought not.'

'I wouldn't have said yes if he'd told me.'

'I guess he learned that lesson from me turning him down then.'

'I suppose he did.' Vivien paused for a moment, wondering. 'When did he ask you to marry him?'

'A few weeks after that day I met you in the coffee shop.' Charlotte's voice sounded reluctant. She knew what she was admitting.

'I see,' Vivien replied. Not only had Max's proposal been all about finding someone to mother a motherless child, but it had come after somebody else had turned him down. She felt her cheeks burn with rage and shame and she turned away from Charlotte so she couldn't see the colour in her face. 'And how long after you turned down his proposal did you set yourself up as his mistress?'

She heard Charlotte stifle a giggle at the stuffy,

old-fashioned words. Vivien supposed that in London this kind of behaviour was all the rage now. It was the Swinging Sixties after all – even if Charlotte was old enough to have swung it all out of her system by now.

'Not for years,' Charlotte replied after a while.

'So you're not denying it?'

'No I'm not denying it, but when he first got in touch again it was the summer after the two of you had married and he did genuinely want to use my darkroom. He had some photographs he'd taken of a party here. I remember that they were beautiful. And then he painted that portrait of you.' Charlotte paused. 'That was really something. He had such a gift and he was wasted at his father's bank. If it's any consolation, he never painted me like that.'

'It's of no consolation at all,' Vivien snapped.

'All right then.'

The silence sat icily between them as Vivien tried to hold herself together. She'd known, of course, that there had been someone else, but it had been better before she knew who that someone else was.

'How long?' she heard herself ask into the silence of the church. 'How long had you and Max been... well... ?' Apparently she did need to know, even if she didn't necessarily have the words to ask.

'After he used my darkroom that summer I didn't hear from him for years. I concentrated on my career, on my photography. It took up a lot of my time. It's not an easy industry at the best of times, especially as one of the only women in the business and, well, I'm hardly Lee Miller, am I?'

Vivien didn't know what to say. She wasn't sure she knew who Lee Miller was.

'Anyway,' Charlotte went on. 'I assumed he'd moved on so I did too and then, about six years ago, we bumped into each other at an exhibition at the National. We went for a drink afterwards and—'

'I don't need to know the details,' Vivien interrupted. She was quite capable of filling in the blanks herself. She and Max had been sleeping in separate rooms by the time he met Charlotte again. They barely spoke about anything that wasn't to do with Gina. She'd had no idea he still went to exhibitions but, she supposed, even Max couldn't be working the whole time.

'We'd been to an exhibition the night he died,' Charlotte said, her voice softer now, sadder. 'An old friend from art school who had become quite famous in America. We were changing trains at King's Cross and he fell suddenly. I don't know what happened. I don't know what made him trip. One minute he was there and then…' As Charlotte's voice faded away, Vivien heard her sniff back her tears. She reached out, taking Charlotte's gloved hand in her own and squeezing once. A moment of solidarity. Charlotte had clearly loved Max in a way Vivien never had. She had yet to shed a single tear over her dead husband.

'I should go,' Charlotte said, getting up suddenly. Vivien said nothing as the other woman walked away, leaving by the same door that they'd entered the church half an hour before. The whole world had turned on its head since then.

Vivien sat for a moment in the chill of the church. She should leave, pay her respects to the people who had come for the funeral, have a cup of coffee with them and then go home to her daughter.

But the stark truth of her husband's other life had shocked her, even though she'd had her suspicions. That Max had asked Charlotte to marry him before he'd asked her was a particular blow. Everything felt shattered somehow, as though neither life nor Vivien herself would ever be the same again.

Secrets have a habit of being revealed, she knew that. But at the same time, when they were, they could blow a life into pieces.

And Vivien knew then that it would be a long time before she would be able to reveal the biggest secret of them all.

How could she do that to her daughter?

32

Montauk, NY – August 2019

'I can't believe it,' Gina said sitting down opposite Isobel, placing the diary on the table between them.

'Which bit?' Isobel asked.

'Any of it. I just can't believe Mum held all of those secrets inside her until the day she died. That she never forced me to take them on when I didn't want to, that…' Gina stopped and turned away, blinking back tears. She'd been doing that a lot since Isobel had given her the diary, since she'd found out the truth about who her biological parents were and about how she came to live with Vivien and Max. 'I wish I'd asked,' she admitted now, as she and Isobel sat on the veranda looking out across the ocean. 'I wish I'd talked to Mum about it when she was still alive, I wish I'd known. I wish I'd made more…' She paused, sighed. 'I wish a lot of things.'

'You had your own stuff going on,' Isobel said, rather diplomatically, she thought. She was trying very hard to be on her mother's side but it was difficult to hear this after the event. She understood her mother's fear of flying, but she'd had plenty of opportunity to pick up the phone whenever she'd wanted. But then she remembered that she had hardly been the perfect granddaughter over the last few years.

She hadn't been the perfect daughter either.

Perhaps we all feel as though we have all the time in the world, and then, when that time inevitably runs out, it takes us by surprise.

'It's not an excuse though, is it?' Gina said.

Isobel decided not to answer that question. 'Would it have made a difference?' she asked instead.

'I don't know. She told me everything on the day I got my A level results, you know. I'd done even better than expected and knew that I'd be off to London to study English in October. I was so excited, so happy and then…' Gina paused.

'That's when Nana told you that you were adopted?'

Gina nodded. 'Oh I understand why, what with me about to leave home and everything, but I went from being so happy to suddenly not knowing who I was within the space of two minutes and well…' She hesitated again. 'I never really forgave Mum for that. But if I'd known more, if I'd known what I know now it might have helped to heal our relationship afterwards. It might have helped me to understand who I was a little better. But if you're asking would I have tried to get in touch with my biological mother, this Evelyn Pugh, then no. It wouldn't have made any difference. I don't think I would have wanted to meet the woman who abandoned me.'

'I don't think it was as simple as that, was it?' Isobel said. 'Not from what Nana wrote in the diary. It sounds as though Evelyn Pugh didn't have much choice. It was 1953 in a small seaside village – she'd have been an outcast if she'd brought you up as a single mother and it sounds as though her family didn't want her to go home until she'd had the baby adopted either. It can't have been an easy choice to make.' She didn't say it out loud but she also wondered about what her mother's life would have been like had Evelyn Pugh chosen not to give her baby up. It seemed to her that a life with Max and Vivien had been infinitely preferable.

Isobel had tried not to read the diary before her mother, even though she had barely been able to stop thinking about what might be in it. She'd kept remembering what Spencer had said in the hospital. How much had Spencer known already and how much had he gleaned from the diary? Had he known the diary existed somewhere? How much had Vivien told him? Up until the point she boarded her plane to America, Isobel had been able to resist dipping into its pages. She'd been so busy in those two days before she left, helping Nick get the house ready for when Spencer came out of hospital, that she hadn't had time to think about it and, at night, she'd fallen asleep before her head hit the pillow – the exhaustion of the previous weeks finally catching up with her.

The night before she'd left for America she and Nick had eaten together and finally talked about what had happened between them and about the last eighteen years. They'd opened their hearts and made themselves completely vulnerable.

'What will you do?' Isobel had asked. 'What will happen to the shop?'

'I'm going to stay here,' Nick had replied. 'I'm going to look after the shop. I want to make a few changes if Grandad will let me.'

'Really?' Isobel had been surprised. 'I thought you might want to move on eventually.'

'Move on where?' He'd leaned forward and taken Isobel's hands in his. 'I'm exactly where I want to be.'

She'd looked up at him then and known it was true. That they were both where they wanted to be, where they needed to be. They might have had to wait eighteen years, but they had finally been given a second chance.

'I'm exactly where I want to be too,' she'd said. 'There's just something I have to do first.'

Nick had nodded. 'Bring your mum home,' he'd said.

He'd stayed the night and they'd slept fully clothed and curled up together on Isobel's single bed on the top floor of Little Clarion. The next morning she'd had to wake early to leave for the airport.

'Let me drive you,' Nick had said.

'No,' she'd replied, reaching out to touch his arm. 'I have to do this for myself.'

It hadn't been until her plane had left Heathrow with little else to occupy her that Isobel started thinking obsessively about the diary again. Her hands had itched to open its pages, to read the story Vivien had written inside. She'd tried to distract herself by planning out the paintings she was hoping to create once she was at the beach house and those she wanted to paint once she got back to Norfolk. When that hadn't worked, she'd tried to plan out the first term of the evening classes she'd promised Lauren that she'd take over.

Eventually, about three hours into the flight, she'd taken her backpack out of the overhead locker, slipped the diary out of the inside pocket and started to read.

'I'm so sorry,' she'd said to her mother when she'd explained what she'd done. 'I know I shouldn't have read it. It's your story not mine.'

But Gina hadn't minded. 'I'd have done the same in your situation,' she'd said.

Gina had put off reading the diary herself for a few days and Isobel had understood why. Knowing that all sorts of things about your life were written in the pages, trying to decide whether or not you wanted to know, was huge. Isobel had felt it herself and, as she'd said, it wasn't even her story. Not really.

'I don't suppose it matters now,' Gina said, reaching for the diary again and turning it over in her hands. 'I've left it too late. Mum and Dad are both dead, the last Lord Harrington died before I was born…'

'Which leaves Evelyn Pugh,' Isobel said. 'She was a little younger than Nana. She might still be alive.'

'You know it's funny but it's not my biological parents I've been thinking about.' Gina leaned forward, placing her elbows in the table. 'I just keep thinking about family – about how Evelyn may have married later, after she'd had me, after she'd grieved George's death and everything. She might have had children. I may have brothers and sisters out there that I know nothing about, and who probably know nothing about me.'

Isobel turned towards her mother. 'I hadn't even thought about that,' she said.

'You and Tim are my family, of course.' Gina paused,

reaching across the table for her daughter's hand. 'Although I know I've not been the greatest mum in the world. I'm not sure I really worked out how to *be* a mum.' Isobel took her hand and gave it a squeeze. She thought about the chrome and glass apartment in London that had never felt like home, the tutors and the babysitters that looked after her while her parents were out or in New York. She thought about how much closer she'd always been to Vivien, and how Vivien had been the one to save her from the threat of boarding school. And, for the first time, she thought she understood.

'The stupid thing is, of course, that your grandmother was a fantastic mum,' Gina went on. 'If I'd just swallowed my pride and asked her for help, even asked her advice from time to time, everything could have been different. I never knew…' She stopped, dabbing her eyes with a tissue. 'I never realised how much my father had bullied her into everything, the lengths he'd gone to keep my adoption quiet. Buying people's silence for heaven's sake, it's so unnecessarily dramatic. I just wish I'd talked to Mum more. I'd have been a much better mother if I had.'

'It doesn't matter now,' Isobel said, because what could they do about the past? 'Moving forward is the important thing. I don't want us to drift apart now Nana's gone.'

'Neither do I,' Gina said quietly.

It could be the moment to mention going back to Silverton Bay. Isobel opened her mouth to start the conversation and then saw the regret in her mother's eyes. She had the best part of a month in Montauk. The question could wait.

'Were you happy?' Gina asked then. 'Were you happy

living with Mum in Norfolk? I never knew if it was the right thing—'

'It was,' Isobel interrupted. 'I was happy. I'm always happy when I'm by the sea, you know that.'

Isobel decided to leave the question of returning to England for a while. Her mother had a lot to process, a lot to work through after reading the diary, and it was best to leave her to do it in her own time. She heard her parents talking late into the night – she couldn't hear what they were saying, only the low rumble of their voices – but she knew what it must be about. One night she heard her mother crying and she wanted, so badly, to go and comfort her. But she also understood her own relationship with her mother enough to realise she had to allow Gina to get through this by herself. They weren't going to suddenly become the sort of mother and daughter who shared everything overnight, in fact they may never have that kind of relationship. But that was all right as well, Isobel thought. Perhaps the most important thing was that they both now knew the truth and could start looking towards the future.

As the summer progressed, the three of them fell into their usual beach house routines. Gina sat on the porch and read, her skin turning golden in the sunlight. Tim fished and drank beer with the locals, he stopped shaving and rarely wore shoes. It was his time, he always said, to let go.

And Isobel painted. This year she really painted. She didn't sit on the beach looking out to sea wondering where her drive and ambition had gone as she had done for the last few summers. She put her brush to the canvas and she painted the horizon, the sea, the sunset, the sunrise. She painted her parents standing together on the shore, she painted the beach house and the main street in the little town where the stayed. She painted Silverton Bay from memory. She painted Nick.

Of course she painted Nick.

She painted all the pictures she hadn't had a chance to start painting back in Norfolk because of everything that had happened with Nick and Spencer, because of what she had found out about Vivien. But now she was more prolific than she had ever been. She couldn't stop thinking about the sea and the light. She had no idea how she was going to get her work home – her father would know the best and safest way – but she just carried on. She felt like a thing possessed.

'Wonderful,' Tim said as he saw her on the beach each day. 'Very Turner-esque.' Not that he would recognise Turner if his life depended on it.

When she wasn't painting, or dreaming or spending time with her parents, she talked to Nick – about the house (the kitchen was in, the study was painted and waiting for her, the rewiring was booked for the autumn and there were men coming to do something to the roof that she wasn't aware had needed doing), about their future and what they would do together when Isobel got home. They talked about Spencer, who was healing quickly and interfering in the work Nick was trying to do on the house. And they talked about a big decision Spencer had made about the future.

'He's selling Odds & Ends,' Nick said. 'And I'm going to buy it from him.'

'And stay in the Bay?' Isobel asked. She could hardly believe it, hardly imagine it. Despite everything he had said before she'd left for America, Isobel hadn't quite believed he would stay.

'It's a good investment,' Nick said. 'Lots of potential.' Isobel's heart sank as she realised Nick hadn't really answered her question. 'But yes, of course I'll be staying in the Bay,' Nick said. 'I told you I would be.'

Isobel smiled to herself. That was all she needed to hear for now.

'Where will Spencer live?' she asked.

'He's got his eye on one of those sheltered apartments where your friend Lauren's grandmother lives,' Nick replied.

There were days when it felt as though summer would last forever, when Norfolk felt as far away as the moon and Isobel's future felt like a nebulous thing she would never really have to deal with. But time passes, however much we might not want it to, and the final days of August approached. Isobel noticed the changes in her father first – he spent less time fishing and more time on the phone as he prepared to go back to New York, back to work. She noticed the days getting slightly shorter, the sunsets a little earlier each day. She noticed the smell of autumn in the air. Soon she would have to go back to Silverton Bay and see what the future held for her.

'We'll miss you when you're gone, honey,' her father said over dinner one night.

'We will,' Gina agreed. 'It's been so lovely having you

here for so long. It's felt right to be honest with you after all these years. I'm so sorry we hadn't told you earlier.'

Isobel didn't say anything for a moment. They sat on the veranda and she noticed the sky was completely clear. She looked at the stars above them, the same stars that shone on Silverton Bay, on Little Clarion, on Nick.

'Why don't you come with me?' she said, feeling the air still around her. 'Why don't you come home?'

33

Norfolk – December 1952

'I'm not going to get better this time, Max,' George said, his voice a hoarse whisper. 'And I need you to do something for me. One last promise.'

'Don't,' Max replied quietly. 'Don't say that. Of course you're going to get better. Everything will be fine, just as it always is.'

Max knew that his cousin had had several heart scares over the years – a result of contracting rheumatic fever as a child. He had a weak heart, yes, but so did lots of people. It didn't mean that this was the end. George had years to live yet, didn't he?

Despite being two years older than Max, George had always been the one who needed looking after.

'Keep an eye on your cousin, Max,' Lady Harrington used to say. 'Make sure he doesn't get too tired.' Or, 'Don't let him stay in the sea too long.' They had been words that were immediately forgotten as soon as Max and George got away from Silverton Hall. Sometimes, on the cliff path,

Max would have to wait for his cousin, who was following behind slowly, breathlessly. Sometimes he'd notice George's lips go blue when they were in the sea and he would suggest going back to the Hall to see what Cook had been baking. But mostly Max never thought about George's health and George himself rarely mentioned it.

Things changed as they grew older. There was the summer Max was thirteen when George was in the hospital in King's Lynn for several weeks and Max had to entertain himself – it had been the first summer he could remember that he hadn't wanted to spend in Silverton Bay as usual because things just hadn't been the same without his cousin. Then there was the seizure that George had had when he was up at Oxford just after the war – Max knew it was connected to his cousin's heart, but he hadn't wanted to think about it. They were both too young, too vibrant, to worry. They had too much to live for.

But this was different, however much Max might try to deny it. He had never seen George look so ill – his face like wax, his eyes red, his lips blue. Perhaps he was right. Perhaps he wasn't going to get better this time.

He felt his cousin's hand on his arm, a grip surprisingly strong for someone so ill.

'I need you to do something for me,' George repeated, breathlessly.

'I know,' Max said quietly, hoping if he could get George to calm down it would somehow save him. 'I know I inherit the Hall and I know there's no money left. Father has already gone through all of this.'

'You need to sell it,' George whispered. 'There's no other way. There's one of those American hoteliers sniffing around.

He'll buy it without too many questions, and quickly too from what I understand. The details are all…' He paused, falling back on the uncomfortable-looking hospital pillows again as he tried to find the breath to continue.

'Everything is in your study,' Max said, smiling softly. 'In the desk drawer. I know.'

George shook his head, his eyes closed. 'But there's something else,' he managed. 'I need you to promise…'

Max watched as his cousin's waxy pallor began to look more and more grey. He gripped George's hand, suddenly realising that perhaps this was it after all. George was the best friend Max had ever had, more brother than cousin. 'Anything,' he said.

'There's a young woman,' George began. 'She works at the Hall, one of the maids. Her name's Evelyn Pugh. She's in a bit of trouble.'

'Oh, George…' Max began. How could his beloved cousin submit to such a cliché?

'It's not what you think, Max.' George tried, and failed, to sit up. 'It's not what you think. I love her, but…' He closed his eyes again, turned his head away. 'I'm not going to be able to marry her now, am I? But you can…'

'You want me to marry her?' Max was horrified.

George smiled. 'Well that would be one solution,' he said. 'But I know what a snob you are and I'm not sure that she would like you very much either.'

Max opened his mouth to protest, but felt George squeeze his hand and closed it again.

'Listen.' George's voice was no more than a faint whisper now so that Max had to bend down to hear him. 'I need you to look after her. I need you to look after the baby.'

'But…how?'

'You'll have to talk to Evelyn. Mrs Castleton will help you. But you'll have to ask Evelyn what she wants to do. You will have to work it out. I can't…' George sank into the pillows again, his breath shallow.

'George, I don't know what to do.'

'I need you to promise,' George whispered.

They were the last words he ever said.

34

Norfolk – September 2019

Nick's truck was outside Little Clarion when Isobel pulled her Citroën into the drive. She wanted to run into the house and wrap her arms around him, she wanted to see all the work that he'd done on the house. She was so excited she barely registered the scaffolding that had sprung up everywhere since she'd left, the men on the roof that Nick had told her about.

Before she'd even shut the car door he was there, at the front door, leaning against the door frame, arms folded across his chest.

'Hello,' he said as she threw herself at him.

'I've missed you so much,' she replied.

'So it would seem.' He smiled, ducking his head to kiss her. 'When are they getting here?'

'Any minute…' Isobel began, but was interrupted by the sound of car tyres on the gravel driveway. 'This is them now.'

It had been her father's idea to take the nautical route

to England from New York, and Isobel had wondered why they had never done that before.

'Oh you know what your father is like about work,' Gina had replied. 'He can never get enough time off.'

But suddenly he could now? And Isobel realised by the look on her father's face that he had suggested this before and Gina had refused. There were many reasons she hadn't wanted to come back to Silverton Bay and her fear of flying had only been one of them.

The truth could be a hard thing to face, as Vivien had written in her diary many times. That was the reason it had taken her so long to tell Gina about her adoption after Max had died. She was scared of what the truth might do to her daughter, to her daughter's friends, to the equilibrium of the village.

But the truth could also change everything for the better, as it had done now. Isobel was glad she'd persisted, glad she'd let her curiosity get the better of her because, on the same day that she had flown back to England, her parents had boarded a ship bound for Southampton.

They'd arrived five days after Isobel landed at Heathrow and, instead of going back to the Bay, Isobel had decided to stay in London to meet them. She'd visited exhibitions at the National Gallery and the Tate – she'd been reading reviews of exhibitions for years and it was time she got back into the habit of actually going to them, of filling her creative well. And she'd reconnected with old friends from art school. The last few months had taught her a lot. She had cut herself off from the things that made her happy and she didn't want to be that person anymore.

And on the morning that her parents' ship was due to

dock in Southampton, she was waiting for them. Because she needed to be sure that they were really there and she hadn't felt she'd be able to be in Silverton Bay for a week worrying if they'd actually arrive, even though she missed Nick so much.

They'd followed her back to Norfolk in their hire car and now, suddenly, they were here. It felt almost impossible and also the most natural thing in the world.

Nick had gone back into the house when Tim and Gina's car had arrived and Isobel led her parents through the front door. There was a huge 'Welcome Home' banner in the hallway that Nick had put up. She felt so happy to be back, so sure that she was doing the right thing. She led her parents towards the kitchen first.

'I haven't seen the new kitchen myself yet,' Isobel said as she opened the door. Nick was waiting for them, standing by the new pine table that he'd had made especially for the kitchen. A table which held a teapot, cups and a very delicious-looking chocolate cake.

'You have been busy,' Isobel teased.

'I'm Nick,' he said, introducing himself. 'I thought you might both be a bit tired and hungry after your journey so I got tea and cake, but if you'd rather I went—'

'No,' they chorused as Isobel went up to him and wrapped her arms around him again.

'This is great,' she said. 'Thank you.'

'The cake or the kitchen?' Nick asked and Isobel could hear what she thought might be nerves in his voice. Was he nervous about what she would think of the kitchen or about meeting her parents for the first time?

She took a moment to look around the new kitchen. It

was wonderful, exactly how she'd imagined – no, better than she'd imagined. Nick had done exactly as he promised and opened up the space into a kitchen-diner. He'd installed a butler sink and the range was on order. The bifold doors might have to wait a little while though.

'Both,' she said quietly. 'Thank you for the cake and the kitchen.'

Isobel introduced her parents to Nick properly as they drank their tea and, within moments, Nick and Tim were talking about buildings, houses and supporting walls.

'You could extend out into the garden if you wanted, Isobel,' Tim said, knocking on the external wall.

'It's a huge house, Dad, I don't need to extend!'

Tim rolled his eyes and turned back to Nick.

Isobel turned to Gina. 'Are you OK, Mum?' she asked. 'What's it like to be back?'

'Wonderful,' Gina said quietly, trying to hide her tears. 'I just wish I'd done it sooner, when Mum was still alive.' She sniffed then, as though pulling herself together. 'And what you've done to this kitchen, Nick, is a miracle. It's unrecognisable!'

Nick grinned, clearly pleased with himself and how well he seemed to be impressing her parents. 'I can show you around the rest of the house if you like?' he said. 'There's still a lot to do, but it will give you an idea.'

'Where's Spencer?' Isobel asked after her parents had left, off to check into Silverton Hall and freshen up before dinner.

'In the pub, can you believe?'

'The pub?'

'He thought you might want some space and time with your mum in the house. I only stayed because…'

'Because I wanted you to,' Isobel said. 'But I thought Spencer was housebound, I thought…'

'He was housebound for exactly two days. Then he learned to use his crutches and was out and about as usual. He's healing more quickly than anybody thought he would too.'

'Wow, that's wonderful news'

'It is.' Nick smiled, looking relieved. 'I was really worried that the fall would have knocked the stuffing out of him, you know? But the man is a machine. He's going to terrorise everyone when he moves to the sheltered housing complex.'

Isobel started to say something, but yawned instead.

'I can go,' Nick said. 'Let you unpack and get some rest.'

'Don't…' she replied, leaning her head on his shoulder. 'Please.'

Nick smiled at her and her stomach flipped. She'd been wondering, for most of the journey home, for most of the time she'd been away, what would happen when she came back, when they were alone together again. She worried that Nick would change his mind, that he would see he had so many more options than hanging around in the Bay running an antiques shop. If she was honest, it was another reason she'd delayed her journey home from London. She'd told herself that she wouldn't hold him back, that she wouldn't mind if he went. But now she was back, now she was with him again, she didn't know if that was true anymore.

'I'm so glad you're home,' Nick said, taking her in his arms. 'I've missed you so much.'

'I've missed you too,' she said, her heart hopeful. 'But I

understand if you've changed your mind about us, or about staying in the Bay.'

'Are you kidding me?' he replied. 'There's nowhere else I want to be. I told you that.'

'Really?'

'Really,' he said softly, pulling away from her a little. 'I've bought Grandad's shop, haven't I?'

'But you said it was a good investment, you said—'

'It will be a good investment. I've got big plans for that shop, but that doesn't mean I'm leaving or I've changed my mind about us.' He paused for a moment, pressing a kiss to her forehead. 'Coming back here has changed my life, Isobel. When I came back from Afghanistan I felt as though I had nothing left to live for. I knew then that I'd never go back to the hospital and I felt as though everything I'd ever worked for had crumbled to dust. My marriage was over and my life felt over. Flipping houses helped. It gave me something to do, a reason to get out of bed, but you…' He trailed off, shaking his head slowly. 'Meeting you again, falling in love with you all over again, has changed everything.' He stopped suddenly and Isobel saw his cheeks colour as he looked away. 'And now I've just laid all my cards on the table without knowing how you feel.'

'Falling in love with me, eh?' Isobel teased and Nick looked away, embarrassed. 'You already know how I feel, Nick,' she said quietly. 'You know I love you too.'

They were back from America in time for the Silverton Hall garden party and were blessed with a gloriously warm day for the event.

'You made it,' Ella said, greeting Isobel with a rather over-enthusiastic hug when she saw her.

'I did and I managed to bring my parents as well.' She still couldn't believe they were here and she kept looking over to where they were talking to Lauren and her husband on the other side of the gardens to make sure they were still there, that she wasn't dreaming it. Lauren's mother, Susan, was coming over from France to see Gina for the first time since Gina had left to go to university and they were busy making arrangements. It was like something out of a movie. 'Mum wants to see the photographs later,' Isobel went on.

'Well she's welcome anytime, you know where they are.' She paused as Spencer arrived next to them, mobile as ever even though he was still on crutches. 'It's good to see you up and about again, Spencer,' Ella said before moving on.

Spencer had brought Bee Burnage with him and as the two of them went to find more champagne and somewhere to sit down, pottering across the garden carefully, neither of them good on their feet, Isobel felt Nick's arm around her waist.

'What do you think is going on there?' he asked, nodding towards Bee and Spencer.

'I don't know,' Isobel replied. 'And I don't much care as long as they're happy.' She turned to Nick. 'I'm more interested in what's going on here.'

Nick bent to drop a kiss on her lips. 'You know what's going on here.'

'I have a proposition to make now that Little Clarion is almost finished.' The roofers had left that week and the electricians were due on Monday. After that there was still quite a lot of painting and decorating to do, furniture to buy and so on, but the bulk of the renovation was almost over. For now at least. Nick already had a long list of projects for the house come spring, once he'd got a head start on the renovation at Odds & Ends.

'Oh yes,' Nick said, raising an eyebrow.

Isobel took a breath. Everything felt as though it was finally coming together, as though her life had meaning for the first time in a long time. She was painting and drawing again and some of her favourite pictures from Montauk were already selling, thanks to the display in Sarah's cafe. She'd signed up with an agency for supply teaching and the art class in the village hall started in just a few days. She felt excited and nervous, as though she was on the brink of something.

Meanwhile, Spencer was soon to move into sheltered housing and Nick was about to start the big renovation at Odds & Ends, completely refurbishing the shop and, eventually, when he had found somewhere to live, turning the upstairs into a gallery for local artists.

What Isobel was about to ask him made sense, but there was a chance that it was still too soon, that Nick was going to say no. But it had been a summer of chances and impossibilities, what was one more risk?

'Well,' she began. 'As Spencer is moving to his new place soon and your flat is going to be pretty much unliveable once you start the renovations on the shop, I was wondering if you'd like to live with me for a while?'

'At Little Clarion?'

Was that hesitation that she heard in his voice? Was he stalling?

'Yes, of course,' she said.

Nick looked down at her and smiled. 'Only for a while?' he asked.

The tension in Isobel's shoulders melted away as she realised what he was saying. 'Well that all depends on how well you behave.'

'Laundry in the laundry basket and toilet seat down,' Nick said. 'I know the drill.'

Isobel stood on tiptoe to kiss him, and as she did she felt him draw her against his body, felt his warmth and his steadiness. She'd been craving this since she was eighteen years old.

'Now,' he said, 'let's go and find your parents and get a picture of you and your mum standing outside the Hall. It is yours in a way, you deserve a picture outside it.'

'How do you mean?' she asked.

Nick grinned. 'You're the last living descendants of the final Lord Harrington.'

'Oh, I hadn't thought about it like that. This could work to my advantage.' She laughed. 'Let's go and find Mum and Dad.'

'After you, my lady.'

Epilogue

Norfolk – September 2019

Gina slipped quietly away from the party, stepping first into the shade of trees and then into the cool of the hotel foyer. It really was unseasonably hot for September.

She could barely believe she was back in England for the first time in over eighteen years. She had finally agreed to Tim's suggestion of the seven-day cruise to Southampton, after making excuses for years, because she had a lot of reasons not to want to return to Silverton Bay. She knew she would never get on a plane again after what she'd seen in New York on that September morning eighteen years before, but she hadn't been able to get on a boat either. In New York she'd felt distanced from it all, from the awful way she'd treated her friends when she'd found out the truth and left for London, from the pain she felt around the lies that had made up her childhood, and from her mother whose very presence reminded her of everything that had happened and how badly she had reacted.

She should have listened to Tim, she should have come back and tried to make amends before it was too late.

But it wasn't too late to make amends with her daughter or the people of Silverton Bay. And that's why she was here.

That was why she'd come home.

She was glad that Isobel had been waiting for them in Southampton. There was a part of her that felt that if her daughter hadn't been there she might have changed her mind, might have chickened out of going back to Silverton Bay and that would have been a tragedy, because now she was here she couldn't understand why she'd grown to hate the place so much.

Everyone had been so kind, making such a fuss of her – people she remembered from childhood, including Susan who she'd spoken to on the phone and who was coming back from France at the weekend, and then there were the people who had moved to the Bay after she'd left but who'd known and loved Vivien. People like Spencer and his grandson Nick. Gina could remember Isobel talking about Nick years ago, when she'd been living with them in New York. She didn't know why they lost touch but was happy to see they'd reconnected. They seemed good for each other. Nick seemed to understand her talented, complicated, sensitive daughter. He seemed to bring out the best in her and Isobel deserved that. Gina wasn't sure that either she or Tim had ever been very good at bringing out the best in Isobel.

She started to walk down the passageway of the hotel that led to the ballroom – at least it was the passageway that had led to the ballroom when she'd been a child. She could remember her mother bringing her down here and showing her where she and Max had used to dance – because she could remember that now she'd read about it in the diary. Surely this new hotel chain hadn't moved the ballroom?

Going back to Little Clarion had been difficult – not as difficult as getting on the ship in the first place, but hard nonetheless. From the outside the house hadn't changed a bit and, from what Isobel had told her when they were at the beach house, she'd expected it to be completely dilapidated inside. But instead it was almost unrecognisable. The upper floors still needed a lot of work, so Nick had said, but while Isobel had been away he had transformed the ground floor. If it hadn't been for the Strawberry Thief wallpaper in the hall, Gina might have thought they were in the wrong house.

She had told Tim that she didn't want to stay at Little Clarion – it was Isobel's home now and Gina wasn't sure what the situation with Nick was – so she and Tim were staying at Silverton Hall. Gina had been thinking about the photographs ever since they first checked in, but this was the first time she'd plucked up the courage to go and look at them.

Here was the ballroom, exactly where it had been all those years ago when she'd come with her mother. Gina walked across the dance floor, which she supposed was used for weddings and Christmas parties these days, her shoes clipping on the polished floor. She tried to imagine her parents – Vivien and Max, because they were her parents, she understood that now – dancing here together. Had they ever loved each other? she wondered. Or had their marriage always been one of necessity, of convenience?

The photographs lined the walls, just as Isobel had told her they would. She walked up to them, running her fingers along the frames, looking for one in particular – the one of her mother in the ball gown, looking over her shoulder. The one that the portrait was based on.

When she spotted it she felt her breath catch in her throat. She'd forgotten how beautiful her mother had been. No wonder Max had noticed Vivien, regardless of his intentions, even in the smog.

'It's a beautiful photograph, isn't it?' a voice said behind her.

Gina turned to see the young woman who was friendly with Isobel. Ella someone or other. She was one of the assistant managers here. She seemed so young to be a manager, but she probably wasn't much younger than Isobel. Everybody seemed young to Gina these days – doctors, lawyers, policemen.

'I've never seen it before,' Gina said, turning back to the photograph. 'Did you know my mother?'

Ella nodded and came to stand next to Gina. 'Yes, she used to come to the hotel for coffee sometimes. She gave us those photographs of the first midsummer party. Your father took them, I believe.'

'Apparently so,' Gina replied. 'There's a painting as well, of this exact photograph.' She pointed to the picture of Vivien looking over her shoulder. 'My father painted it. He went to art school after the war but had to give it all up to work in his father's bank.'

'Have you seen the other photographs?' Ella asked, moving towards a display of older pictures that Gina had bypassed in her haste to find the photograph of her mother. She followed Ella.

'This is the Hall when it was still owned by the Harrington

family,' Ella said, pointing at the appropriate photograph. 'And this is the last Lord Harrington.' She turned and smiled and Gina swallowed. 'He's the guy who spent all the money, ran everything into the ground and then died young.' Ella rolled her eyes. 'As you can see, he liked golf.'

Gina stared at the picture of the young man in the plus fours standing on the steps of Silverton Hall. If everything Vivien had written in her diary was true, this was her biological father, the man who died before she was born, the man to whom Max promised everything. She'd known, of course, that his picture was here in the ballroom – Isobel had told her – but for some reason she hadn't really believed it. The fact that George Edward Harrington, an actual lord, was her father still didn't feel remotely real.

Ella was still talking about what a wastrel the last Lord Harrington had been, but Gina knew the story wasn't quite so black and white as that. Silverton Hall, like so many English estates, had been falling into decline since the First World War and George himself had been ill for most of his life. He'd known his heart would fail eventually; he must have spent his short life waiting for that to happen. Gina blinked back the tears that were threatening to come. She would cry for the man who had been her father later, when she was alone.

Ella had moved on to another photograph. 'This is all the staff who worked at the Hall before it first became a hotel,' she said. 'This is a Mrs Castleton who I believe your mother knew.'

Gina smiled and nodded. She would recognise Mrs Castleton anywhere.

'And this is my grandmother,' Ella said pointing at a

young woman in a dark dress and white apron. 'She started at the hall as a housemaid when she was just fourteen.'

Gina found herself peering closer. A housemaid who had been at the Hall since she was young. It couldn't be, could it? Surely not.

'What happened to her?'

'After the Hall was bought, you mean? Well, she moved to Nottingham, the rest of her family were there then. She married and had eight children.' Ella grinned and Gina found herself thinking about those eight children. Were they the brothers and sisters she'd imagined when she'd first read Vivien's diary? No, of course not. She was being fanciful now. 'The eldest of her children is my mum,' Ella went on.

'What was her name?' Gina heard herself ask in a voice that didn't sound like her own. 'Your grandmother, what was her name?'

'Evelyn,' Ella said, turning back to the photograph again. 'Evelyn Pugh.'

Nick and Isobel's Playlist

'Reptilia' – The Strokes
'Blue Monday' – New Order
'A Day in the Life' – the Beatles
'Driftwood' – Travis
'Walls Come Tumbling Down' – The Style Council
'Never Tear Us Apart' – INXS
'Me and Julio down by the Schoolyard' – Paul Simon
'Love is a Battlefield' – Pat Benatar
'Boys Don't Cry' – The Cure
'The Safety Dance' – Men Without Hats
'Shout' – Tears for Fears
'Love Will Tear Us Apart' – Joy Division
'(Stranded on) the Wrong Beach' – Noel Gallagher's High Flying Birds
'Blinded by the Sun' – The Seahorses
'Lucky Man' – The Verve
'Leaving on a Jet Plane' – John Denver
'Jump' – Aztec Camera

Acknowledgements

Silverton Bay is fictional, as is the story of Silverton Hall, but the Bay itself is based on Old Hunstanton on the North Norfolk coast, location of many wonderful holidays both as a child and now. I had the initial idea for Silverton Hall whilst staying at The Caley Hall Hotel, a place I highly recommend for great food, beautiful surroundings and for being dog friendly. It may not have the beautiful ballroom of Silverton Hall, but parts of it date back to 1648 and the Caley family were recorded in the Domesday Book.

This novel was one of those books that took a long time to write and made me doubt myself on more than one occasion so, as always, my first thank-you goes to my long-suffering agent Lina Langlee, who not only encouraged me to keep going but had to put up with a lot of moaning emails on the way there (she will also tell me that this sentence is too long).

Thanks, of course, to everyone at Aria and Head of Zeus: Rachel Faulkner-Willcocks, Bianca Gillam, Laura Palmer, Nicky Lovick, and all the team.

I've always found the 1950s fascinating – that sort of in-between time after the war and before the 60s started to swing and am grateful to two books for helping me with my research: *Having It So Good* by Peter Hennessey (one of a brilliant trilogy of post-war analyses) and *1950s Life in London* by Mike Hutton. Also, Harriet Salisbury's *The War on Our Doorstep* gives some fascinating accounts of London during the Blitz.

I'm also grateful to Brenda Knight for her first-hand account of what it was like to live in London at the time of the Great Smog.

Thank you to my husband, my beta-reader, proof-reader and general cheerleader; Sarah Bennett, my WhatsApp partner-in-crime; and my incredibly patient family who put up with me when my head is in the clouds.

And thank you to you, my readers both old and new. Without you none of this would be possible.

This book is dedicated to my beautiful ginger cat, Vesper, who passed away while I was working on my structural edits. She would sit with me, quietly, by my writing desk until such a time as she felt like breaking into a wardrobe or scaling a bookcase. Her chaotic energy will be hugely missed in my office. Fly high, little girl.

About the Author

RACHEL BURTON has been making up stories for as long as she can remember and always dreamed of being a writer until life somehow got in the way. After reading for a degree in Classics and another in English Literature she accidentally fell into a career in law, but eventually managed to write her first book on her lunch breaks. She loves words, Shakespeare, tea, The Beatles, dresses with pockets and very tall romantic heroes (not necessarily in that order) and lives with her husband in Yorkshire. Find her on Instagram and Twitter @RachelBWriter.